SILVERHILL

SILVERHILL

Phyllis A. Whitney

Doubleday & Company, Inc., Garden City, New York

SILVERHILL

I

The wind whipped at my brown summer skirt, snatched at my white straw hat as I came down from the plane and started across the field of the small New Hampshire airport.

Flying in, we had circled Mt. Abenaki, and as I crossed the open field I had a clear, stunning view of its rocky head and sloping, pine-covered flanks where they rose isolated above the rolling countryside. My mother had always called it "The Mountain," capitalizing—and that was the way I thought of it, this peak that I had seen only once as a child, and then never again. Now I was bringing Mother home to New Hampshire for the last time, and she would never gaze upon any of this loved landscape again.

As I crossed the macadam, holding onto my hat, I saw the long black waiting vehicle, which could be intended for only one purpose. All the anxiety and uncertainty I had tried to deny while I hurled myself toward catastrophe increased as I glanced hastily at the few people who stood beyond the gate.

I had sent Grandmother Julia Gorham a telegram to let her know—defiantly—that I was bringing her daughter Blanche home to Shelby. I was bringing my mother home to bury her in the family plot as she had wished. I warned her as well that Mother had wanted me to visit Silverhill. It had not been necessary to add that this was also my wish —or perhaps more a need than a wish.

No answer reached me. In grief that was laced with indignation I sent another message announcing the time of my arrival, trusting that all arrangements would be made. I would not take my grandmother's silence as refusal.

Now, reaching the gate and looking toward the waiting black car, I wondered which, if any, of my unknown family would be here to meet me. Grandmother Julia, who was nearly eighty, would be unlikely to come. Nor would Aunt Arvilla be here. My mother's older sister was my first reason for visiting Silverhill, though I planned to remain quiet about this for a time. I knew that Arvilla Gorham was a deeply disturbed woman. I knew as well that my mother blamed herself to some degree for Arvilla's state of mind. In her last urgency before she died, Mother had charged me with a difficult mission as far as Arvilla was concerned. Difficult because, as Mother warned me, Grandmother Julia would oppose what I must do.

There still remained my cousin, Gerald Gorham, and my aunt by marriage, Nina Gorham. Perhaps they would come.

But no one near the gate looked at me inquiringly as I passed through. No one waited near the passenger cars to welcome me. Not until I started across the graveled area of the parking lot did a man turn from talking to the driver of the black car and glance in my direction. I knew that he could not be my Cousin Gerald, but at least he seemed to expect me.

He wore rough brown country corduroys, with brown patches at the knees, well stained from use, and his jacket was of light tan tweed. Scarcely the formal dress of a man about to attend a funeral. Nevertheless, he watched openly as I approached, and when I hesitated he came toward me.

"You're Malinda Rice," he said with assurance. "I'm Elden Salway from Silverhill. Your grandmother sent me."

He was a squarely built man, probably in his early forties, muscular, and brown-skinned from the outdoors, his body a bit short for his massive, well-shaped head. His sandy hair had a coarse look to it, and thick, tawny eyebrows drew down above pale blue eyes—all giving him a rough, scowling appearance that contrasted with a mouth surprisingly well formed and sensitive.

He made no offer to shake hands. "The gray Bentley over

there belongs to Silverhill," he said. "You might as well get in and wait for me."

As he would have turned away I touched his arm quickly. "Is everything arranged? Will any of the Gorhams be at the cemetery?"

His pale, intent gaze focused upon me again—more with curiosity than sympathy, and I was aware that he looked me up and down with a quick sweep of his eyes, letting his scrutiny stop at the scar on my cheek before I could make my instinctive gesture of covering it.

"You look a lot like pictures I've seen of Miss Arvilla when she was young," he said. "But you've got your grandmother's eyes. Amethyst, they're called—historically. I suppose you know that. No, none of the family will be coming to the cemetery. That's why they've sent me. Here's a note your grandmother's written you."

I took the envelope from him. So it was to be like that. No welcome. No one to greet me, although my mother was Julia Gorham's youngest daughter.

"Are you one of the family?" I asked, nettled and on the defensive—not for myself, but because of the insult to my mother.

The tawny eyebrows came up and his mouth tightened into a wry grin. "I'm the gardener, Miss," he said, touching his forehead in a mock gesture of respect before he went off toward the plane, meaning clearly that he considered himself no ordinary gardener.

I held the stiff envelope of Gorham notepaper with something like repugnance as I walked toward the gray Bentley. Was I expected to get into the back seat and ride in formality to the cemetery, driven by this odd gardener-chauffeur? My eyes burned with unshed tears. I had been through ten dreadful days, culminating with my mother's death, and my nerves were raw. I knew I had better watch myself. If I was to accomplish this unhappy mission, I had better learn all I could about the present atmosphere at Silverhill.

Firmly I opened the front door of the car and got in beside the driver's seat. Tense and keyed up, I was afraid to open my grandmother's note at once. Instead, I sat very still, examining white gloves for travel stains, looking down at tan suede shoes for dust marks, tucking a strand of blond hair beneath my hat, even repinning the French twist exposed at the back.

All busy little movements that meant nothing, but were made because I could not sit still and because I was resentful for my mother, defiant on my own account, and just a little frightened besides. How could I possibly carry out what she had begged me to do?

Outside the air-conditioned plane, the June afternoon was hot and I opened my compact and dabbed my shiny nose with desultory effect before I powdered quickly over the scar on my right cheek. That was what the compact was for, really. Otherwise, I'd not have bothered. Sun came through the open window, touching the deep crescent beside my mouth—lighting it as brilliantly as any studio spotlight might have done—or as lamplight in a restaurant had exposed it so cruelly and deliberately when I had gone dining with Greg that night nearly two weeks ago.

I was ready now to turn my cheek toward the kindness of shadow, as I had not done on the night when I had realized the truth about Greg. I could not blame him. He had fooled himself as much as he had fooled me, but the awakening had shocked me, made me a little ill. This time I had forgotten my own rules and trusted too much. It was better to carry my head high, and take sympathy from no one. I didn't need it. I had a good deal of the Gorham confidence—or at least I was good at bluffing—and I need not be soft and foolish and weak.

I snapped the compact shut, hiding the mirror, and put it away. My hands, at least, were unmarred. I pulled off wrist-length gloves and stared at them for comfort. Long-fingered and strong of bone they were—not small and plump and dainty like my mother's. "Hands of character as well as beauty," Mr. Donati used to say as he watched me pose them before a camera with the famous Donati rings heavy upon my fingers—rings that would be dramatically advertised in national magazines by these same praise-worthy hands.

At least I had learned to use my hands well. They had come to our rescue when Mother's failing health had forced her to leave her work in a dress shop some years before and I had found the only opening that offered itself. I had never liked modeling, yet I had learned to be good at my job. In that I could take some pride. I had kept busy, I had worked hard. No one had thought of photographing my face, however, until Greg came along. It was he who claimed that I was wasted on all this photographing of hands. It was Greg who had said, "Let's try her face," and had produced those amazing pictures that I could hardly believe I had posed for.

I shivered and tried to shut off my thoughts. Enough trouble faced me in the immediate present without any futile aching over what was past and done with.

From behind the car I heard slow footsteps and turned. Four men bore the gray casket toward its waiting carrier, and I swallowed hard at the sight of it. I had begun to miss my mother dreadfully. She had been only fifty-eight—a gentle person, with a sweetness and prettiness that had lasted to the end. All the Gorham women were beauties, people said. But I was not a Gorham, I told myself fiercely. I was Mallie Rice. I belonged to my father's name, even though he had died in France during the Second World War, and all his family was gone. In many ways he was more real to me than the Gorhams because of my mother's loving memories and all the stories she had told about him. So I would be a Rice and independent of the Gorhams. As soon as I had carried out my promise to my mother, I would return to New York and go back to modeling. My hands could earn me a living any time, as Mr. Donati often said. But I would not return to any studio where Greg might be working.

The casket had disappeared from sight and Elden Salway came to the Bentley and got in beside me.

At once he saw the unopened envelope in my lap. "Aren't you going to read your grandmother's letter?"

I resented the curt question. "Must I? Does it make any difference whether I read it or not, since I'll be going back to the house with you afterwards. No matter what she says."

He touched the starter and the engine whispered elegantly. "With me?" he echoed. "Oh, no you won't be! She'd have my head if I took you back. Not that she doesn't take it off about twice a week anyway. And I'm still here and functioning. But this time she's practically livid—so this I won't chance doing."

The black car had started ahead and we slipped smoothly after it, leaving the airport to follow the highway toward the town of Shelby, New Hampshire. I turned to study Elden Salway. The old retainer with family privileges—was that it? Or just a rather crusty New Englander? Living all my life in New York City as I had, I certainly knew nothing about family retainers, or about people who lived in mansions, for that matter, and he matched no one I'd ever met in a novel, or seen on the stage. He was a blunt-seeming man, not particularly courteous, yet not entirely unkind either.

"If she's determined not to see me, then I don't need to read her letter," I said. "But how can she be so heartless? Doesn't she care at all that her youngest daughter has just died?"

He threw me a sidelong look from beneath shaggy brows. "Your mother walked out of Silverhill before I came there with my own parents when I was a year old—so I'm not exactly aware of what went on. But I gather Blanche Gorham left of her own accord, and under her own steam—and that she returned there only once."

I touched the scar on my cheek, tracing the deep curve of its outline with a finger. I knew about that last visit Blanche had made to Silverhill when I was four years old. Mother had never forgiven herself for taking me there, because of the accident that had scarred my face.

"She was only seventeen when she ran away to marry my father," I protested. "Why should they hold a grudge against her all these years? She was a kind, gentle, generous person. As long as I knew her, she never deliberately hurt anyone, so how could her family want to disown her? Since I was born late in her life—eighteen years after her marriage, why should anything that happened so long in the past be held against me?"

Elden Salway's hands were quietly in control upon the wheel as we followed the black car along a curving road lined with pine woods.

"You don't know your grandmother," he said. "Mrs. Julia lost her youngest daughter a long time ago, and I guess she lost everything else that counted at about the same time. Your branch of the family can't mean anything to her now. Her life goes along the way she wants it. She doesn't need an unknown granddaughter coming here to stir up old troubles. Your mother wrote to her, you know. Wrote a week or so ago. I thought the roof would blow right off the house—though she's been close-mouthed about that letter. Hasn't given out a peep about what was in it."

I knew Mother had written, though I had not seen the letter. "This is between your grandmother and me," Mother had said. "There are certain things you need to know about your family and I mean to see that you're told before I die. Then you'll be armed to go back there and do what must be done for your poor Aunt Arvilla."

Arvilla had been the real beauty of the family, Mother

had always said. She was the daring one, the exciting one, who had run away and defied the Gorhams to go on the stage back in the Twenties. Mother had told me stories about her when I was small—thrilling tales about the big sister she had so admired and could never be like. "Fritzie Vernon," Arvilla had called herself on the stage for the brief time when she had startled and shocked the whole Gorham clan by becoming an overnight rage, a musical comedy star on Broadway. Yet what good had her daring rebellion done her? Julia Gorham had eventually sent her son Henry, who was the middle child, to bring his sister home, and Arvilla had stayed home ever since. When Mother returned to Silverhill after my father's death, she was shocked at Arvilla's state. During the years afterwards she had brooded over her sister, but I had little knowledge of whether Arvilla had improved or deteriorated since then.

"How is my Aunt Arvilla?" I asked Elden Salway.

His face seemed to darken, as though the thought of her disturbed him. "Crazy as a coot," he said and closed his mouth firmly upon the words.

"I want to see her," I told him. "I'm still going to Silverhill, whether my grandmother likes it or not."

He gave me a sidelong look and said nothing.

Rebelliously I flicked the letter with my finger. I must begin to take stock, I knew. I was twenty-three years old, with a shattered romance that had injured my pride, but probably hadn't broken my heart permanently. Perhaps marriage was not for me. Perhaps children were not for me. Nevertheless, there was a future I must work out for myself, and I meant to make it as satisfying as possible. First, I would see Silverhill. I would talk to Aunt Arvilla and deliver my mother's message. What's more, I would have a look at the background that had bred me. Even though I had grown up far away from Mt. Abenaki, the region that circled the mountain was in my blood. Silverhill had created me, too, and I had the strong feeling that the

hurtful matters my mother had refused to talk about must
be unearthed, clarified. If I was honest, it was not only because of poor Fritzie-Arvilla that I wanted to visit Silverhill,
and I would not be bullied by Julia Gorham as my mother
had apparently been. I had to find out about *me,* and I
knew well enough how to stand up to buffetings. So let her
do her worst.

"Got a lot of your grandma in you, haven't you?" said
Elden Salway in my ear.

I glanced at him, startled, and saw the grin tighten his
mouth again. He was actually enjoying my misery. What
a curious way he had of smiling—not spreading his lips,
but pulling them into a grimace. His mouth, in repose, was
that of a thoughtful, sensitive man, yet he constantly
pressed it into something far less attractive.

"What do you know about me?" I demanded. "How can
you say a thing like that?"

"Chips all over both your shoulders!" he said. "And your
chin's a lot like old Mrs. Julia's, as well as your eyes. Might
be entertaining if you come out to Silverhill, at that. Maybe
a good stirring up is what everybody out there needs, including your Cousin Gerald. Too much of the time they sit
around and let Mrs. Julia tell them how to breathe. All
except me."

"What are they like?" I asked him. "What are they all
really like?"

He grunted. "Come and see for yourself—but don't tell
Mrs. Julia I said that. Anyway, there's the house now, if
you want to look. Best view of it to be had around here."

I turned my head quickly and looked out the window.
We were following the road at a moderate pace, the black
car moving decorously ahead as it curved around the edge
of a lake—or a pond, as it was called in New Hampshire.
Across a blue surface that repeated the sunny June sky,
green lawns rose gently, spreading wide to reach thick woods

on either hand. Where the hill leveled stood the house—that
gray ghost of a house with silver birches framing it: Silverhill! Behind it rose Mt. Abenaki—a grand and fitting back-
drop, deep blue-gray in the distance.

There was no more than a glimpse to be had of acres of
lawn and trees, of the strange hybrid architecture of the
house, but the reality bore out the long implanted picture
in my mind. From my mother's accounts I knew what to
expect. The Gothic-towered central house rose in square,
solid dignity to its mansard roofs and dormer windows, just
as Grandfather Zebediah Gorham's father had originally
built it. I knew about its strange inner wall, the result of a
still older feud in the family. And I knew, too, how Zebediah
—Diah, as they called him—with his dashing, irreverent,
world-traveled ways, had added on the wide, two-storied
wings that spread out from either side at the back, as if
they would lift the solid older house frivolously off the
ground. In the beginning the result had been considered
an atrocity, but Silverhill had grown at last to be all of one
piece. It belonged to itself in its individuality and was now
exactly as people expected it to be—as I, in my young
imaginings, had always known it would be. Neither ugly nor
beautiful. A silver house spreading wide among its silver
birches, and still housing a woman who had once been a
fabulous beauty, who still ruled autocratically without set-
ting foot off her land. I wondered why, at the sight of it,
I experienced no elation, no sense of belonging, but only
a slight feeling of dread. How much I had to dread, I could
not of course know at that point.

I must have made some sound, given a long sigh that
drew Elden Salway's attention. Perhaps he interpreted it
as approval, for he nodded as if in agreement.

"Wait till you see the garden," he said. "Wait till you
see what I've done with the garden around in back." There
was a note in his voice that answered any puzzle about
why he had stayed all his life at Silverhill. He loved the

place, just as Mother had loved it long ago. Somehow I did not think I would ever love it.

"Grandfather Diah built a conservatory too, didn't he?" I said. "With a glass dome, and—"

His grunt was louder this time and it had a disgusted sound. "If I had my way I'd tear down that whole monstrosity. Arvilla's turning into a hothouse plant herself, nursing all that unhealthy growth."

For no reason at all a chill seemed to touch me, as though there was something here to frighten and threaten me. Something my conscious mind did not recognize, but that some inner part of me knew—and feared.

"We're getting into town now," the man beside me said. "Shelby's only fifteen minutes from Silverhill by this road. A fellow gets out in the country fast in New Hampshire. We'll go straight to the cemetery."

I seemed to know the old streets we followed, overhung with meeting branches of oak and maple. The village green with the white courthouse at one end, and the steepled white church at the other, seemed familiar. Perhaps I was bred to all this through my mother's affectionate telling.

"Will no one at all be at the cemetery?" I repeated, my heart sinking a little at the nearness of what must now be done.

"Your grandmother has sent her minister, Dr. Worth. Nobody else."

"Then she might have sent him to the airport, at least," I said tartly. "Or her lawyer, or family doctor."

A growl of laughter issued from Elden Salway's throat, startling me again. "Instead of me, you mean? Or at least I might have dressed up, don't you think? But remember, we all have our orders. The idea is to insult you, offend you, send you packing as fast as you can go. Make you understand just how much they don't think of your mother, *or* of her daughter at Silverhill. Doc Martin lives at the house, you know. Or maybe you don't. But nobody's dared to tell him. Not after Mrs. Julia gave her orders. He's the only one who might get up on his high horse and talk about principles and family duty and such. Dr. Wayne Martin's the one old Mrs. Julia won't fight with—because he holds the power of need over her. He could take his boy and move out anytime. Or he could say to her, 'All right—no sleeping pills. You don't need 'em anyway.' But she does—with that mind of hers going ninety an hour as if she were a young girl at a ball. She's never found out about age—that one. But she can't do a thing with Wayne. Quiet marble, that's what he is, when he wants to be. The only mystery is why he stays there at all."

"I'd like to meet him," I said. "I'd like to meet anyone who has the courage to stand up to my grandmother."

"Oh, he's got that all right. And he's the best doctor around here, besides. Comes in handy with Arvilla. There're some who say he has to be a good doctor to make up for that father of his. Old Doc Martin is dead, but there aren't many old-timers who have a good word for him. Well, here we are."

The black car had turned off the road through a wide gate. The old cemetery sloped downhill toward the river, where weeping willows hung above the banks. The higher levels were rimmed by old pine trees, and the headstones that marched away down the slope in neat rows had a look of age about them. Some were moss-grown where they turned their backs to the sun, and others had crumbled around the edges from age.

The fight went out of my spine. I was in the painful present which I had tried to thrust away in spite of the black car moving relentlessly ahead. I fought hard against tears. Not for anything would I show weakness that could be reported to Julia Gorham.

Events moved with swift efficiency—and all too heartlessly as well. Dr. Worth was elderly and correctly kind, but a little cool. He too had been instructed by my grandmother. The granite shaft on Grandfather Diah's grave dominated the Gorham plot, rising even more importantly than his own father's, or his son Henry's—placed there undoubtedly by Julia herself after Diah had died so tragically at Silverhill. The name ZEBEDIAH made stern New England letters on stern New England granite—though all the tales I'd heard of Diah were of a warm, loving, passionate man—a man devoted to living. To him alone of these forebears did I feel any kinship. It had to do with the cause of his death that Mother had sent me here.

My mother's grave formed a dark oblong on the far edge of the Gorham plot—as though all these sleeping relatives had turned their backs upon her. A remote place had been set aside for her, without honor, or love, or any decent respect.

There was no need to fight my tears now. My eyes were dry because I was angry again. I stood without weeping as the casket was lowered into the pit and Dr. Worth murmured words I did not trouble to attend. How could such words mean anything when he had never known the gentle person who had once been Blanche Gorham? I shut him out and said my own quiet prayer. Elden Salway stood beside me, and for the first time I sensed grudging sympathy in the man. He was Gorham-oriented, but he could look outside as well, wryly grinning, both at himself and at Silverhill.

It was over quickly. Ordinarily the mourners would have gone weeping away in their cars, leaving the grave to be filled in unobserved. Dr. Worth held my hand for a moment with professional sympathy and wished me a good flight home. I said stonily that I wasn't going home, and he took his hand away as though I had pinched him. I did not watch as he left the cemetery.

"What are you going to do now?" Elden Salway asked. "Anything more I can help you with?"

Clearly he did not want to leave me rudderless. Clearly

some sense of injustice troubled him and for a few minutes we stood together while shovelfuls of earth rang upon the casket. Then he spoke to me gruffly.

"I've got your suitcase in the back of the car. Picked it up at the airport. Where do you want me to leave it?"

"Take it with you," I told him. "I'll call for it at Silverhill."

He gave me a quick salute, a look that had a certain respect in it, and went off to where the dignified gray car waited—a car that matched the house at Silverhill. I heard it go purring away, but I did not follow it with my eyes. I moved from the graveside and walked about the lonely, peaceful enclosure with its marble and granite markers, its grassy slopes, its dandelions and buttercups growing heedlessly among the grass. Here was none of the studied tidiness of a city cemetery. There was a scent of pines on the light, warm breeze, and everywhere a sense of peace. One could not feel anguish for the untroubled sleepers in such a place.

It was the sight of flowers here and there upon the graves that brought my tears at last. The gravediggers had finished and gone away, and there was no one to see me cry. I returned to sit on the grass near my mother's grave, and now I wept without restraint because Blanche's mother had sent not even a rosebud for her lost daughter, and because I had taken no time for flowers myself. Bare earth seemed rough and ugly. My mother did not deserve to be left like that.

The soft thud of someone running lightly over the turf and down the slope between the graves reached me and I looked around to see that a boy about nine years old had come into the cemetery. He was an angular boy, with ankles that had a tendency to grow too quickly out of blue denim jeans. His light brown hair stood up in an unruly cowlick on one side of his head, and in one hand he held an assortment of wilting wild flowers. These he carried to a grave not far from me and laid them gently upon the low mound. For a few moments he stood very still beside its stone marker, his back toward me, his young shoulders spelling sorrow. Then he straightened himself with a deliberate effort—and turned about to see me for the first time.

He seemed a solemn child and the look of his brown eyes was sober and faintly surprised as he regarded me. I noted the angular triangle of his small face as he came toward me—a face with wide cheekbones tapering to a pointed chin. Generous freckles sprinkled a nose that was still a child's nose, lacking character and shape, yet faintly impudent in contrast to eyes that seemed too gravely adult. His brown eyelashes were amazingly thick and long.

"Hello," I said, and brushed away my tears to smile at him.

He came close to me, still staring. "Someone has died." It was statement, not question, as he flicked a glance at the raw mound of earth and then fixed his unblinking look upon me again. His eyes noted my cheek and did not turn away, but I never minded the regard of a child. Later he might ask me straight out why my face was marked, and I would not mind that either.

"Yes," I agreed. "Someone has died. My mother has just been buried here."

He nodded his understanding. "My mother is over there."

"I saw you bringing her flowers. Where did you get them? I haven't any for my mother's grave."

"If you don't mind wild flowers, there are lots all around. I'll show you, if you like."

"Wild flowers are best," I told him. "Flowers I can pick myself."

He knew all the hidden corners of this place. I shut away Julia Gorham's letter in my handbag and followed as he led me to the stone wall. It was a low wall and we climbed over easily and filled our arms with Queen Anne's lace and daisies and buttercups. When we returned to scatter them across the dark earth I felt a little better for making this offering of love, and because I had been helped by someone who had shown me sympathy.

The boy was still curious, however—not staring so boldly as at first, but still stealing quick, studying looks, as though I puzzled him greatly.

"I'm waiting for my father," he said. "He's coming in a little while to drive me home. Do you care if I stay with you until he comes?"

"I'd like that," I told him simply.

He sat crosslegged on the grass, with me beside him, and blinked his long fawn's lashes, studying me again. Soon, I thought, he would ask about the mark on my cheek. But he did not and his sudden question startled me.

"Do you like birds?" he asked.

He could scarcely have spoken stranger words, considering my long-endured phobia about caged birds. Wild birds —birds that sang from the branches of a tree and never came near me—these I did not mind. But with caged birds I always had the curious, unreasoning fear that they might get out, and if they did they would fly at me, hurt me in some way. Once when I was about ten and we had gone visiting a friend of my mother's, the woman had taken her parakeet out of its cage and let it fly about the room. The harmless little creature had lighted on my shoulder and I had gone promptly into hysterics. There had been still other times—once when we'd gone into a pet shop to look at puppies, and there had been birds all around, safely shut in their cages. Mother had needed to get me out of there fast, before I repeated my ridiculous performance.

Sometimes I had the feeling that my mother knew very well why I reacted this way, but for some reason she would never tell me. I had come to suspect that my bird fear was connected in some way with the scar on my cheek—but she would not answer my questions, and became so nervous and upset when I tried to talk to her about it that eventually

I desisted. On each occasion she promised that we would discuss the matter "another time"—but of course that other time never came. I seldom thought of this old childhood fear anymore. When I visited friends who owned birds I simply stayed away from the cages and suppressed the foolish quivering that ran along my nerves.

Now this small boy with the cowlick and the solemn look had asked me out of a clear sky whether I liked birds. For a moment or two I could only gape at him blankly, so that he sensed my bewilderment and tried to reassure me.

"It's just that you look so much like Aunt Fritzie," he said, as though this explained everything.

This was as startling as the question about birds, and in the face of my continued astonishment, he hurried on.

"Of course her name isn't really Fritzie, but she likes me to call her that. And she isn't really my aunt. But she likes that, too—and I don't mind."

"Is your Aunt Fritzie by any chance Arvilla Gorham?" I asked.

"Yes, of course," he said. "Do you know her?"

I shook my head. "Not yet, but I hope to. How do you happen to know her?"

"I live at Silverhill where she lives," he answered. "My name's Chris Martin. After Mom died, Dad and I went back there to stay. It's where he grew up after his own parents died, you know. So of course I see Aunt Fritzie all the time."

Elden Salway had spoken of a "Doc Martin" who stayed at Silverhill. This boy must be his son. Very soon the father —the man who had not been told of my coming lest he side against Grandmother Julia—would be here. A possible course of action began to stir in my mind.

I snapped open my bag and took out my grandmother's letter. Chris Martin watched me while I slit the creamy envelope and removed the folded sheet with its richly engraved

SILVERHILL at the top. I had seen similar notepaper before, though without this heading. Gorham Notepapers were known all over the country, but this was clearly private stock.

The black handwriting was strong, forceful, and she had used a pen with a broad nib—no sleezy ballpoint. The words told me exactly what I expected to hear from her: that she no longer recognized Blanche as her daughter. Because Blanche's name had once been Gorham, and because Zebediah would have wished it, she was to be allowed burial in the family plot. But that was where all obligation ended. I was expected to go home at once and make no claim upon the family.

I stiffened as I read. Here was something more than I had expected—words far more cruel than had ever been spoken to me before.

"If you've come for money," she wrote, "you are wasting your time. When I die, Silverhill, and everything in it, every cent I own, will go to my grandson Gerald Gorham, the son of my son Henry. There will be nothing for you. If you have come here to attempt blackmail because of your mother's absurd fabrications, then I shall deal with you as blackmailers deserve."

Warmth burned my cheeks as I read the outrageous words. The paper in my hands trembled with the fury that flashed through me. How dared she—oh, how dared she? Blackmail? As if my mother had ever intended anything of the sort!

"You sure look mad," said the small boy who watched me. "Your eyes are just about shooting sparks, the way Mrs. Julia's eyes can do. And your face is awfully red—except for that little new moon thing on your cheek. That's white. Are you angry with me?"

This time it was harder to smile. "Of course not. I—I'm upset—"

"Here comes Dad," the boy said. "You can ask him, if

something worries you. He can always figure out what to do."

I turned to look up the slope of hill toward the cemetery gate, and put my right hand to my cheek. Moving without haste, the man came toward us and I had time to see him clearly as he approached. "Quiet marble" when he was angry, Elden Salway had said. Yes, he could be that, I thought, though he was smiling at his son now, as he came toward us between the rows of stone angels and bodiless cherub faces.

He was a big man and tall—taller than I—and his shoulders had breadth under his lightweight summer suit. His head was bare, with a thick dark shock of hair that tumbled in a peak above a tanned forehead. His son's cowlick in reverse. His eyes had a gray, steady, measuring look, his mouth was wide, his chin marked by a deep cleft. I had the feeling that this was a man who would not be easily fooled, and who would pamper no malingering patient with a bedside manner.

He returned my stare as he approached, as if he too took inventory, his look so intent that I felt suddenly confused and ill at ease. Sooner or later I would have to take my hand from my cheek, and that was something I always hated to do. Astonishingly, he did it for me. Without speaking he bent and pulled my hand away, staring without subterfuge at the deep scar—almost as if he expected to find it there. Then he smiled at me with warmth and kindness, and with neither pity nor sympathy. There was recognition in his look and nothing of marble.

"You can't be anyone but Mallie Rice," he said. "I'm Wayne Martin and the last time I saw you I was fourteen, and you were four. You've grown up looking the way your Aunt Arvilla must have looked when she was young."

He did not do the thing I was so accustomed to, and that I always waited for in a new acquaintance. He did not look, suddenly frozen, at my cheek, and then quickly take his eyes away, not permitting them to stray toward that part of my face again. I was used to that distressed avoidance which pretended no mark was there, but this man simply studied the scar with interest, and when his eyes moved in that direction he looked at it again—as he looked at my hair, and my eyes, and my mouth. I had a sudden feeling of having known him very well back in those days when I was four, of having found, unexpectedly, an old friend who would stand beside me now. I gave him warm smile for smile and I did not put my hand to my cheek again.

"Her mother died," Chris said, explaining me. "I've been helping her get flowers for the grave. But why does she look so much like Aunt Fritzie?"

"Because she's Aunt Fritzie's niece," Wayne Martin said. "And that means she's Mrs. Julia's granddaughter." He looked at the raw grave with bright wild flowers carpeting it, and already beginning to wilt. "I'm sorry about your mother, but I don't understand. No one told me. Mrs. Julia knows you're here, of course? You've been out to Silverhill?"

"I haven't," I said. "Mr. Salway met me at the airport with instructions from my grandmother to bring me here and then tell me to go away as soon as possible. She has written me a letter to that effect, besides. She seems to think I've come here to blackmail her in some way."

The look of annoyance in Wayne Martin's gray eyes was gratifying. "Julia knows I've always been against her absurd feuding," he said. "I suppose that's why I haven't been told. She knew I'd lecture her. And I'm going to."

In spite of his reassuring words, I wondered fleetingly how much he knew. "Feuding" seemed too light a word for the source of the trouble that had sent my mother running from Silverhill, and had left her with a feeling of horrified self-blame for the rest of her life.

"What do you mean to do?" Wayne Martin went on. "Are you going straight back to New York as she wishes?"

"I mean to visit Silverhill," I said. "My mother wanted me to go there—and I shall, if it's possible."

"It's possible," he said.

I caught that sense of marble now—cool and very quiet. Hard, too, unyielding, implacable. I suspected that his patients would do exactly as he told them—and no nonsense. At the same time I had the curious wish that he would always be on my side and never turn this cold implacability against me.

"I'll bring you there myself," he promised, as if the matter was settled.

I had to test him. "Perhaps you won't if you read my grandmother's letter."

He did not take it from my hand. "I don't need to read it. I know the ruses she can figure out, the tricks she can play. Her mind has lost none of its agility in her old age. Wait for me here while I go down the road and make a phone call. When I come back I'll drive you to Silverhill. I have a house call to make out that way, and I must take Chris home." He looked at the boy. "Stay with her, will you, son? She's an old friend and I don't want her to get away."

He went off with a long stride which indicated purpose not likely to be defeated.

When he had gone I went with the boy to stand beside that other grave, where grass had grown thickly over the mound. There was lettering on the small headstone and I bent to read. The words ANN BELOVED had been inscribed simply on the stone.

"It's been two years," Chris said, "but I still miss her."

A fresh mistiness crossed my vision, though now the tears were for another loss besides my own.

Together we walked toward the gate of the cemetery. There was no one about and we sat on the low wall and waited. I had a strong sense of everything placed in capable

hands—hands which would set misunderstandings and injustice to rights. I no longer felt either angry or afraid. Chris
and I smiled, accepting each other in liking and good will.

"One thing—" the boy said, "—if you come to stay at
Silverhill now, you'll be in time for the wedding. It's going
to be very exciting. Mrs. Julia's going to have the ceremony
performed in the gallery that Mr. Diah built. She may
even have people in from town. Hardly anybody comes to
Silverhill anymore."

This seemed a startling bit of information. As far as I
knew there was no one very young at Silverhill. My Cousin
Gerald was about Elden's age—in his early forties—and long
a bachelor. The women were old.

"Who is getting married?" I asked.

Chris started to answer, and then wrinkled the freckles
on his nose in an apologetic grimace. "Dad says I talk too
much. He said I wasn't to mention this away from the house.
I forgot."

"That's all right," I assured him, wondering if it might
be his father who was remarrying. But the boy did not
sound sufficiently involved, if that was the case.

"Elden Salway says it will be the death of somebody if
they do get married," the boy went on. "But Elden always
talks that way—so I haven't really told you anything, have
I?"

I shook my head and agreed that he had not. Nevertheless, the word "death" rang unpleasantly in my ears. There
had been too much of violent death there among the birches
and I wondered who it was that Elden—that dark, sardonic
man—might threaten, and whether my coming would in-
volve me in more than I bargained for. My brief moment
of feeling that I could relax because all my problems were
in capable hands had faded. My problems were ones that
no one else could solve. I closed my eyes to bright sun-
light and a strange, faint pulsing of wings seemed to sweep

through me, stirring old fears, old memories I could never quite grasp.

In a nearby pine tree a squirrel chattered. The sun shone and the boy beside me whistled tunelessly. I did not move and gradually my senses quieted. Unpleasantness might very well await me at my mother's home—but certainly nothing more. I was no timid girl to turn and flee simply because no one had made me welcome—or because I had as a child been afraid of birds.

Chris said, "Bet I can throw a pine cone farther than you can."

I flung off the sense of wings, the memory of white trees around a silver house, and took up his challenge.

II

Wayne Martin's car was neither sleek nor gray, and it did not run in elegant silence. Its color was a dusty black; it was several years old and it complained on every hill. Now and then the doctor talked to it coaxingly and it seemed to respond.

Chris sat between us in the front seat, alert to everything on the road. I could feel his slight body, boy-warm in the summer heat, one bare arm slightly damp against my own. It was a long while since I had been as close as this to a child and I was surprised at the feeling of tenderness for someone young which sprang up in me.

Before we got into the car Wayne Martin had asked about my baggage and I told him I'd persuaded Elden Salway to take it out to Silverhill. That was the first time I heard Wayne laugh. It was a warming sound and no pinched-in city laughter that was afraid to call attention to itself.

"Julia may have her hands full with you, at that," he

said. "But don't be too hard on her, Mallie. Remember your grandmother's an old woman and life has dealt her some crushing blows. We have to admire her spirit and courage."

I made no promises, felt no sympathy. Not after that letter and the final unkindness to my mother.

"Of course you may not meet her at all," he warned as we followed the same curving road I had come along only an hour before. "She says she won't see you, won't talk to you. But you are to spend the night at least at Silverhill, and her daughter-in-law—your Aunt Nina—will make you understand your grandmother's wishes. This will give you a toe in the door. After that we'll count on her curiosity to do the rest."

I glanced at him over Chris's head, noting the clear line of his profile—the strong-bridged nose, the set of his jaw. Dr. Wayne Martin would make a powerful friend, even in a court made up of Gorhams.

"How did you manage this?" I asked.

He shot me a quick look and I knew there was humor in him, as well as purpose and strength. "I have my secret methods. I only twisted her arm a little."

This was my chance to ask questions, as I had wanted to ask them of Elden. "Is the house still like a museum? When I was little Mother used to tell me about the way Julia and Diah would take off for Europe on buying sprees, and how they'd come home with a mixture of all sorts of things—from Chippendale chairs to tapestries from Valenciennes. Mother didn't know till she was six or seven that not everyone else lived in the midst of museum treasures just the way she did."

"I expect it's more like a museum than ever," Wayne said, "with your Cousin Gerald as curator. He has a more professional approach than your grandparents ever had. I gather they liked to use their treasures and live with what they bought. Gerald is more interested in labeling and preserving—and I suppose that's a good idea too. There's a lot of valuable stuff out there."

I nodded, remembering. "Mother started taking me to the Metropolitan and other museums around New York almost as soon as I could walk. She said I had to understand about such things as knowing the difference between Chippendale and Sheraton, for instance."

"Preparing you for Silverhill?" Wayne asked.

"It always seemed that way, even when there was so little possibility that I'd ever go there. I'm afraid I wasn't an apt pupil. I liked the mummies and suits of armor better than I liked all the furniture and art objects."

Chris broke in eagerly with his own contribution. "Dad, Uncle Gerald has brought out all that old jewelry Mrs. Julia would never let anyone touch before. I'll bet Mallie'd like to see the things those old-fashioned ladies used to wear."

I was more interested in my cousin than in old jewelry.

"How does Gerald manage?" I asked. "I mean—I know he has something dreadfully wrong with his right arm."

"Mainly he manages to hide it and himself," Wayne said, sounding less sympathetic than I would have expected a doctor to be. "He has always made too much in his own mind of the fact that his father was a tremendously vigorous man physically. Henry was a notable athlete in his younger days and won all sorts of cups for his swimming and running, to say nothing of being a whiz on the tennis court. I gather he was disappointed in his son from the first, and Gerald knew it. Henry wanted him to be an all-round athlete like himself. Nevertheless, Gerald has a brilliant mind—if he'd be satisfied with that—and he has done a great job with the Gorham collections. His writings on the subject have been published in journals around the world."

Mother had told me about Gerald's arm when I was ten or so, and I had used it to develop a little drama of self-pity I used to play out before my bedroom mirror. I could remember standing before the glass, talking out loud to Cousin Gerald, of whom I had no memory. "The cursed Gorhams," I used to call us companionably, if melodramatically—though his handicap was one of birth, not accident like mine, and a great deal more serious.

"It's time Gerald got on with living his own life," Wayne said impatiently.

At once I found myself on the defensive. There seemed a special kinship between Gerald and me—more than the relationship of blood. It was not always easy for the marked to get on with living. I looked at Wayne Martin over the top of his son's rumpled head, resenting his abrasive words about Gerald.

"Aren't doctors supposed to be kind and considerate— develop a bedside manner?" I asked tartly. "Do you frighten your patients into obeying you?"

"Saves a lot of time if they do," he said. "I've never thought self-pity helped anyone."

That made me wince, since I was not always guiltless of the tendency.

Fortunately Chris went on with his news of Silverhill. "Aunt Fritzie got into the jewelry today. She stole the moonstone necklace and gave it to Jimmy. Jimmy hid it—so there's been a lot of excitement. You should have heard Mrs. Julia! They still haven't found it. It's of amethysts and moonstones, Uncle Gerald says, and was made about a hundred years ago by a very famous jewelry designer in Europe."

His father groaned. "No wonder old Mrs. Julia's in a temper, what with one thing and another." He glanced at me. "This is plunging you into a difficult emotional atmosphere, I'm afraid."

I wondered about the wedding Chris had mentioned and whether, judging by Elden's words which Chris had quoted, that might not add to the difficult situation. But after the boy's warning, I dared not ask.

"I expect it will be difficult anyway," I said. "Why doesn't someone tell Jimmy to give the necklace back?"

Chris snickered. "Because Jimmy's a macaw. You know —a kind of parrot. He talks a little, but not well enough to say what he's done with it. I'm supposed to help look for the necklace this afternoon because I know some of Jimmy's hiding places."

So there was a pet bird in the house, I thought uneasily, remembering that sense of pulsing wings I'd felt only a little while ago.

"We're on Gorham land now," Wayne said. "The first Gorham planted these Norway pines. The acreage has shrunk a bit as parcels have been sold off, but there's still enough land to keep unwanted neighbors from springing up nearby. It's a good thing none of us get lonely."

I had not noticed when the car left the highway, but now I watched the finely graveled dirt road curve ahead, following a narrow aisle between tall red pines. There were no fences along this private way, and one could easily leave the road to walk among the well-spaced trees.

"Imagine owning a private forest!" I said.

"In the old days the Gorhams owned a good many forests. That's where all their paper came from. But now the mills have moved farther north and there's not much manufacturing done around this area. The main sales office is still in Shelby, but that's about all."

We wound into the open again, along the edge of a pond, and I saw we were on the Gorham side of the same water I had seen before; on the side where wide lawns sloped gently up to the silver-gray house. The drive crossed at the foot of the lawn, following the water, then turned up the hill toward the rear, where hundreds of birches stood out white against the darker pines. Wayne did not drive to the double garage behind the house, but turned again and drew up in an oval space before the entrance.

When he opened the car door for me I got out and stood

for a moment looking up at the tall forbidding central tower that fronted the house. It stood out foursquare, protruding from the rest, with windows running three stories up, and no rounding of its shape until it reached the roof and sloped to a high pitch. From the very peak an eagle weather-vane commanded the world. The rest of the old house stood back a little from the entrance tower, its immensely tall windows rising from floor to ceiling in the lower rooms. The newer wings Diah had built were farther back and I could see little of their extension from my place before the front door.

"I'll take you in," Wayne said.

I hesitated for an uncertain moment and then went up the steps.

Chris was ahead of us at the wide door of handsome black wood, intricately carved. A door, surely, that had been transported intact from some European palace. From its center a bronze lion's head snarled at us, offering the ring in its teeth as a knocker. Chris did not touch it. The door was unlocked and he opened it to let us into a square foyer the width of the tower, with a black and white marble floor and dark-paneled wood all around. Along one wall stood a great medieval chest with a brass candelabrum set upon it, while on the opposite side a huge carved wooden chair reared itself—a chair from some monastery, perhaps. Near it a full suit of armor stood guard, gleaming brightly from its helmet to the lance held in a mailed hand.

Chris tapped upon the closed visor as though he expected it to open. "This is Mortimer," he said. "Sometimes he talks to me."

His father smiled. "I know—he used to talk to me too. Maybe you'd better run along and hunt up those moonstones before Aunt Fritzie gets into any more trouble."

"I'll see you," Chris told me gravely, and disappeared through the right-hand door of two that opened off the tower base of the foyer.

"I often wonder how good this place is for the boy," his father said, looking after him. "I grew up here, but I got away a bit more than he does—especially in summertime. Things weren't quite so elderly then."

"Why do you stay?" I asked bluntly.

"Old debts to pay, perhaps. But that's a long story. Let's save it for another time." An unhappiness seemed to cloud his eyes.

I stood beside him at the left-hand door, conscious that he was indeed a good bit taller than I, though I was a tall girl. Conscious too of how unexpectedly comfortable I felt with him—as though I had known him very well for a long while, so there was no need to wear a chip on my shoulder, no need to hide the scar he had seemed to expect, and did not mind.

"We never lock our doors out here," he said, "but today we'll be formal and have ourselves announced. Are you ready?"

I wasn't ready of course. There was no way in which I could be prepared for whatever lay beyond that door, though even then I could not know how little prepared I was. I could only remind myself that my grandmother Julia had been wickedly rude and unfair and that there was no reason why I need be afraid of her, or need take anything from her, for that matter.

Wayne seemed to realize that I braced myself, for he smiled at me as he put a finger to the bell. "Why did your mother want you to come here?"

I answered in a rush, lest the door open on my blurted words. "Because of Aunt Arvilla. Because there's something I must talk to her about, tell her."

This seemed to surprise him. "Arvilla? You won't get far with her, you know. Fritzie's only wish is to forget everything about the past. Her mind seems to have provided her with an escape from the painful. Something human brains sometimes manage when life becomes more than we can cope with. When she has spells of remembering, there's the devil to pay. So if you go stirring her up, no one is going to thank you—including me."

"But is it right to leave her like that?" I asked.

His dark brows quirked and his eyes seemed to challenge my words. His chin with the cleft in it appeared to harden against me. "Are you in any position to know what is right for Arvilla Gorham? Or to know what has been done for her?"

Here was marble again, I thought, and knew that I ventured on dangerous ground if I wanted Wayne Martin for my friend. Yet I dared not back down.

"My mother must have known," I said. "It's because of her that I've come here."

For a moment longer the marble held against me. Then he relaxed, shrugging. "I don't suppose it matters. They won't permit you to see her anyway. Mostly she stays on her own side of the wall—*the* wall, you know—built into the structure when the house was built. She'll be kept out of your way, I'm sure."

Footsteps sounded in the hall beyond and the door was opened by a young woman, perhaps in her mid-thirties. She smiled at Wayne in welcome and gave me a quick, bright look out of brown eyes that seemed a little wary. Her neatly trimmed brown hair matched her eyes and waved softly back from a good forehead. Her aqua blue uniform showed the gentle rounding of her figure, and a crisp nylon apron was tied about her waist.

"Hello, Kate," Wayne said. And then to me, "This is Kate Salway. Kate, this is Miss Malinda Rice."

Salway? Somehow I was surprised. Elden had seemed a solitary man. The girl's left hand was bare of any ring, so she must be his sister, though there was no resemblance between them.

She gestured us toward the open door of a large room

across the hall that seemed more drawing room than parlor. "I'll go call Mrs. Nina," she said. "She's out in back trying to calm Mrs. Julia."

"The moonstones?" Wayne asked.

"The moonstones and—" She glanced at me, then quickly away, and hurried off down the long hall to disappear through a door at the dim far end.

Wayne stood for a moment at the foot of a flight of stairs that curved upward on our right. With a sense of recognition my eyes followed the expanse of wall that rose beside the stairs.

"This must be *the* wall," I said. "Mother used to tell me about it when I was little. About how those first two Gorham brothers didn't speak, and built their house so they needn't communicate."

Wayne Martin nodded. "The wall cuts the house exactly in half and nobody has ever troubled to break through it. Of course Diah built a gallery out in back, connecting the two sides, but in the house proper the only entrances are by way of the front door and tower balconies."

He led the way through a wide doorway with its wings folded open, and into a room that was astonishingly beautiful, and must be very little changed from the days when my mother had lived in this house. It was a large enough room to hold two sofas gracefully—one a Duncan Phyfe with thunderbolt and drapery-swag carving across the back; the other a graceful Chippendale, upholstered in pale gold damask. Satin draperies with a softly faded design in gold and amethyst hung beside enormously high windows, and the rose and blue colors of the two Persian rugs had muted to soft beauty over the years. Overhead hung two crystal chandeliers, with tall white candles set in their holders. The wallpaper was done in a tiny all-over design of gray-blue petals, and the wood moldings had been left in their original golden chestnut, richly beautiful. No one had lightened rooms with white paint in the days when this house was built, or wished to hide the luster of finely grained wood.

After a quick look around, my eyes sought the space above the brown and white marble of the mantel. Just one portrait hung there, however, instead of the two I expected. That a second had hung beside the first was evident in the faint outline left on the wall, and by the off-center position of the remaining picture.

"That's Julia Gorham, isn't it?" I said, and stared in wonder at the young face of my grandmother.

"She was twenty-four when that was painted," Wayne said. "There's another of your grandfather that was done at the same time which is supposed to hang beside it."

The girl in the picture had been a year older than I and long married. She was dark-haired and wore a fluffed pompadour and a great chignon at the back of her slightly turned head. Her dress was of garnet silk, and a deep "V" showed the lovely column of her throat as it curved to meet the clear line of the chin. Full lips smiled faintly, secretly, as if she thought of something wickedly pleasing, and the great amethyst eyes—beneath dark brows—were dreamy. The artist had caught her in a relaxed and almost quiet moment —yet not altogether so. The long-fingered hands in her lap—hands like mine!—had a certain tension about them, so that I half expected her to lift them in some quick, commanding gesture. The portrait was three-quarters, with pale, neutral draperies behind the dominant figure—but it was the face that held the observer. A young face caught forever by the artist as Julia Gorham must have looked around 1911—all those years ago when she was twenty-four and known both here and abroad as an impetuous beauty.

I looked at the portrait, marveling. She was a complete stranger to me—then and now. Yet, because she had lived, I lived.

On the bare, polished floor of the hallway footsteps came softly hurrying, and a small woman rushed into the room, breathless and seemingly eager. Aunt Nina was hardly more than five feet tall, trim and neat, almost ageless in appearance, though she was near my mother in years. She wore her gray hair close-cropped and curly about her small head, and though she was not a pretty woman, she possessed an arresting look of alertness, due perhaps to the way she constantly lifted her chin to look up at a taller world about her. Her mouth might have been her one beauty, but she appeared to have pinched it in so long that tiny lines rayed upward from the lips and gave her a slightly disapproving look, belying the apparent eagerness of that tilted chin. Beneath thin brows that belonged to an age of plucking, her eyes were pale gray and anxious. She seemed a woman of uncomfortable contrasts, Uncle Henry's wife, Nina, and not at all the sort who might marry a famous athlete.

For a moment she stood in the double doorway surveying the room, glancing first at Wayne, and then uneasily at me, as though she hardly dared allow her gaze to rest upon her husband's niece. As if in relief, her look swept on almost at once to the wall above the mantel, finding there something she could deal with in the missing picture.

"Oh, no!" she cried, and turned toward the hall. "Kate! Where are you, Kate?"

At once Kate Salway appeared at her side and they both stared at the empty space of wall.

"Not again!" Kate wailed despairingly.

"How are we to stop this?" Nina Gorham cried. "Do something about it, will you, Kate? Before Mother Julia sees what has happened."

"I'll try," Kate said, sounding doubtful. "But you know how upset Miss Arvilla is today."

When she had gone off down the hall, Aunt Nina turned to me for a more searching look, as if she could put me off no longer. This time I recognized the quick lighting of her gaze upon my cheek, the quick darting away—and old resentment seethed in me. How dared she look at me that

way—she who had never bothered—not once—to help when
my mother was ill?

"You shouldn't have come here," she went on in a little
rush. "Whatever it is your mother put you up to, your
grandmother won't allow it. I am to tell you—"

During the drive with Wayne Martin I had calmed a
little, but now my hackles rose in quick antagonism. "I
want to see my grandmother," I said boldly. "I want to hear
from her exactly what she thinks I am up to, as you say."

Aunt Nina's small pinched mouth seemed to grow even
smaller, the pale look of her eyes more uneasy. "That
isn't possible, of course. She has no wish to see you. At her
age she has won the right to do as she likes, and she owes
you nothing—nothing at all."

Words were being repeated, I knew. Words Aunt Nina
had been instructed to speak, but as she said them I grew
aware of some emotion so strong that one could almost
smell it emanating from her small person. Suddenly I knew
what it was. Nina Gorham was afraid. She was possessed
by as deadly a fear as I had ever encountered, though I
had no idea toward whom, or what, it was directed. Surely
she was not afraid of me, though the very intensity of her
emotion touched me with its contagion and I was made
uneasy too, and fearful of some intangible quality about
Silverhill—as if it not only rejected me, but seemed to
threaten me in some way.

Wayne came to my help, quietly, firmly. "Let's not worry
about that now, Nina. Mallie is to stay for the night, and
I think she ought to meet Gerald, since he is her cousin,
and be shown around the old ancestral home. If I had
time, I'd do it myself. But I've got to have a look at the
Palmer boy's boils, and Mrs. Nestor's latest allergy rash."
He held out his hand to me, and once more his eyes were
kind. They told me to relax, not to be hurt, to take it easy.
"I'll see you later," he said as his son had done, and went
out the door, before I could so much as thank him for

bringing me here. I had a sense of loss at his going, as though a hand I had clung to had been taken away.

Nina Gorham reached for a tasseled red velvet bell pull that was an antique in itself and I heard a clamor somewhere in the depths of the house. She did not speak to me again, but turned her back as if in repudiation and faced the door.

No one had asked me to sit down, and I went idly to an octagonal table and picked up a magazine. Not until I turned the pages and it fell open to a Donati ad did I realize what I held in my hands. Never, never could I look at this particular picture without wincing. The hand photos I did not mind. They were my job, and one I had learned to do well. But here before me was my face in three-quarter view—far more beautiful than reality could ever be, thanks to Greg's clever lighting. Only the left side showed itself in detail from the pale gold of my hair to the curve of my chin. The other side faded into delicate, smoky shadow, and there was no scar visible. A heavy Donati costume piece in Florentine design circled my throat, and the visible ear wore dangling imitation emerald. I could still feel the weight of the pendant on my earlobe. I put the magazine down quickly, allowing the pages to close, wondering if anyone in this house had seen that picture and knew who had posed for it.

Kate Salway must have been far away on the other side of the house, for it took her a while to reach us and she was slightly out of breath when she came.

"Will you show Miss Rice to her room, please, Kate," Aunt Nina said. And then to me, "You will join the family for dinner at seven. Until then, perhaps you'd better remain in your room." She rushed off in her breathless way, without another glance, and Kate Salway did not look at me as she spoke.

"Your room is ready, Miss Rice. The guest rooms are on the third floor."

She led the way up the stairs and I followed, looking at everything along the way, since this might be my only chance to acquaint myself with Silverhill. I noted faded, wine-colored wallpaper, carved banisters and the graceful half-oval the stairwell made, rising beside the dividing wall.

Kate went ahead of me along the second floor, where I glimpsed a sitting room and adjacent bedroom. "Mrs. Nina's rooms," she murmured and started up the last flight.

I did not miss the fact that glass doors opened on each floor upon the tower balconies that fronted the house. Arvilla Gorham lived on the other side of the wall, Wayne had said, but I had known about these communicating doors even before he had mentioned them. At the back of my mind rebellious plans were in the making.

"It will be quiet up here," Kate Salway said, and gestured me into a bright front room. An odd remark, since everything about Silverhill seemed quiet.

The mansard roof caused the walls to slope upward in a steep pitch, leaving plenty of headroom. There were three dormer windows, cushioned with seats set deeply into them. Tieback curtains were of white dotted swiss, and the bedspread on the fourposter was of dotted white chenille. On the floor at the foot of the bed my suitcase waited for me.

"I see your brother has smuggled in my luggage," I said wryly.

Kate's brown gaze rested briefly on my face and then hurried away, though I had the feeling that her avoidance of a direct look was not because of my cheek, but because of some restraint that others had imposed upon her. Apparently Silverhill had set its curious blight upon her too, for she was another who stayed here mysteriously, as though the house had invisible tentacles which held relentlessly unless escape was quickly managed.

She ignored my remark about the suitcase and ran an exploring hand across the top of a well-polished highboy.

There could hardly have been dust on that shining surface, but she looked critically at her fingers.

"We have such a time getting maids out here," she said, speaking nervously now, as though she feared silence—or perhaps feared whatever I might say. "Girls from town never want to come this far out, and they won't live in anyway. It's too quiet and the house has a reputation besides."

This interested me. "A reputation?"

Her glance flicked my way momentarily. I wished she would relax and accept me, but I suppose the atmosphere of disapproval Aunt Nina had shed made that impossible.

"Oh, it's to be expected," she said and took a cloth from the pocket of her apron to run across the top of the highboy. "We aren't exactly like other people out here, you know."

I sensed a perverse sort of pride in her words, as though Silverhill's difference was somehow laudable.

"You grew up here, didn't you?" I asked. "Yet you never ran away?"

Her eyes met mine in the mirror, and held for the first time. For the first time she answered me simply. "Once there was a period when I meant to be a nurse, but I gave it up in my first year of training and came home. Your grandmother has been wonderful to Elden and me. We've neither of us really wanted to live anywhere else."

This seemed strange, inexplicable, considering that she was young and attractive and could surely make a better life for herself away from this house. She seemed to come to some decision and turned from the mirror to face me directly. I liked her calm wide brow, the generous width of her mouth. She did not look like a woman who would engage herself in fighting unkind, unreasonable battles.

Her next words were unexpected. "I remember the time your mother brought you here. You were such a bright, pretty little thing. And curious! You were into everything the minute anyone turned his back. I was only sixteen at the time, but I remember you very well."

My hand reached toward my cheek. "Then—you must know how this happened to me?"

A hint of alarm touched her eyes and she looked quickly away. "You mean you don't remember? You mean your mother didn't tell you?"

"It made my mother ill to talk about it," I said. "She felt that what happened was best forgotten—an accident. But I think I'll never be free of what it did to me until I know exactly what occurred."

Abruptly she was the housekeeper again, rather than a young woman who might be my friend. "It's not for me to talk about," she said primly. "Your grandmother warned us ahead of time. There's to be no talking, no offers of—of friendliness."

I understood her wariness now, her earlier care in dealing with me, her reluctance to look me straight in the face. Candor, I suspected, was far more natural to her.

"Yet you're telling me this," I said. "Do you think such orders are right or fair?"

With a hint of spirit she echoed my words. "Right? Fair? What do such things matter when it becomes necessary to live with what really *is* and make the best you can of it?"

I wondered what reality in her life she found it so difficult to live with that this was her philosophy.

"I suppose I'm not very good at making the best of things I don't like," I said. "Not even with this." And I touched my cheek. "I suppose I'm given to rushing at things to make them better. Or trying to at least."

"Even when trying is a way of breaking your heart?" This time she had flung aside her self-effacing role of housekeeper and relapsed into speaking as a woman.

She stood near the door, and I across the room, and we looked at each other openly, each trying to read the other. Kate Salway was no more the usual housekeeper than her brother was a typical gardener. Both were more family than servitors. There was in this young woman a quiet determination which would be a good thing to have on my side —had her loyalties not been so thoroughly engaged elsewhere.

Her eyes dropped first, and uneasiness repossessed her. Clearly she wanted to escape me, to end this tentative approach between us.

"If there's anything you need, you'll find a bell near the head of the stairs," she told me and turned toward the door.

She would have gone quickly away if I had not stopped her. "Wait a moment, please. Would you mind telling me whose rooms are where, so I won't blunder around when I leave this room? I know Aunt Arvilla is on the other side of the wall—"

She complied reluctantly. "Yes, her rooms are on the first floor on the other side. Chris and Dr. Martin are on the second floor on that side. The third is used for attic storage now. Mrs. Nina's rooms are on the second floor, this side, as you saw coming up. Mrs. Julia—we always say 'Mrs. Julia' and 'Mrs. Nina' to avoid two Mrs. Gorhams—has her apartment in the left wing that was built onto the house soon after she came here as a bride. And Mr. Gerald's rooms are in the right wing. But you're not supposed to go wandering around the house, Miss Rice."

I smiled at her. "I'm not a proper guest, I'm afraid. This is my grandparents' house. It's where my mother grew up. Will you tell me one thing before you leave? Dr. Martin's son spoke of a wedding coming up shortly. Who is going to be married at Silverhill?"

My words could hardly have had a more shocking effect. The healthy rose of her skin paled and her brown eyes turned suddenly stormy. I would not have expected such passion in this quiet girl.

"Chris spoke out of turn!" she cried. "There isn't going

to be any wedding—never, never!" And she flung herself about and rushed off downstairs.

I stood for a moment staring after her in astonishment. Then, since I had no clue to her vehemence, no answer to why the thought of some possible marriage should so disturb her, I turned back to my own affairs.

I lifted my suitcase to the bed and, as I hung up the few things I had brought, my mind was busy with troublesome problems. How was I to see Aunt Arvilla, and what was I to say to her if I managed such a meeting?

How was I to approach a half-demented woman and assure her that her long-held belief in a responsibility for her father's death was false, and that her sister Blanche knew what had happened that day and had charged me with information intended to free Arvilla of all sense of guilt? How could I know what effect such word, coming at this late date, might have upon Arvilla Gorham? Was it about this rejected truth that Mother had written in her secret letter to Julia Gorham? If so, why had the old lady spoken of blackmail and fought so indignantly against the idea of seeing me? What else that I might not know lay behind Grandfather Diah's death? He had fallen on the attic stairs —this Mother had told me, and everyone except my mother had held poor Arvilla responsible; had claimed in fact that she had pushed him deliberately.

What I needed was time—a chance to remain at Silverhill for a few days in order to talk to whoever would talk to me; a chance to meet Aunt Arvilla quietly, get to know her a little before I tried to carry out my mother's wishes. At the moment it seemed unlikely that I would be allowed to remain here after tonight. No time was to be allowed me.

Once I tiptoed into the empty hall and tried the double glass doors of the balcony. They opened easily and let me out upon a glassed-in tower enclosure that gave me a marvelous view. Through its windows I could see far out over Silverhill's lawns and across glassy blue water to where late

afternoon traffic sped by on the highway I had earlier
traversed. The cars seemed remote, and far removed from
a house engrossed thoroughly with its own past.

I had not come into the tower to look at the view, however, and I turned to the duplicate glass doors that led
into the other half of the house and tried their knob gently.
Though it turned, something held the doors locked on the
other side—a bolt, perhaps, or a hook that could not be
raised from this side. The glass panes were curtained and
I could not see through into the dim upper hall of Arvilla's
side of the house.

I gave up my attempt and went back to my own room.
Thoroughly spent, I flung myself full length on the bed
and tried to think of nothing. But my thoughts would not
be quiet. At once Greg's face was before my eyes, wearing
the look I had seen on it that night in the restaurant. I did
not want to remember. I wanted to wipe all that from my
mind forever. But I knew the time had come to look clearly
at Greg and at myself. Only then could I be free of him.

III

There was always the danger of responding too eagerly to
kindness, the danger of trusting too much. There had been
boys in school who liked me well enough and had sometimes taken me out, but often they were the boys other
girls my age did not care about. Grasping for superiority,
I told myself they were more sensitive, more perceptive,
more interesting than the handsome, popular boys. Quite
possibly this was true, but just as the boys I wanted to date
looked for girls who were superficially pretty, so I did not
want to date the dreamy, sensitive, shy ones who would
accept me.

Of course so suspicious and contradictory an attitude

led inevitably to humiliation, but I was too young to see how foolish I was being. When I met Greg all that changed. I let down my guard and rejected suspicion. Greg loved all that was beautiful. If he could love me, then, ergo, everything must be right with me.

In the studio he took a sensuous delight in rich contrasts of light and shadow, in the use of color, the arrangement of space. Until Greg came, I had earned a living for my mother and myself by posing my hands for Mr. Donati's jewelry, as well as for a few other firms interested in nail polish or skin cream ads. But Greg could whip up his own sort of creative storm and he told Mr. Donati that he was blind not to be using me to better effect. He demanded that he be given a try at photographing the new fake-sapphire Donati dog collar—using me!

There were cries of consternation, but Greg performed his magic with the emphasis on one half of my face, where practically every pore was visible, and faded out the other side so delicately that the beholder never guessed he was being fooled. In fact, he succeeded so well, and so repeatedly, that I was able to earn more than I had earned before, and his own reputation was enhanced besides. We helped each other, and out of this work relationship grew more than liking. Inevitably we began to go out together on evening dates, and my Pygmalion began to believe in what he had created. My guard was lowered. I trusted him, and I began a bit tentatively to fall in love.

Perhaps I was only in love with love, and responding as I could not help but respond to a perceptive man who was blind to the mark on my face. How was I to know? How could I tell the difference when the pain of old rejections had gone so deep and there was nothing else against which I could measure my new feeling of response to admiration and approval?

It was months, however, before I noticed that Greg always managed to place himself on my left side, whether we were in a theater, or a restaurant, or walking on the street. I believe he did this instinctively, scarcely aware of it himself. At other times, when my face must come full into his view, I think he simply did not look because he could not bear to accept the flaw my cheek presented. How far we dreamed ourselves into unreality—the two of us!

I cannot now remember what caused my awakening—perhaps it was no more than a slow adding up of signs. But awaken I did, with a sudden, hurtful awareness of what he was doing. At first I did not want to believe and I gave him every chance to prove me wrong. But on that last date we had together I forced myself to try him out. In the restaurant where he took me I refused the usual seat on his left, and sat opposite him with my face boldly exposed to lamplight. No matter how much it hurt us both, I had to know. I even talked about the mark on my face and told him of the times when I had been wounded because of it. I told him of a woman who had come from Shelby to visit my mother when I was eleven, and of how she had said, not knowing that I listened, "What a tragedy, your daughter's scar—when all the Gorham women have been so beautiful!" I hated my face more than ever after that, though Mother had been furious with her friend, and angry over so shallow a remark. As Greg listened, I saw his sick expression, and I grew a little ill myself. After dinner I begged off and let him take me home. There I found my mother in bed and too ill herself to comfort me ever again; able to struggle only for the last thing she wanted of me—help for her sister Arvilla. I did not know it at the time, but her letter to my grandmother must already have been on its way.

Now, lying in my room at Silverhill, I could live over the experiences of these last ten days, with all their hurt and loss, in order to accomplish a grim realization and acceptance. Never again would I be so vulnerable. I knew very well that I was too ready to hurl myself impetuously into the center of a situation, with frequently resulting hurt to myself and others. It was time I learned to move more slowly, with a more thoughtful approach. How easy it always is to make good resolutions.

At the studio next morning, Greg had found that he could not photograph me properly. Someone less skilled had taken over, but profile shots were not the same, and in a day or two I was posing again for my usual hand spots. That was when I left my job and stayed at home. Mother was ill and needed me, I told them, but I knew I would never go back.

Of course I was aware of the good advice that could be given me. I had read my psychology books and knew the trouble must be mainly with me. Only I didn't quite believe it. I supposed there were men in the world who would not weigh me by such standards that a marked cheek put me outside the pale. Yet I neither knew how to find a man like that, nor how to be free of myself. I began to see that a larger shadow lay over my life than the one created by lighting and a camera. A shadow that had its origin under the mansard roofs of Silverhill. By coming here, I had an opportunity to expose those shadows to bright, rational daylight and cure my own inner confusion. I must try to help myself as well as poor Arvilla. Perhaps I would help neither of us—but I must try. I would not let them send me away until I had managed what I'd come for.

Having made my resolve, I relaxed and fell asleep. The shadows grew long upon the lawns beneath my windows and when I awoke to look outside, I found that the white birches seemed to have gathered in around the house. Surely they had not crowded so when I had looked at them earlier. What a curious illusion!

It was nearly seven when I realized the time. I turned on a light and hurried into a mauve pink sheath that left my arms bare. As I wound the mass of the French twist more neatly at the back of my head I suddenly realized that this style of wearing my hair was not very different from the way young Julia Gorham had worn hers when that portrait downstairs was painted. Except that her hair was almost black, while mine was golden fair. Gorham hair, my mother always called it, her own being exactly the same, soft and fine, and best worn long if it was to be managed easily. Only my eyes were not Gorham—not that bright, clear Gorham blue, but with more of a violet cast, the off-blue of an amethyst, with the pupil very dark in the center. My grandmother's eyes.

I turned abruptly from the mirror and went to the door. I would leave a light burning in the room, I thought, since it would be night when I returned and I might not fancy coming up here to the darkness of a strange room.

No one was about as I followed the barrier wall downstairs. Partway down the last flight I paused on a whimsical impulse and pressed my ear against wine-colored wallpaper, wondering what went on beyond the dividing wall in this strange house. What I heard startled and chilled me. In some opposite room a woman was laughing. The sound was not one of mirth, but a high, foolish chuckling that made my scalp prickle.

I drew hastily away, half inclined to run back upstairs and make no further effort to see Arvilla Gorham. But I did not—I would not. Before falling asleep, I had resolved to accomplish what I had come for before I allowed myself to be driven from Silverhill. Wayne Martin had helped me to get this far, however doubtful he might be of my purpose. Now I must get the rest of the way myself. Nearly everyone who lived under this roof would oppose me—discounting only Chris Martin, and perhaps Aunt Arvilla herself. But I had the promise I had made my mother, and the later promise I had made myself. I meant to keep them both if I could.

Without further hesitation I went downstairs to the first floor. The long drawing room was empty and its pale blues and muted gold, its underlying carpet hues of faded rose were softly beautiful and inviting. Through double doors at the rear I glimpsed a walnut-paneled dining room, where a maid was placing silver upon linen damask. The girl slanted a quick look at me, curiosity in her eyes. The town would have plenty to talk about tonight, I suspected.

As I walked down the room, however, I had eyes for only one thing. Grandfather Diah's picture had been restored to its place on the wall beside Julia's and I warmed to it immediately, as I had not toward my grandmother's portrait. Were he alive now, I doubted that Julia's letter would have been sent to me.

He had been twenty-eight, Mother told me, when these two portraits were painted in England. The artist had caught his dashing good looks and something of his vitality in the very way his mane of blond hair lifted in a thick crest from his forehead, in the intensity of blue eyes, in the impetuous nature of his mouth. But there was more. In Grandfather Diah's face I sensed not only the drive of great energy —which was in Julia as well—but also a lively generosity, a kindliness, that seemed absent in hers. They were both vital and impetuous, these two who had been husband and wife, but one felt a serener spirit in Diah, for all his adventurous nature. In the portrait he wore a gray business suit, with the high collar and chain-looped vest of that day —yet I could easily imagine him in more romantic garb, his hand resting on a sword hilt, a cloak about his shoulders, and swashbuckling boots encasing his legs.

The voice behind me spoke in a low tone, but the words reached me clearly enough. "What do you think of our grandparents, Malinda?"

I whirled to meet so reasonable a facsimile of the portrait that I felt inclined to blink. But even as I regarded my Cousin Gerald in surprise I knew the resemblance had only to do with his good looks, thick blond hair, blue Gorham eyes, a nose and mouth rather like Grandfather Diah's—and with nothing else. One sensed that Diah was muscled and fit. Gerald, at forty-one, had allowed his body to turn flabby. There was another dissimilarity.

My cousin wore well-cut brown trousers and a light tan jacket, with the right sleeve neatly pinned at elbow length so that it hung loosely from his shoulder, concealing whatever lay within. What happened to me at that moment was curious. I looked at his pinned-up sleeve, and then compulsively away. I did exactly what every stranger did with me, and was at once ashamed. Gerald, at least, was more relaxed than I. He looked straight at my cheek and shook his head ruefully.

"Mother has exaggerated," he said. "There's nothing much to it, really, once you know the scar is there. But between us, we haven't been lucky, have we, Cousin Malinda?"

I was tempted to tell him of the dramatic little game I used to play before my mirror, after I had been told about his arm, but I did not dare. I must tread softly, since I did not know yet whether my cousin was as antagonistic toward me as his mother and grandmother, or whether—just possibly—he might be a friend.

"Well—what do you think of them?" he repeated, gesturing toward the portraits with his left hand.

"They must have been a good deal alike—and very different," I said cautiously. "I wonder how they got along together?"

"You've a perceptive eye, Cousin. The difference, of course, lies in the stuff of which they were made. Both must have had dash and elegance in those days—but with Gran it was the elegance of fine steel, with Grandfather Diah, of rich velvet. They got along fine as long as steel had its way, I imagine."

"And now that the velvet is gone—what has the steel become?"

"Rapier sharp," he said. "And sometimes dangerous."

Was he too warning me? I wondered. Stiffening inwardly, I launched into my attack.

"I want to meet my grandmother," I told him. "I'm here because of her, and I have the right to see her at least."

"Here—because of her?"

"Literally, I mean. As you are too. Because those two in the portraits lived, we live. There's a tie, whether she likes it or not. I can't break it until I've seen her, spoken to her."

He shook his head at me. "You're flinging yourself at the rapier point," he said. "If you keep on, you're the one who will be damaged."

"I won't be put off so easily," I said.

"I can see that." He studied me more warily before he continued. "We've been talking you over, you know. It seems your mother sent Gran a letter that has upset her thoroughly, though she's being secretive about what it said."

"I've heard about that letter, though my mother didn't show it to me."

However inactive Gerald's body had become, his eyes were brightly alert, giving indication of keen intellect behind. Nevertheless, there was a disturbing quality in the man that seemed to grow from some hidden ferment. The same sort of ferment that motivated his grandmother? But there would be a difference, as I knew very well. Julia had been beautiful and much admired. Disfigurement could twist a drive in strange directions. I still could not tell whether Gerald would prove an ally, or whether he might meet me with real opposition. So far, he seemed neutral. A mere reporter, an observer of conflicts outside himself.

"I don't understand why my grandmother should be so upset by my coming here," I said.

He answered readily. "Nor do I. But the immediate problem is to get rid of you as quickly as we can. Gran doesn't mean to see you at all. However, no one will put you out in the dark among Silverhill's haunted birches tonight, Cousin, so you might as well enjoy our dubious company while you have the chance. Why don't you sit down? You give the impression of resting on coiled springs."

I chose Chippendale and settled upon pale gold cushions, but I did not relax. How softly he spoke—so that I had to strain a little to catch the rather formal words—as though by speaking softly he called as little attention as possible to his physical self. It was the words that troubled me, however. With every new announcement that Grandmother Julia would not see me, my resolve to see her grew stronger. Possibly there was a little steel in me as well. The difficulty was to find a way. I could hardly go battering at her door.

Gerald did not seat himself at once, but moved about the room, touching a Venetian glass goblet on a corner shelf, the porcelain figure of a German shepherdess in a cabinet, pausing before a Girandole mirror to adjust its candle arms —all done with loving concentration, so that I was aware of the care and pride he lavished upon these things. Not until he put his hand on the shield back of a small Hepplewhite chair near the fireplace and bent to examine the striped blue satin of the seat did his expression change to displeasure. Carefully he studied the fabric, then flicked a finger across it as if he had discovered a flaw that pained him deeply.

Someone came into the dining room behind us and began to speak quietly to the maid. It was Kate Salway. She had changed from uniform and apron to a dark green, full-skirted dress that went well with her brown hair and flattered her rounded figure. Gerald looked up at the same moment and regarded her questioningly.

"We won't need a place for Mrs. Julia at the table tonight," she told him in answer to the look. "There will be just yourself and your mother and Miss Rice."

"You see?" Gerald said to me. "I didn't think she'd appear, with you at the table. Kate—has the necklace been found?"

She came through the double doors into the drawing room, her pleasant face troubled. "Chris has searched everywhere, but so far it hasn't turned up. Of course we'll keep trying. Your Aunt Fritzie says she doesn't know a thing about it since she gave it to that bird."

"At least you've brought back the picture," Gerald said. "Where did she take it this time?"

"She had it in her bedroom. It's hardly small enough for her to hide."

Gerald waved an exasperated hand at the Hepplewhite chair. "Look at this, Kate! She must have climbed on the chair in her shoes to get the picture down. And only yesterday I caught her using an Imari bowl for a bird bath. She behaves like an irresponsible child—and I don't know why we have to put up with it forever, just because she was once Grandfather's favorite child and Gran has a guilty conscience."

A guilty conscience? My attention was caught. But Gerald sounded like a petulant child himself, even though, with his head bent above the chair, I could see the start of the heavy jowls he would wear before long. Was this the key to my cousin—that he was a middle-aged man who was still a child and concerned himself mainly with precious toys, rather than with living?

Kate came anxiously into the room to look at the chair. "I'm sorry, Gerald. There's no way to keep her locked out of this part of the house without confining her completely, but I'll try to keep a closer watch."

"Gerald," she called him, easily, naturally—not "Mr. Gorham." But of course they had grown up together in this house and she would use the more formal term only in speaking to a stranger like myself.

He gave the chair seat a last brush and smiled at her more kindly. "Do that, will you, Kate? Today has been upsetting, what with one thing and another."

She nodded, understanding. "That means no writing,

doesn't it? But everything will be quiet again soon. Sometimes I think Miss Fritzie has antennae out, even when no one tells her a thing. She senses it when something out of the ordinary is going on. She's disturbed and restless now. You know she doesn't do things like this when everything is quiet."

"Has she been told that her younger sister is dead?" I put the question boldly.

Gerald looked startled. "Oh, no—we'd never tell her that. We try not to remind her of the past. She gets out of hand the moment she begins to remember happenings that have hurt her. That may be what's the matter now—with your coming."

"Is she at all dangerous?" I asked.

"Certainly not!" This time Kate answered, clearly shocked. "She's a dear, really, and she'd never hurt a fly."

Gerald snorted. "And you, Kate, are a soft-hearted pushover for anyone in trouble. We don't know whether or not she's dangerous because she's been kept in cotton batting for years. But there have been times in the past—" He glanced at me. "Of course Malinda was only four when she visited us then, so I don't suppose she remembers Aunt Fritzie."

I shook my head, sensing an undercurrent. "I don't remember much about that visit. Mother never wanted to talk about it because of what happened to me while I was here."

A light, breathless voice spoke from the dining-room door. "It would have been better if she had never brought you to Silverhill that time," Aunt Nina said, "and never come back here herself. Better for you and for all of us."

She stood in the doorway, a trim little woman in a rose-figured silk dress, the lift of her chin as eager as though she rose on tiptoe to meet the world—while everything she said belied such eagerness.

"Kate, Mother Julia wants you right away," she went on, and there seemed an asperity in her tone, until she turned to Gerald. "We can sit down at the table now, if you like. The new maid hasn't learned to announce dinner."

Kate fled, her cheeks pink, as though she had been caught in some guilty act. Gerald's observant blue gaze seemed to note his mother's manner, but he made no comment as he seated us at the table, and took the chair at one end. Fine linen reflected a gleam of candles from its frosty surface. The heavy silver was old. Red roses glowed in a bowl of delicate Stiegel glass. Down the long expanse an empty high-backed chair at the far end imposed its empty presence upon us in clear reproach.

Aunt Nina tinkled a brass bell at her place and at once the current town girl rushed through the swinging door from the kitchen. Aunt Nina made a slight motion of her head and the girl flung herself at tall windows standing open to the cooling evening air. To my surprise she pulled green draperies vigorously across each window, and then fled back to the kitchen. I had a quick impression of pale birch trees pressing close to the house in the fading outdoor light, only to find themselves shut out by those drawn curtains.

Gerald noted my look. "Our evenings are usually cool here, and we like privacy," he said. By candlelight his eyebrows seemed as light as his hair and almost invisible when he raised them sardonically, giving his forehead a pale, bald look.

"Privacy?" I echoed. "Who would be out there—except the birches?"

He smiled a bit wickedly, observing Aunt Nina. "Exactly. They always make us a bit nervous at night, don't they, Mother?"

"Gerald, please," Aunt Nina said, but I saw that her concern was more for the girl who had returned with a tray of soup plates than for her son's words.

Gerald went on, clearly indifferent to the help. "You should know about our family legends, Malinda. I warn you, the birches are haunted."

Aunt Nina glanced at the maid. "Mr. Gorham is teasing, you know. Don't let him frighten you."

The girl managed to place the soup plates without accident and fled once more to the haven of the kitchen.

Aunt Nina shook her head despairingly. "You can see why we have trouble keeping help."

I looked at Gerald. "Who walks under the trees at night so that you have to close the draperies and hide from view?"

I tried to keep my tone light, as if I took none of this seriously, but Gerald's soft laughter increased my uneasiness.

"Do you think the Gorhams haven't their share of ghosts, Cousin?" he said. "There's Grandfather Diah on the attic stairs, though only Aunt Fritzie sees him. Then there's the child who cries at night and hides among the birch trees. We don't know whether it's a girl or a boy, but we think we hear the wailing."

I glanced at Aunt Nina, expecting to find her lips prim with disapproval of this fantasy with which her son was trying to frighten me. Instead, the sight of her face shocked me more than any ghost story could. The pinched-in look was gone from her mouth, and her lips were parted slightly —as though she were a young girl listening eagerly to some marvelous tale told by her elders. Now that the maid was gone, her eyes admired her son and denied nothing of what he was saying.

"Who is this child supposed to be?" I asked.

Gerald shook his head. "Who knows? Diah and Julia planted those trees when they were young—that's white birch out there, not the gray birch that springs up everywhere in the woods like weeds. The trees have had a lifetime of growing and Gran claims they creep closer to the house every year. She says they'll smother us someday. But she and my mother and Kate never see the child. Only Aunt Fritzie and I have the gift. Perhaps you'll have it too, Cousin Malinda."

"What about Elden?" I asked. "Does he play this game?"

Gerald's teasing mood changed to sudden irritability. He had been baiting both his mother and me, but now I sensed annoyed withdrawal, as though I had said something that offended him.

Aunt Nina, quickly aware of the change, tried to launch into a new subject, but her words were broken off by the sound of a tremendous and violent crash. From somewhere on this floor came a loud metallic ringing, a reverberating clatter, that seemed to go on for minutes, filling our ears with booming noise.

Gerald and Aunt Nina flung down their napkins and jumped to their feet. For an instant they looked at each other in alarm—then rushed into the hall toward the front door. I hurried after them, to meet Kate running down from upstairs. Gerald pulled at the door to the foyer and we crowded into the opening.

Bracket lamps on either side lighted the space and for a moment I could see nothing wrong. Then Gerald and Aunt Nina pushed through the doorway, while Kate and I stood together looking at what lay strewn across the marble floor. The armored knight had fallen. Mortimer's helmet, with its ridged skull and slotted visor had rolled off to crash against the leg of the monastery chair. The neck gorget on which the helmet sat lay near the front door, looking gruesomely headless. A fluted breastplate had fallen in the center of the floor, while gauntlets and leg greaves and lance had been scattered in a jumble of shining steel. The stand which had supported the suit of armor stood in its place undisturbed.

"This was deliberate," Gerald said, his voice tight with suppressed anger. "The thing didn't fall over by itself."

Kate began to pull at the heavy pieces, attempting to get them out of the way and into a corner heap. I tried to help, picking up the flexible chain mail of the skirt.

"It could have been an accident," she said. "Miss Fritzie loves Mortimer. She'd never try to hurt him."

Aunt Nina stood with her hands to her mouth, staring down at the knight's scattered armor.

"Mischief!" she whispered. "More wicked mischief! Oh, when will it stop?"

Gerald had recovered first. "Leave it for now, Kate. Nothing is hurt. This stuff has seen jousting and battle action. Tomorrow Elden can put it back together."

Kate agreed readily. "Chris knows every piece. He can help."

"I thought you were going to keep an eye on her, Kate." Gerald was curt.

For once Kate stood up to him. "Elden and I were having our dinner, and I'd just come back to the house. I was looking for her when I heard the crash. I can't be everywhere at once. Now I'll find her and get her to bed."

She hurried off to Aunt Fritzie's side of the house, and Gerald returned to the dining room. Aunt Nina gestured me ahead of her and we followed him to the table. Once we were seated, she did her best to provide a new subject to discuss while we went on with our meal.

"I do like what you've done in displaying the jewelry collection," she told her son brightly. "Even without the moonstone and amethyst necklace, you've made a lovely show of Mother Julia's treasures."

I stared at my cooling soup, embarrassed by her urgent endeavor to coax him into better humor. Gerald, however, permitted himself to be distracted and spoke willingly enough of the fine pieces in the collection.

As his voice ran on, soft as silk, I wished fervently for Wayne Martin's presence at the table to counteract the unpleasantness of the mood in which we dined. It seemed, however, that Wayne kept to his rooms on the other side of the house, except when he was invited here or came over for some special reason. The crash of tumbling steel continued to ring in my ears and my will to act was like something suspended apart from me. How could I do anything

in the face of the mischievous madness of which Aunt Arvilla was capable?

When we finished our soup, the roast lamb was brought
in. Gerald was served his meat cut into small squares and
he managed neatly, skillfully with his left hand. As he ate
he asked if I would like to see the collection in the morning.
At once his mother threw me one of her quick, hostile looks.

"Malinda will be taking the early plane back to New
York," she told him, "so there will be no time. Your grandmother has already arranged for Elden to drive her to the
airport tomorrow morning."

Here was the opening for which I waited, and I managed
to close my ears to the echo of tumbling armor, and revive
my will to act. When the maid had brought strawberries
and cream, placed a silver coffee service beside Aunt Nina,
and disappeared into her burrow, I spoke directly to Gerald.

"I'd like very much to see the jewelry collection and anything else you care to show me tomorrow. I shan't be leaving until after I've seen Grandmother Julia, and apparently
that may take a little time."

Though it must have cost her an effort to keep her hands
steady, Aunt Nina filled a Spode cup from the silver coffee
urn and passed it to me. When I had taken it, she pressed
her fingers upon the tablecloth on each side of her dessert
plate and bent toward me in her earnest way.

"Listen to me, Malinda. Your grandmother feels that you
should be sent away at once. She won't sleep a wink with
you in the house, and I may have to sit up with her. Surely
you can see how your presence has disrupted our quiet
lives. Nevertheless, in spite of her wish that you should be
told nothing, I think you must be warned that your Aunt
Arvilla once tried to injure you seriously, and she may try
again, if she discovers you are here. You were lucky to get
off with no more than a scar on your cheek after her attack
upon you the last time. We all remember this, and we are
doing everything possible to keep you out of her way. For

your own protection, as well as hers, we want you to leave Silverhill early tomorrow and forget about this place and about us, as we must forget you. The past can't possibly be righted. Your grandmother has worked out a way for all of us to live in a bearable fashion. If you try to disturb this equilibrium it may be at your own cost. There's nothing for you here—nothing at all!"

Even if her words had not carried such a ring of conviction, I was ready to believe the shocking things she claimed about Arvilla. Still, I must persist, or give up for good.

"If Aunt Arvilla doesn't remember what happened at that time, how can it matter?" I asked.

Gerald broke in impatiently. "There's no telling what she remembers, or how quickly she forgets. You've seen the trick she has just played. Why? What sensible reason could possibly lie behind such action?"

I had no answer to give him.

"If Mother Julia wants you gone, you'd better go," Aunt Nina persisted.

"What Mother means," Gerald put in, "is simply that Gran controls our lives. My life is here at Silverhill and I have to recognize that. If I'm to keep everything as I like it, Gran must be pleased. You, dear Cousin, are taboo. So what can we do but turn you out?"

I stared stubbornly at my plate and said nothing. My silence made Aunt Nina nervous. Her hands moved busily among the things on the table before her as she tried again to persuade me.

"There's not the slightest chance of your grandmother changing her will, Malinda. If that is what you hope for—"

Gerald laughed softly. "She wouldn't be so foolish, Mother. If there was any chance of Malinda's inheriting what should come to me, I wouldn't be sitting here with her so amiably. Though it's not the money that interests me most, Cousin, or even the sacrosanct Gorham Notepaper business. These things are already in competent hands as far as their management goes. What I care about is the house itself, and all that's in it. I know and understand our collections better than Julia or Diah ever did. Gran knows that. She'll never give them to anyone else, even if I block her in this notion she's got into her head."

"I—I'm not sure about that!" Aunt Nina's voice seemed to crack as she spoke, and once more I could feel the deep-seated fear in the woman. A fear of me? But that was fantastic.

Gerald's brief amiability vanished. "My hand won't be forced on this plan of Grandmother's, no matter what she does," he told his mother. "She's bluffing, anyway. Nothing is going to change."

I managed to find my tongue. "Of course it isn't—as far as I'm concerned. I'm not a threat to anyone. I'm sorry my coming here has disturbed you and I'll go away as soon as I can. But first I must see my grandmother. I must see Aunt Arvilla. And I want to know the truth about the time when Mother brought me here and the accident happened that scarred my cheek. So—unless you put me out bodily—I mean to stay until these three things are accomplished."

Aunt Nina took prompt offense at my words. She put her napkin to her lips with a trembling hand and excused herself from the table in a voice that shook. Gerald rose to see her from the room. Then he came back to the table wearing an expression of wry amusement. I knew that he would never believe my disavowals, any more than his mother did. Both were sure that I had come for much more than I claimed.

When he spoke, however, his words took me by surprise.

"Gran's famous ruby ring would look well on those long fingers of yours, Malinda. You've the same handsome bones. You must try on the ring sometime. It may be that our grandmother will even settle a few gifts upon you, Malinda. Gifts of some value—if she is properly persuaded."

I could see his obvious direction and I was thoroughly angry. "And I suppose you would persuade her?"

"It's possible, Cousin. Sometimes she listens to me."

"The bargain being that I would then leave Silverhill without causing any more trouble?"

"Why not? There's nothing for you here. As for seeing Gran and Aunt Fritzie—that would be a waste of time, even if it were possible."

I started to push back my chair, wanting only to escape his outrageous offer of bribery. But Gerald moved the coffee service blandly across to me.

"Pour me another cup, will you—and help yourself. Then let's go into the drawing room for a while. We mustn't send you off to bed on this note of unpleasantness."

I poured coffee with a hand that was anything but steady, and we carried our cups into the lamplit room. Someone had already closed the opaque summer curtains, though there could be nothing out there on Gorham land except the white birches. The trees reminded me of Gerald's earlier remarks and I tried to recover my temper in further questioning.

"What did you mean about Aunt Arvilla seeing Diah on the attic stairs?"

"Isn't that the reasonable place to see him?" Gerald asked lightly. "After all, that's where he died—and Aunt Arvilla was responsible. Though I hardly think he'd be vengeful."

By an effort, I kept my tone casual. "What is supposed to have happened?"

"We know well enough what happened," Gerald said. "Fritzie had a breakdown after my father brought her home from her Broadway triumphs. What a girl she must have been in those days—before Grandmother Julia broke her spirit. I was born around the time it all happened, so I never knew her then. She went to pieces and nearly died, I understand. Then, when everyone thought she was recovering, she had a quarrel with Grandfather Diah and pushed him down the attic stairs. He was killed in the fall, and no one here has ever fully recovered from that disaster. Fritzie has been a wreck of herself ever since, and Gran lost everything she cared about in life when she lost Diah. She has stayed as far away from Fritzie as possible ever since, though she's a woman who knows her duty and she has seen that her daughter was cared for and given a home. Of course stiff-necked Gorham pride would never let her put Fritzie away in an institution where she belongs. Old Doc Martin, Wayne's father, used to keep an eye on her—and now of course Wayne lives on her side of the house and watches out for her to some extent. But we've all been defeated and weighed down by having a demented old woman on our hands. There—now you have it, Malinda. I suppose you'll think me callous, but I don't believe we should all be sacrificed to someone who will never be well again."

I took a slow breath and spoke in a tone as soft as Gerald's own. "What if it was all a mistake? What if Aunt Arvilla never really pushed her father on the stairs? Wouldn't there be hope for her again if she was told the truth?"

Gerald regarded me without astonishment, without denial. "So that's the fabrication Gran keeps talking about. If that's what your mother told you, and if that's why she sent you here, then there's even more reason to turn around and go back to New York at once. The one thing Fritzie remembers clearly about that time is what she did. To tell her something different now would never change her mind and it certainly wouldn't clear up the rest of her confusion. Let her alone, Cousin Malinda. Don't make everything worse."

There seemed an almost ominous ring to his words, though I suspected that he was far more concerned for his inheritance than he was for Aunt Arvilla's sanity.

I finished my coffee and set the cup on a low table. I had nothing more to say. If I could meet Arvilla myself, perhaps I would understand what I must do. Surely Aunt Nina's talk of danger to me was overrated at this late date. She only wanted to frighten me away—as did Gerald.

My cousin offered me a cigarette and I refused, watching him put one in his mouth and light it singlehanded with a monogrammed lighter.

"What was your own father like?" I asked, and the question was not altogether idle. Any clues out of the past which would help me understand these extraordinary relatives might be useful in solving my several problems.

Gerald drew deeply on his cigarette. I sensed a stiffening in him and knew I had chosen a somehow provocative subject. What Wayne Martin had said about his father's being an athlete returned to my mind.

"He died when I was fairly young," Gerald said, "in spite of that health kick he was always on. I hardly remember him, though I gather he was pretty much the All-American boy of his day. Mother will show you the trophies he won, if you ask her. Cups for everything from the hundred-yard dash to some championship tennis matches. In fact, that's where he met my mother—on a tennis court. Can you picture that? He was having an off day, or didn't think her worth exerting himself for, and she beat him a couple of sets. Naturally, he had to put her down—and I suppose the best way to do that was by marrying her. Especially since she had a good family name herself and was considered a catch. Henry Gorham would hardly overlook that."

I listened uncomfortably to the rancor in his words. He seemed to have a distaste for both his parents.

"You can see what a disappointment a son like me must have been to Henry," he went on. "I suspect he loathed the sight of me. Since it was mutual, it probably didn't matter. Of course he gave up sports when he grew older and became a proper businessman in the Gorham enterprises. Very satisfactory for everyone, I'm sure, though I think he bored my grandmother. He was certainly no Diah. You've seen the modest stone in the cemetery?" Gerald reached out and ground his half-smoked cigarette viciously into an ashtray. "Mother never remembers to dust his silver trophies," he added. "Rather revealing, don't you think?"

It was Gerald himself who stood revealed, I thought, aware that he had tried deliberately to shock me. Apparently he wanted me to think the worst possible of every member of the family. I hated to imagine what a man like this might do if ever given reason to take vindictive action—toward me. Now, though he did not believe it, he had no reason for such action, but at least I knew he would be no ally for me in this house.

My guarded expression must have left him dissatisfied, for he stood up abruptly, once more changing his course.

"Since there's no one around to interfere, why shouldn't I show you the jewelry collection this evening?" he asked.

This at least was an invitation I could accept with alacrity and I followed him to the rear of the front hall.

"This is where the back door of the old house used to be," he said, putting his hand on a china knob. "Now it leads to the section Grandfather Diah built onto the house. Careful—there are three steps down. The moon is up by this time, so I'd like you to see the gallery without any indoor lighting."

He took my hand and I went down the steps into a long room with windows running along the opposite side. Or what I thought were windows, until I saw that one of them reflected the dimly lighted hall behind me, while the next one threw back an arch-framed reflection of the moonlit garden beyond: a mirror reflecting a mirror that reflected a window in endless pictures that were more than a little confusing. The true windows overlooked what must be the garden Elden Salway had mentioned to me, and I could see its white paths winding between blossoms that were washed of all color by moonlight—yet I could not be sure whether I looked at reality or reflection. Even when I glanced down at pale Chinese carpets at my feet, I found that shadows lay across them—the graceful shadows of arched windows and curiously wrought pilasters, increasing an effect that was dreamlike and unreal. Everything was different here. Even my cousin seemed altered, gilded perhaps by the mirrored illusion.

"The gallery changes constantly under changes in lighting," Gerald told me. "Grandfather Diah might have been an artist if he cared to be, but he chose to do his painting with light and shadow and the use of mirrors and windows and space. When I was a child they used to let me play in here because I was careful never to break anything. Sometimes I think the place has bred a confusion in me about what's real and what isn't. Perhaps I've even come to prefer the illusion."

There was something wry in Gerald's words, and even though I could not like him, I felt a kinship with him, understanding very well how easy it might be to choose illusion rather than reality—how seductively easy!

The realization made me look quickly about for a real window among the mirrored ones and I went to stand before it in order to clear the fogginess from my senses. Grandfather's gallery left me with a troubling feeling of inner confusion. I did not really want illusion. I did not want to be like Gerald and retreat from what lay outside in the real world, however much it might hurt me. The gallery was unbelievably beautiful in its magical patterns of light and dark, with moonlight silvering the Chinese carpets, yet it concealed too much that might lie hidden in ugliness underneath. I had a sudden urgent wish to cover the mirrors, to open all the windows.

I knew it was necessary to turn outward to the real world, and do it soon. Perhaps that was why I had come here—to rid myself of shadowy imitations of life. Once I knew the truth, whatever it might be, then I could choose with assurance between reality and illusion, between retreat and a more courageous venturing.

From the window I could see a picket fence, shining white beneath the moon—a fence that encased the garden all around, holding back the pines and birch trees from their encroachment. Here, at least, the birches could not crowd the house, or look in at these gallery windows. Off to the left a space had been opened among the trees to allow a clear view into the distance, and I saw that Diah had painted with the outdoors as well, making the natural view a part of the house. There in the opening, with its head reaching black and rocky into a moon-white sky, stood Mt. Abenaki—"The Mountain" of my mother's childhood. This, at least, was real and hard and unyielding, yet at the same time it lifted my heart to see it, as if it promised me the healing of old pain.

Behind me Gerald touched a switch and amber light brought the long gallery to life. In an instant the outdoors became no more than black paneling where the true windows stood. Mirrors now reflected the interior back and forth, imitating one another, so that I had a sense of standing in a hall of vast proportions, its cabinets and tables, its crystal vases and jade ornaments, its porcelain and brass and ivory, repeating themselves forever, just as Gerald and I were repeated. Here must have been collected some of the most precious items that Grandfather Diah had acquired. Yet the room was a corridor too, leading right and left to doors that opened upon the living quarters of my grandmother and of my cousin. A rich and sumptuous corridor!

Looking about me, I remembered what Chris had said at the cemetery about the coming wedding that was to be held here in the gallery at Silverhill, and I tried once more to find the answer to that particular puzzle.

"Dr. Martin's son mentioned that Grandmother Julia plans to hold a ceremony here in this room—a wedding ceremony. But when I asked Kate about it she seemed upset and told me no wedding would be held."

Gerald turned abruptly and went to a glass-topped case that stood against the rear wall. When he spoke his back was toward me and I could not see his face.

"Kate is right," he said softly. "This time Gran has bitten off a lot more than she can chew."

"But why is everyone so secretive? Who is getting married?"

"It's no secret. It's my marriage she's trying to bring about." He swung around to face me, his eyes bright with challenge. "What do you think of that, Cousin? Our charming grandmother is so greedy for descendants—heirs! —that she would force me into marriage. A man with an arm like mine!"

I could feel the self-laceration of his words along my own nerves. "Don't!" I said. "I know how you feel, but it's senseless. There's no reason why you shouldn't marry."

He laughed unpleasantly. "Thank you, but I'll ask for no unsavory mixture of sympathy and revulsion from any woman, Cousin."

There was nothing more to be said. I understood very well indeed.

When I was silent, he appeared to relent. "Perhaps we've both inherited Gran's sharp tongue. Come here, Malinda. This is what I wanted to show you."

He touched a switch beneath the cabinet, so that soft lighting glowed under the glass. I went to stand beside him where I could see the array of necklaces, earrings, brooches, bracelets—even hatpins—that had been spread out to stunning effect upon a ground of black velvet. The shine of brilliants caught the light, and the fire of precious stones as well. Faceted diamonds and emeralds, rounded cabochon rubies, winked at me.

Not all the pieces were Victorian. Gerald showed me a very old and fragile necklace of silver filigree, said to have belonged to Queen Christina of Sweden. There was a breast-pin of Catherine of Russia's, resplendent with emeralds, and there were other pieces which had been owned by lesser notables such as actresses and singers. A lovely golden diadem studded with rosy coral had belonged to Jenny Lind.

He pointed out a handsome parure to me—a matching set of necklace, earrings, brooch and bracelet done in Florentine mosaic. Next to it lay a pair of Creole earrings woven of gold strands and human hair.

"The Victorians used every sort of decorative substance possible," Gerald said. "They were innovators who didn't depend entirely on precious stones. That's why some of their creations have never been broken up, as those of great value have. That blue set over there is made of blown glass. The space next to it should be occupied by the moonstone and amethyst necklace that Fritzie's taken from the case. It's part of a parure too, as you can see, and the craftsmanship is superb. The set was made by one of the great designers of his day—Castellani."

I studied the display, thinking ruefully of the costume pieces of which Mr. Donati was so proud, machine-made and cheap in both quality and design.

"Gran used to wear all these things," Gerald told me. "She was famous for her beautiful neck and shoulders, her lovely hands and graceful head. Imagine her in a Merry Widow hat with one of those ivory-headed hatpins thrust through the crown to hold it on!"

Suddenly he bent toward the collection of long, old-fashioned hatpins, their fanciful heads fanned out to show them off.

"Look!" The exclamation was angry as he raised the glass lid of the case. "She's been into the hatpins too! The pin with a crescent head of garnets is missing. Nothing's safe from her—nothing! And that hatpin isn't a toy. She mustn't be left with such a thing in her possession. I must get a man out from Shelby to put a lock on the case. Of course, the priceless items must be kept locked now that Grandmother has let them out of her safe."

I stood beside him, staring at those long slender pins of another day—some with chased silver heads, one with a knight's helmet like Mortimer's, some jeweled, some inlaid —all delicate in their craftsmanship. And with that revealing space between, where the garnet pin had been taken from its velvet case.

"Watch your fingers," Gerald said, and lowered the glass lid carefully into place. Then he gestured toward a pier-glass mirror that stood between windows in the center of the gallery on the opposite side. "That's the door to Fritzie's conservatory. That's why I can't keep her out of the gallery. She practically lives in there. Diah was plant-mad at one time in his life and he brought in all sorts of exotica from around the world. Now Fritzie looks after the plants the way I look after the collection."

I stared at glass that did not appear to be a door, and which reflected me as I stood before it. My bare arms felt chilled, as though a draft blew upon me, and I knew I was looking at something I had seen before, something which had once frightened me.

Gerald watched me curiously. "You might as well have a look in there tomorrow," he said. "See if it tells you anything. That's where it happened, you know—the accident that caused your scar. If you can call it an accident, considering that Fritzie was to blame."

Without warning I began to feel physically and emotionally depleted. I could not endure this place. I could not bear to stand looking into that mirror that was really a door. I must have grown dizzy for I reached toward a black Regency chair to steady myself.

"Off to bed with you," Gerald said. "You look as though you've stood all you can take for one day. You know the way into the house, don't you? I'm going to stay here and make sure nothing else is missing. And I'll have a look for that necklace and hatpin myself."

I said good night a bit bleakly and went up the three steps into the old part of the house. At the front of the hall the stairs waited for me, dimly lit where they ran up beside the wall. No one was about and I did not climb to the upper floor. Now that I had escaped the gallery, my strength of will had returned and I went instead to the door that led into the foyer with its marble checks and medieval chest. Two lights still burned in copper sconces and the door to Aunt Arvilla's side of the wall invited me. I stepped around the heap of armor that was the fallen knight, and put my hand on the knob of her door. In this place of supposedly unlocked doors, this door, like the one upstairs, had been secured against any intruder. Perhaps deliberately secured against me?

From the floor Mortimer's helmet seemed to watch me suspiciously through the slit in its visor and I gave the thing a tap with my toe, wondering if it would talk to me as it had talked to Chris and his father. Perhaps not—in its present humiliating position.

At least the massive black wooden panel of the front door opened easily and I went through, leaving it slightly ajar behind me. Gravel crunched under my feet as I crossed the drive and while a carriage lamp burned near the steps, it cast a meager glow, and only moonlight illumined wide lawns sloping toward the silvered pond. I stepped out upon the grass and moved well away from the house, so that although its dark bulk rose behind, I could see ahead of me only sky and trees and grass and water. Here I could breathe more freely the cool night air of the country, scented by pines and by leaf mold and the burgeoning earth of June. My sense of weariness lessened, and for a few moments I could shed the oppressive atmosphere of the house.

Yet not altogether. Something of it stayed with me, even

here. Through the soughing of wind in the trees I could imagine Arvilla's laughter as I had heard it through the wall. The mark on my cheek seemed to burn and I did not like to think of a woman who had laughed like that, a woman who could mischievously push over a heavy suit of armor, stealing about the house with a garnet-studded hatpin in her hands. If she had meant to hurt me once, would she want to again? What had I done to so anger her that she might not forgive me, even now? No answers came to me about anything. The time was not yet ready for me to know just how dreadful the truth had been.

IV

As I stood on the grass, trying to shake off the spell of the house, I began to think of my mother. When she was a child Blanche Gorham must often have stood in this very place. I wished she were with me now. I could not yet accept the fact that she was no longer waiting for me, concerning herself with my problems, as she had always done. If I had spent the night in Shelby I might have gone to the cemetery to sit on the grass beside that raw mound of earth and try to comfort myself with a make-believe sense of her nearness.

This, I was beginning to discover, was one of the unexpectedly wounding things about deep loss. I went through the necessary activities of the day, I met the problems that presented themselves in whatever way I could, and I thought of other things. I was distracted. And for a time pain remained in the background. But when everything quieted, when I found myself alone, then without warning the sense of loss returned, cutting, thrusting, leaving me awash with pain and loneliness. It was my mother who slept quietly now, and I who missed her.

For all of my life we had been good friends and understanding companions. The availability of each made any trouble that beset the other more bearable—up to a point. As I became older we inevitably grew a little apart. I could not bear to be told that I was throwing myself too much into my work as an escape, that I was turning my back on life. I resented her words, feeling that she did not understand how hard I worked—for both of us!—resenting any criticism, as the young always do. Nor could I tell her about the disillusionment with Greg. Since she had begun to pin her expectation upon him, I was all the more unreasonably piqued by her very hope. Yet while I could no longer be easily comforted and counseled as a child can be, now that I had lost her I longed perversely for that very counseling. At Silverhill, her home, I needed her most of all.

How empty of companionship the moonlight seemed— how terribly quiet the night. The wind had hushed and the very birds were asleep, except for the occasional hoot of an owl. The underlying sounds of night insects merely emphasized the stillness. Now and then a distant car flashed by along the road far across the wide pond, its headlights gleaming yellow for a few moments, then vanishing into the dark shield of trees. I was not accustomed to such quiet. Perhaps I missed the sound of city streets that were never still. Tonight in the city it would be hot in those streets. Concrete and stone held in the day's heat and threw it back in the night hours—while here the air was deliciously fresh and a little chill. Behind me, if I looked, I would see the birches tall and slim, and close to the house. I would not look.

The thick carpet of grass, soft as a Chinese rug, must have muffled the footsteps behind me for I did not know anyone was near until Elden spoke my name.

"What do you think of Silverhill now, Miss Rice?" he asked.

I turned and at once the house filled the horizon, blocking out all else, standing as silver by night as it did by day, with its Gothic tower thrusting high, and two pale wings stretching out to either side.

"At least I've begun to meet some of the people who live here," I said.

"Not Miss Fritzie, I'll bet. Kate says they're keeping Miss Fritzie locked away from you. But she'll know. She can tell when something's up, and she's already playing tricks on everyone, the way she does when she's stirred up. I heard about the armor. That must have sent Mrs. Nina half out of her wits."

He sounded as though he rather enjoyed the thought. I did not want to discuss either Nina or Aunt Arvilla with this man. As he had done earlier, he left me questioning and uneasy. He was not at all like his sister, and though he had the New Englander's easy manner toward those who employed him, I had no confidence in him as a friend, either to me, or to the family. The sound of his laughter, low in his throat, reminded me again of a growl, and I winced at the sound. There was too much mockery in this man—a mockery that must have its roots in some deep-seated bitterness. I could not guess its source, since Julia Gorham had given him a home, an education, a living. Why should he then be resentful?

"So his nibs showed you the gallery tonight?" Elden went on. "Quite a guy Zebediah must have been in his day—with all that money to spend, and fine expensive tastes. They used to let Gerald play among all that stuff when he was small, though my father wouldn't have him in the garden because he never had any sense about trees and plants. He'd as soon tear off a branch that got in his way, as go under it, or trample the flowers if he wanted to chase a ball. What with having only one arm to catch with, he had to do a lot of chasing when we were kids."

There seemed something especially antagonistic toward Gerald Gorham here—though why this man with two good arms should resent a man with only one I did not know.

"You grew up together, then, did you?" I asked.

I could see Elden's massive, well-shaped head move in the pale light as he nodded. "We grew up hating each other's guts—if that's what you mean by together."

"Why?" I asked bluntly.

He growled again. "Because he wouldn't let me alone. I had two arms and he never forgave me for that. He always had to try my games, and if I objected he'd fight me. Can you think what it was like—trying to hold off a kid with one arm when he was bent on knocking your block off? It always looked as though I was picking on him, yet I couldn't let go and let him have it. Except once. Just once I knocked him down and gave him a good black eye and a nosebleed. It was worth it in spite of the hoorah that followed. You'd have thought I'd committed murder to hear Mrs. Nina screech. She's never forgiven me to this day. If she'd let him alone, Gerald might have been all right after that—he knew he had it coming. But she kept telling him what a bully I was, and—well, we don't have much use for each other by this time."

The story made me uncomfortable. There was no clear-cut side to take, and I found myself suddenly more sympathetic toward Elden than toward my cousin, though I wasn't sure my feeling was justified.

"Why do you stay—you and Kate?"

He looked away from me. "I don't need much. A garden, food, a roof over my head. Kate deserves better than that. I'd take her away from here in a minute if I could."

"Why can't you then?"

"You ask too many questions," he told me, "—though maybe you've got more gumption than any of them, except old Mrs. Julia. I don't know what you can do that will change anything—but maybe it's good that you've come. Maybe you'll bring a few things to a head. Mrs. Julia has a favorite word she likes to use—'catalyst.' Maybe that's what you are. And if you're going to be around a while, maybe you'd better know what you're up against."

I could hardly see myself as a catalyst. "I like your sister," I said, "but she runs away from me. I suppose I've asked her too many questions as well."

He looked at me again and the fixity of his gaze made me uncomfortable. "I think she likes you too. But she's afraid. She's walking a tightrope now and she doesn't know which side she'll fall toward." His hands, hanging loose at his sides, tightened into fists. "Do you think I wouldn't take her away in a minute if I was able? Do you think I like to stand by and watch while they try to bring off this marriage?"

"I've heard Gerald say he'll never marry anyone," I told him.

There was suppressed violence in Elden's manner. "He'd better mean it! I won't have him marrying my sister. But it's the old lady we've got to deal with. She'll bend everybody to her will, if she can. You'd better watch out for what she'll do to you, if you stick around."

He swung away from me and went up the slope and toward the side of the house where the grove of birches crowded close. He, at least, was not afraid of the birches by night, for he disappeared among the tall white trunks, leaving me to stare after him in astonishment.

So this was what Grandmother Julia planned—Kate's marriage to Gerald Gorham—with both Kate and her brother bitterly opposed to the union, to say nothing of Gerald's own objections. And probably his mother's, considering Aunt Nina's manner toward Kate. But surely, if there was such opposition the girl's hand could not be forced. Poor Kate, I thought—more a pawn in my grandmother's game than anyone else, being perhaps the only woman available for Julia Gorham's purpose; one she knew she could manage.

I followed the slope of lawn toward the house and stood

for a moment looking up at the dark central tower, with lights scattered on each side. Lamps still burned in the drawing room, glowing faintly behind drawn curtains. Above, in Aunt Nina's rooms windows stood open and the lights were brighter. Apparently she did not fear the birches up there. In my own room on the third-floor front no light burned, though I remembered putting one on before I came downstairs. Perhaps Kate, or one of the maids, had gone in to turn down the bed, and had frugally switched off the light. The explanation was simple enough, and I did not know why uneasiness once more touched me.

On Aunt Arvilla's side downstairs the front rooms were dark, though a faint glow shone through, as though some source of light illumined the back of the house. Above, on the second floor, a lamp shone in the window, so Wayne Martin must be there, or the boy, Chris. I wished I might talk to the doctor, but there seemed no unobtrusive way into that side of the house.

It seemed a very long while since Wayne had brought me to Silverhill, and I longed for the quiet strength of his presence, of his clear thinking and lack of subterfuge. He alone had held out a hand to me. Everyone else I had met seemed deep in one sort of intrigue or another, ingrown and narrow in their family concerns. Even Kate and Elden, who were not family, were all too deeply involved. Wayne Martin lived as much in the outer world as he did here, and I was sure he would never be bound by the illusory life created by the gallery, nor would he be given to the fantasy of the birch trees.

For the present, however, I could only return to the room which had been assigned me. When I went up the steps I was half afraid that the front door might be closed against me, but I found it ajar as I had left it, and I slipped through and ran upstairs. Apparently no one but Elden had discovered that I was outside. This time I did not pause to press an ear to the wall. If anyone laughed on the other side of the house, I did not want to hear that sound again.

I stole past Aunt Nina's closed door, wondering if she had gone down to still another conference about me in Grandmother Julia's wing. The upper stairs were steeper and the hall above seemed empty and dim, lighted only by a wall bracket where the steps turned, and by another near my room.

My door stood open upon darkness, though I was sure I had left it closed. Someone had certainly been here. Quickly I reached for the switch and the old-fashioned overhead fixture came on, shedding a cold light upon the room, hiding nothing. There was no one here. Nor had anyone been in to turn down the bed. But as I stepped into the room I caught the rosy gleam from something on the counterpane. A glow of dark red jewels. When I came closer, I saw that a long hatpin with a golden crescent head, garnet-studded, spiked the pillow, pinning to it a folded square of paper.

This was surely the missing hatpin from the collection downstairs, and its presence meant that Arvilla Gorham must have come into my room. I did not like the thought that she could reach me, though I could not reach her. My fingers were not altogether steady as I pulled the hatpin from the feather mound into which it had been thrust, freeing the square of familiar Gorham notepaper. It crackled, parchment-stiff in my hands as I unfolded it. The message was scrawled in blue ink in a slightly backhand script that wandered across the page with the untidiness of a child's writing. The words were few:

"Please come through the tower to the other side. And bring this hatpin with you."

There was nothing else—no salutation, no signature—but it was meant for me, and Arvilla Gorham had left it here. I closed the door to the hall and sat down in a low slipper chair, the hatpin in one hand, the cryptic note in the other.

If I were wise, I supposed, I would take both straight downstairs to Gerald. I would certainly never set foot in the other side of the house where Arvilla Gorham waited for me, secretly and alone. The incident of hatpin and note seemed uncanny, since everyone claimed that Aunt Arvilla did not know I was here at Silverhill. Still, as Kate had reported, she had been "disturbed" all day, had sensed something in the air, so perhaps she was somehow aware of my presence.

This chance, if I took it, would give me the opportunity to accomplish what I had come here for. Aunt Arvilla had apparently given those who watched her the slip and such an occasion might not happen easily again. If I saw her now, if I delivered the promised message from my mother, I would be free to leave tomorrow and take up my life again in any way I pleased. This, surely, was what I most wanted to do. So why did the prospect not elate me? Why did I have the feeling that if I fled from the unpleasantness of Silverhill, with all its antagonisms and veiled threats, I would leave with a part of my life forever clouded? Would that really matter? Or did I feel this way because I would never see Wayne Martin again, never learn what role he had played in my childhood—was it this that left me with a sense of something unfinished?

I weighed the hatpin in my hand, feeling the heaviness of the jeweled head, testing the sharpness of the point. Such pins had been used to skewer on broad-brimmed mounds of feathers, ribbon and lace that were gracious to view when a lady went driving in her carriage. These great hats had gone out quickly enough with the coming of the automobile, but when they were commonly worn, every woman possessed within easy reach a vicious weapon with which to guard her person. I smiled to myself, though a pin like this was no laughing matter. At least it would be in my hands, not in Aunt Arvilla's, if I went to her now. How mad she might be, I did not know, though the sound of her laughter had made me shiver. Long ago in the past she had once tried to hurt me, but there seemed no reason why she should harm me now.

I made up my mind and went into the hall, taking the hatpin with me. The double tower doors on my side opened easily and I found that the empty space which duplicated the foyer downstairs was filled with pale moonlight flooding through windows all around. This time the doors on the other side stood unbolted and partly open. I pushed them wide cautiously and looked into a hall that was a twin in architecture to the one on my side of the house—yet, unlike the other, this was a dusty, neglected place.

No one was in sight, but halfway down the length of the hall, opposite the balustrade that guarded the stairwell, a door stood open and light wavered in the aperture. Surely the flicker indicated candlelight. I could still retreat. I could return through the tower and bolt the door on my own side. Instead, I held to my course, irresistibly drawn toward wavering light that shone through the open door.

As I came opposite the stairwell, the hall itself took my attention in some strangely intense way. I was aware of everything about me. Of cobwebs strung in neglect between the balusters, of dust upon the mahogany rail, and of the most unusual wallpaper I had ever seen. The design was darkly ornate, with a large-figured gold and black and cinnamon floral pattern, gloomy and depressing, except where it was strewn at intervals with roses of a surprising Dresden blue. Judging by the strips that hung in loose peelings here and there, the walls had worn this dress for a good many years, yet the lack of light had preserved the blue of the roses. Apparently no one bothered to keep this floor in good repair, as was done everywhere else in the house. It seemed an abandoned place—strangely so in a house where good housekeeping was everywhere in evidence. A forbidden place? I wondered. One to which servants would not come, and others preferred to avoid?

I glanced over the rail and down upon steep stairs, knowing with conviction that this was the place where Diah Gorham must have died in the fall supposedly precipitated by his elder daughter. Naturally Grandmother Julia permitted no one here. I felt cold, chilled to the bone. It was as though past violence, the very memory of death and following anguish, had left some psychic stain here which the years could not eradicate.

There was no sound, no sign from the candlelit room, though I now stood opposite its door. Anything was better than to linger beside these chilling stairs, and I went to the door and pushed it open more widely. Inside, tall white candles were set upon a mantel in twin pewter holders, their flames dipping to greet me at the draft from the door. There were no bulbs in the overhead light fixtures and the room was unfurnished, with only storage boxes and trunks set about.

On the bare floor before an open trunk knelt a woman dressed in a ruffled gray chiffon robe, with a matching nightgown underneath. Her pale gold hair hung down her back in a thick braid and she had the white, faintly crumpled skin of one who has stayed too much indoors. As she turned to look at me I saw that her blue eyes were amazingly beautiful, the full lids unwrinkled, their glance youthful and eager, arrestingly alive. However I had expected Arvilla Gorham to look, it was not like this.

My hand went to my cheek as I remembered that it might not be wise to remind her of my scar.

"I knew you'd come," she said and gave me a smile that seemed surprisingly open and friendly. "You brought back my pin, too, didn't you?" She held out her hand for it—a thin hand from which the flesh had receded.

I put the hatpin behind my back with a sense of stepping into a world where all the rules were different and I could not even know what game I was playing.

"You wanted to see me?" I asked.

"Of course I wanted to see you!"

She did not seem to mind that I would not immediately surrender the pin, but bent again over the trunk and began flinging things carelessly out upon the floor: green satin slippers, an old corset, a bunch of artificial violets crumpled and faded, a feather boa, its white fluff yellowed with age.

"Ah—here it is!" she cried, and pulled out a woman's gown of a style that belonged to early in the century—a frock of heavy silk, as blue in color as those Dresden roses in the hall, and so full in its skirt that it must have been made of yards of cloth. A huge lace bertha overlaid the top, and two small black velvet bows decorated the front of the high lace collar.

She heaved the gown at me delightedly. "There you are —put it on!"

The thing came sailing at me through the air so that I had to reach out with both hands in order to keep it from falling to the floor at the impact. The heavy folds enveloped my arms and the lace speared itself on the hatpin.

"Why?" I asked, still groping for reason in a foreign landscape. "Why do you want me to put it on?"

She rose as lithely from the floor as any young person, not troubling to brush dust from her chiffon robe, or the smudge from her nose. Standing, she was as tall as I, and her astonishingly clear blue eyes came level with my own. I found myself already changing my ideas about "poor Arvilla." Her quality was one of engaging youthfulness, and I was caught by her direct manner, her way of cutting through to the core of matters, untroubled by any need for subterfuge.

"Of course I should explain," she agreed reasonably. "After all, I've been thinking about you ever since you arrived today. I saw Dr. Wayne bring you here in his car this afternoon—and I knew who you were right away."

She took my breath—this tall, slim wraith who carried herself with the air of an attractive young girl, and who seemed far more assured of manner than I would have expected her to be.

"Who am I, then?" I challenged her.

She put a light hand on my shoulder. "You're my own young self come back to me," she said simply. "I watched you this afternoon from my window and when I saw you coming up the steps I knew I saw myself, just the way I used to be."

I smiled at her, understanding. "Yes—everyone has told me how much I resemble you when you were young."

"Blanche's daughter," she said and her hand moved from my shoulder to my chin, turning my head. "You've hurt your cheek, haven't you? Now how did you do a thing like that?"

I breathed more easily. Apparently the scar meant nothing to her. "I don't remember much about it."

"On a stage it wouldn't show," she said, studying the mark judiciously. "Makeup would easily cover it across the distance of the footlights. Do put on the dress, dear. I'm all wrong for it now—I haven't tried it on for years. I was playing a Balkan princess in a period musical comedy when I wore that frock. It was my street costume in the second act. There's a hat here somewhere."

She bent over the trunk again while I shook out the dress, examining it. Why shouldn't I indulge her by putting it on? Here was a way of making friends with Aunt Arvilla, of getting to know her a little better before I launched myself into delivering a message from the past.

With some excitement she was again flinging articles recklessly to one side and the other until she found the hat. Luckily it had been quite flat in the first place, with a shallow crown, or it would have been hopelessly crushed under all that now lay upon the floor. As she held it up I saw that the frame was covered with yellowed Irish lace, hanging gracefully in inch-deep scallops all around the wide flat brim. A large black velvet bow graced the top and she made an attempt to perk up the bow before she rose and gave me the hat.

"Here—put it on, dear. What's your name? I knew it once, I'm sure, but I've forgotten."

"Malinda," I said, "but Mother always called me Mallie."

I took the hat and set it upon my head. She tipped it this way and that until it sat straight upon my head in the style of another day.

"Now then—the hatpin," she commanded, holding out her hand. "Mother gave me that pin on my eighteenth birthday and it's the one I used to wear in this very hat when I brought down the house with my last song in the second act. The song I sang to my American, you know, when I told him I didn't want to be a princess anymore. This sounds very old-fashioned now, doesn't it? Though of course it was beginning to sound old-fashioned even in the Twenties. Perhaps that was the last of the sentimental, romantic shows everyone used to love. All those dreadful young novelists were beginning to appear and influence everything—Hemingway and Fitzgerald and Dos Passos and Dreiser. I never liked them, really. I liked George Barr McCutcheon much better."

This time I gave her the pin and she worked it gently into the crown. "There—you must do it the rest of the way, so I won't prick you."

I had lost all concern about the hatpin and I did as she bade me. She stood back to regard me with her bright, excited blue gaze and I felt completely lulled and charmed, all my uneasiness gone. I was beginning to think I knew her very well, that I had nothing to worry about—though of course I was wrong. So terribly wrong.

"Now the dress!" she cried. "Hurry—do! Someone is sure to look into my bedroom downstairs and find me gone. Kate thinks she got me safely to bed. There'll be another hullabaloo and everything will be spoiled. Besides, it's cold up here. All the house is cold so much of the time—but especially up here."

I could not disappoint her. In a moment I had unzipped my mauve-pink sheath and got out of it without disturbing the hat. She helped me eagerly as I stepped into the heavy silk dress and drew it up about me, thrusting my arms into loose bishop sleeves that were inset with slashes of silk which had grown fragile with age.

"Turn around," she said. "There are hooks all the way up the back. No zippers in those days. My gowns used to drive my dressers wild—all that hooking and unhooking that had to be done quickly because I would be on again early in the third act. But everyone loved me in this dress. Now I can look at you and see how I must have appeared to an audience."

Her fingers were skillful at the hooking, though she clucked a bit over the tightness around my waist, and the absence of a proper corset beneath. Besides, I was thin in the wrong places to do the dress justice, she said. Nor did she approve of my nylon slip.

"There should be petticoats—flounces of petticoats to hold out the train. But there's no time for that now. You'll have to do as you are."

Do for what? I wondered, but I did not want to spoil her fun by asking.

When the last hook was fastened, she ran across the room to a covered bonbon dish set between the pewter candlesticks on the mantel. She brought it back to me and lifted the cover. I stared in dismay as candlelight shone upon a coil of moonstone and amethyst. She plucked out the necklace and held it up, tossing the candy dish into the trunk. It was an amazing thing—a wide fringe made up of graduated stones that hung pendant four rows deep from a slim gold collar. I could not speak as she came behind me to hook the gold clasp at the back of my neck.

The pendant stones glowed against the ecru lace of the high-necked bertha.

"Of course I didn't wear it with a street costume like this," she said. "It was for my ball gown in the third act, when I was supposed to give up my American and marry a prince I didn't love. In the last scene I took off the necklace and used it as a bribe, so I could escape the palace and run away with my handsome hero. As a matter of fact, I detested the man who played the lead as the American. He was a scene stealer, if there ever was one. My duet with the prince really went over much better because we were *en rapport*. Of course in real life I would never have let the necklace go for anything. Lanny Earle gave it to me. He found it in an antique shop in New York and knew it should belong to me. I always wore it for him in the last act."

Lanny Earle? The name had a vaguely familiar ring. So Aunt Arvilla had enjoyed a real-life romance in her days of being on the stage—and good for her! Nevertheless, I had now been told two stories about the necklace and I had to bring her back from this fantasy in which she tried to recapture lost emotion through me.

"Cousin Gerald says the necklace belongs to your mother," I told her. "He says you took it from the collection."

"Of course I took it—as it was taken from me!" There was still spirit in Arvilla Gorham. "When my brother Henry brought me home that time, Mother said the necklace was too valuable to keep, and highly improper for me to have accepted as a gift. As if I cared about that! But by that time it—it couldn't be returned, and it has been in Mother's hands ever since. She wanted it because the amethysts match her eyes." Aunt Arvilla peered at me, suddenly doubtful. "Your eyes are the wrong color. They're like hers!"

"I'm her granddaughter," I said.

She accepted that and went on. "As soon as young Chris

told me Gerald had the jewels out to catalogue them, I knew I had to get the necklace back. And of course the garnet hatpin—though I didn't think of that till later. Did you hear the lovely crash Mortimer made when I toppled him over on that marble floor? I knew everyone would rush to the foyer and give me a chance to get to the jewelry case out in the gallery. I already had the necklace, but I wanted the hatpin as well, so I could be ready for you. I hid the necklace in the bonbon dish, and told everyone I had given it to Jimmy, my pet macaw."

I had to laugh at the very reasonableness of her actions. Except for a childlike quality, there seemed to be nothing wrong with either her memory, or her wits, and I began to side against my grandmother to an even greater degree.

Aunt Arvilla stood back and studied me with evident satisfaction. "You look absolutely ravishing! You look just the way Lanny said I looked in that dress."

"I wish I could see myself," I said.

At once she was all purposeful action. "Of course you must see yourself! We'll take care of that at once. There's a cheval glass in my room downstairs. Come along, Mallie dear. We'll go down there at once. No one can stop us now."

I gestured toward the articles scattered across the dusty floor. "Shall we put these back into the trunk first?"

She paused, regarding the confusion about the trunk in perplexity, a finger to her lips. "I came up here to look for something. I know I did. There was another dress— something white, embroidered with blue roses. I remember I was doing the embroidery myself—but I—I never finished. Every now and then I look for it, but I can never seem to find it." For the first time her high spirits wavered.

I waited, eager for anything she might tell me about the past. But she shrugged, her look bright and intent again.

"The blue roses were for luck, you know. I used to put them on everything. You'll find one embroidered inside the crown of that hat you're wearing, and inside the bodice of the dress. I used them because of the wallpaper roses out in the hall."

I wanted to keep her here longer before we went downstairs. I had said nothing that I had come here to say, and the opportunity for an opening seemed to be slipping away. Already she had drifted into the hall ahead of me, moving gracefully, afloat in her cloud of gray chiffon. I followed her more awkwardly, the blue skirt hampering my legs, its train apparently possessed of a rebellious life of its own. She glanced back at me and laughed.

"Now you spoil the illusion! You could never walk across a stage like that. Pick up the train, dear. Just behind, where the fullness comes. If you want to learn how to walk, watch Mother. She's the one I learned from. She was always an actress, really, though she would never have anything to do with the stage, and she'd be angry if you said that to her."

Again I tried to bring her back to the present. "What about the wallpaper, Aunt Arvilla?"

Halfway down the chill length of the hall she paused. Even in heavy silk, the cold seemed to penetrate here, and I could feel it myself as she shivered.

"If you want to be my friend," she told me, "don't call me Arvilla. Those I like always call me Fritzie. I'd like to be rid of Arvilla forever, though she always sneaks back when Mother is around."

"Then I'll call you that too, Aunt Fritzie," I said.

She gave me her bright, beautiful smile and reached out a hand to touch one of the blue roses that appeared here and there in the depressing gold and black and cinnamon pattern of the wallpaper.

"Blanche used to be afraid of these roses," she said. "Blanche was afraid of so many things. Is she still a scaredy-cat?"

I seized my opportunity. "Mother died a few days ago.

That's why I'm here, Aunt Fritzie. She was buried this afternoon in the Gorham plot in Shelby."

She wavered and put a hand to the wall. I watched her uncertainly, not knowing what the effect of my words would be, or whether I had done something dreadful in speaking them out so abruptly.

"Blanche!" she said, and the word was a soft cry. "Henry used to laugh because she was afraid of all the little ghost faces the roses made when we came up here to play. Henry was always unkind when we weren't sensible and proper, the way he was. So I made up a little story for Blanche about the roses being lucky—so she wouldn't be afraid. And after a while I believed it myself, and I began to use them for my lucky charm. But I wonder if they were really lucky. I wonder why I wanted to put them on that dress I was making. A white dress embroidered with blue roses."

She approached the head of the stairs and then paused again to reach back and take my hand. Already she seemed to have forgotten Mother's death.

"We must go down quickly," she warned me. "This is always the dangerous part of coming up here—the stairs. He fell all the way down this flight, you know. Backwards. So he waits for me here sometimes. Tonight you may be in danger too—because you're wearing my dress and you look the way he'd remember me. Hold my hand tightly. I loved my father when he was alive. Even when he was angry and disappointed with me, I loved him. I never meant to lose my temper and push him down the stairs. Here, Mallie— hold my hand and come with me quickly!"

Her fear was infectious and some touch of horror came with me as I ran down the stairs clutching her hand awkwardly, impeded by the unwieldy skirts of my dress. But when we reached the second floor she laughed around at me like a guilty child.

"There! We fooled him again, didn't we? Perhaps he didn't know which one of us to push. So I'm safe for an-

other time, and so are you. Though someday I know it
will happen. Someday they'll find me just the way they did
Diah Gorham."

I was beginning to see why Mother had charged me
with this mission. I could see how very much needed to be
done for Fritzie Gorham. When was I to have the chance?
When, other than now?

"Wait!" I called softly, as she would have run ahead of
me down the hall to the next turn of stairs.

She stopped and I clung to her hand again. "Please listen,
Aunt Fritzie. Mother sent me here to tell you something.
She wanted you to know—"

The thin hand twisted out of my grasp, and her bright,
youthful eyes seemed suddenly venomous.

"Hush!" she said. "You've come to tell me more lies. I
know—and I won't listen. My sister died a long time ago.
For me she died when she turned against me and—and—"
She faltered and her voice broke. She covered her face with
her hands. "No—I can't remember. I don't want to remember!"

I had done all I could for the moment. Perhaps the Gorhams were right and only disaster would result in the de-
livery of my mother's message.

"Never mind, Aunt Fritzie," I said, coaxing her now. "We
were going to find a mirror—so I can see how I look in your
dress."

She seemed to recover quite easily and to fling off disturbing thoughts of the past. But the same girlish quality
that had engaged me at first was beginning to distress me
now. She became too young at times and remembering her
eerie laughter, I understood why it had distressed me. It
was a child's laughter, coming from the mouth of an
aging woman.

I followed as she tiptoed ahead, and saw that double
doors stood open upon a room lighted by a single green-

shaded lamp that stood on a library table. Aunt Fritzie put a finger to her lips and beckoned to me. I went to stand beside her, looking into the room.

Wayne Martin had clearly been reading aloud to his son. Tieless, and in shirtsleeves, he sat in a deep green leather chair, with the boy upon his knee leaning against him. Both were fast asleep, with the book fallen to the floor. Wayne's head, as darkly tousled as his son's, lay back against the chair, and all pain and concern, all hint of the stringent quality I had glimpsed in him at times seemed wiped away. His mouth wore a faint, tender smile, and his lashes lay thick and dark upon his cheeks, resembling his son's. Even the cleft of his chin, seen thus, gave him an unguarded look, instead of that more usual air of invincible strength. I liked his strength, but I was a woman and I liked this too. I had never seen a man asleep before in just this way, and the sight, with his son in his arms, touched me. The boy's head rested against his father's chest and his lips puffed in tiny, repeated snores, so that he too seemed unguarded and all too vulnerable. The sight brought an unexpected stinging of tears to my eyes.

Gently Aunt Fritzie drew me past the open doorway, but before I was out of sight Chris stirred in a dream, and his father wakened, opened his eyes and stared at me without astonishment—as though I were a part of both their dreams and not in the least surprising in my 1903 costume.

Self-consciousness seized me—and dismay. Not only was I in fancy dress, but I was in Arvilla Gorham's company, where I should not be. Some explanation was certainly called for.

"This is—is the street costume of a Balkan princess," I told him brightly, and the statement seemed no more strange than anything else that was happening to me.

"I know," he said. "Her name was Zobelia. You remember the song?"

How could I not remember it? I flung Aunt Fritzie a

look of astonishment. So it was she who had made that old song famous? How little I knew—about anything!

Chris stirred against his father, but did not waken, and Wayne stood up, lifting his sleeping son in his arms. Aunt Fritzie, hearing his words, popped back into view, her expression one of delight.

"*She* is Zobelia now!" she cried.

"More likely she's Fritzie Vernon," Wayne said. "Anyway, suppose both you Balkan princesses come in and sit down, so we can talk over this re-creation of history. But first I'll put Chris to bed."

I liked his calm, faintly amused acceptance of a situation which had been thrust so suddenly upon him. If he had reservations, he was at least giving me the benefit of the doubt. This was not a man who would go in for such petty rages as I had sometimes witnessed with Greg when very small matters went wrong. With due cause, I was sure he could be an angry man, but he would not be unjust, or condemn me without a hearing. I was trusting again, I thought in sudden discovery. Trusting too soon—and somehow I did not mind.

I followed Aunt Fritzie into the room, while Wayne carried Chris off to bed. These, clearly, were a doctor's quarters, and not at all like the rest of the house. His black medical bag was set open upon a table, with a stethoscope spilling out of it. Near the telephone lay an appointment book. The thick volumes in the bookcase had to do with his profession, and there were laboratory reports with their printed headings topping the papers on his desk. All the furniture seemed commonplace and a little shabby, in contrast to the rest of the house—as if this room belonged to a man who had forgotten, or tried to forget, everything but his work.

Aunt Fritzie crossed the room to stand before the old-fashioned rolltop desk, open and crammed with papers and envelopes in every pigeonhole. She patted the scarred oak with an affectionate hand.

"This used to be old Dr. Wayne's desk. Wayne's father was always good to me. He was kind, even when my parents weren't. He kept me from dying when all those dreadful things happened."

Wayne had returned to the room. He slipped Fritzie's hand gently through the crook of his arm and led her to a black leather sofa. Shabby russet cushions were strewn its length, matching the equally russet patches where the leather had worn through. I had a feeling that most of these things were his father's, brought here long ago because he felt comfortable with them, perhaps even as a young medical student returning to the only home he knew at vacation time, and later as a young man perhaps wanting to fill the shoes of the country doctor who had been his father. At least Grandmother Julia, whatever else she was, had given Wayne Martin this home.

"Let's sit down and talk things over," he said, and motioned me to a place beside him, with Aunt Fritzie on the other.

The train of my costume wrapped itself about my ankles when I walked and I was glad to sit down and rearrange its folds at my feet. Wayne watched me, amused, and not nearly so condemning as I might have expected.

"Now suppose you two tell me all about this escapade," he said. "How did you happen to meet?"

Aunt Fritzie ducked her head to look around him at me. "I wrote Mallie a note and pinned it to her pillow with my garnet hatpin. I asked her to come and see me. So she did."

"Eminently simple," Wayne said. "And apparently not disastrous." He glanced at me again, and this time his eye was caught by the luster of moonstones. He reached out to touch the fringe of jewels about my neck. "Where did you get this?"

"I loaned it to her," Aunt Fritzie explained cheerfully.

"I found it in the collection this morning and of course I took it away because it's mine. I climbed on a chair in the drawing room and got the picture down too—the portrait of my father. But someone has already discovered that and taken it back."

"Why do you keep taking it away?" Wayne asked, his tone mild and uncritical.

"Because I can't talk to him on the wall of Mother's drawing room. When he's up there beside her, he won't listen to me. When I get him away alone, then I can talk to him. I can try to make him understand that I never meant what happened. If I could just get him to listen to me, perhaps I'd stop having the feeling that he waits for me on the attic stairs."

"Do you think such make-believe is really going to help?" Wayne asked. "You have work that keeps you busy and happy—why not forget about the past?"

"Because it won't forget about me," said Aunt Fritzie reasonably.

She spoke with unexpected wisdom. Events that were past did not always let you alone just because you wanted to forget them. Wayne, too, knew better than that.

He took her hand into his affectionately. "Sometimes you are a scatterbrain, Fritzie dear, and sometimes you are a very wise woman. You make me wonder if the scatterbrain is real, or if you just hide behind her to keep people from getting at you. Right now, however, I'm not talking to a character in a play. I'm talking to you. In order to keep peace in the family and a roof on the house, you'd better give that amethyst-moonstone thing back to Gerald. And the hatpin too. You don't really have any need for them these days."

"But the necklace is mine!" she assured him, growing excited again. "Lanny gave it to me. He would have come for me, you know—no matter where they hid me, or how many doors they locked. He'd have come for me eventually —if he had lived. Mallie—" she turned to me in entreaty, wanting me to believe, to help her, "—Mallie, let me tell you. Lanny Earle was a very well-known motion picture actor at the time. He had to go back to Hollywood to make another picture, even though we had fallen in love and he wanted to stay in New York for as long as my show would run. He left me only because he had to. And then— there was an accident. His car went off an ocean cliff out in California one night—and everything ended for me. Everything!"

Wayne tightened his grasp of her hand. "Don't keep saying that, Fritzie. I've been there too and I know it's futile. Things don't end. We pick up and go on—the way you've done. You can't tell me you're miserably unhappy these days. But you will be if you indulge yourself in these romances concerning a time you can't recall. That's what you've done tonight, isn't it—dressing Mallie up in your old stage clothes because she resembles you, trying to recapture something that's been gone for a good many years?"

Perhaps the quiet reality of what he was saying might have reached her, in spite of her keyed up mood, but just then we heard the sound of footsteps coming up the stairs. The steps of more than one person.

Wayne rose and went to the door, and though he moved without haste, I saw by his grave look that real trouble was upon us. Some sort of confrontation was about to take place and a feeling of near panic seized me. I wasn't ready! But then—would I ever be ready?

There was nothing to do but wait for whoever was about to walk through the door to Wayne Martin's room.

V

Nina Gorham came through the doorway first and paused to stare, shocked to see Fritzie and me sitting together on the long couch. Undoubtedly shocked at my costume, my hat, and the moonstone necklace about my throat. Her lips parted and she flung a frightened look behind her, but no words came. She was clearly speechless with alarm.

Kate Salway was next, and just after her, leaning upon her arm, came a tall, white-haired woman dressed in a long wine-colored gown that molded the lines of her fine, full figure. When she saw Aunt Fritzie and me sitting side by side on Wayne's leather couch, she pushed herself free of Kate's support and crossed the floor with a firm, graceful step. From the top of her high-piled white hair to the buckled black satin slippers on her feet she carried herself with regal bearing. I had never seen greater poise, or finer posture, than my grandmother Julia displayed in her seventy-ninth year.

Kate let her go and stayed near Aunt Nina just inside the door, clearly anxious and uncertain. Wayne went to the rolltop desk with an air of not interfering, of removing himself from the family picture.

As her mother neared us, Aunt Fritzie, who had sat frozen beside me, uttered a soft gasp and got quickly to her feet. I could not help myself when she pulled me up beside her, so that we stood like two naughty children awaiting punishment. I hated to meet Grandmother Julia like this, with all the disadvantage on my side, yet I found myself momentarily commanded by eyes that looked briefly into my own, and then away, as though what she saw repelled her. If age betrayed none of its outward signs in her carriage, in the proud lifting of her chin—it was there in her face. The fair smooth skin of the portrait downstairs had crumpled into tiny lines raying out from her eyes, from her mouth, even running down the column of her throat to flaw its once smooth beauty. Yet out of this wreckage, and somehow denying it, her astounding blue-violet eyes —amethyst eyes!—looked at us, smoldering with the undamped fires that still burned in Julia Gorham and would not be quenched until her death.

If my costume surprised her, if my likeness to her daughter when Fritzie was young, came home to her, she gave not the slightest sign. Her brief look dismissed me as being of no consequence, and I could feel myself shrink in my own estimation, even while I resented the diminishment. Her attention was given fully to Aunt Fritzie, who shriveled into a wizened child before her eyes.

"Look at you!" Grandmother Julia said, flicking a hand in distaste at her daughter. "You're filthy with cobwebs and dust. And your face is dirty. You've been in the attic again, haven't you?"

Aunt Fritzie flung out hands that looked more bony than her mother's and her words tumbled over one another as she tried to speak.

"I—I had to look for the white dress. The one with the roses done in blue. I know it must be there. I know—"

Julia Gorham whipped her into silence with a word. "Hush!"

Fritzie hushed and hung her head in shame like a beaten child. I stared at my grandmother with sudden hatred and slipped an arm about Aunt Fritzie's drooping shoulders. A gesture her mother ignored.

"Listen to me, Arvilla," Grandmother Julia said, and her voice betrayed no least quaver of age. "There never was a white dress. You haven't worn one since you were a little girl. This running away to search the attic is further evidence of a behavior that grows uncontrollable. What you do with your father's picture, the stealing of the necklace and the hatpin, pushing over that suit of armor—all this is part of the same pattern. Where do you think this sort of thing will end for you?"

Before our eyes Aunt Fritzie began to weep helplessly, and I hated my grandmother fervently for doing this to her, hated the breakdown, the disintegration of a person that her cruel words were causing.

"Take her back to bed," Grandmother said to Kate Salway, and I was glad, at least, to see the gentleness with which Kate put an arm about poor Fritzie and led her away.

No one said anything until they were out of sight, and then Aunt Nina spoke nervously. "The attic must be locked. This sort of thing can't be allowed to continue."

Grandmother Julia ignored her as though her son Henry's wife could not possibly say anything worth listening to. All her attention was given suddenly to me and I found myself stiffening in an effort to stand up in my own right and with a will of my own in the face of her wilting stare. Why hadn't Wayne Martin stopped the wicked attack upon Aunt Fritzie? Why didn't he help me? But I dared not look around to see where he was, what he was doing. All my strength must be given to the clash with my grandmother that was now upon me.

"You hardly wear that costume with a flair," she told me, a new challenge snapping through her words, shining in her eyes. She enjoyed a battle, this woman. I was a young, unknown quantity and she must be aware that I would not be as easily dismissed as Aunt Fritzie. After all, I was here against her wishes, and others would have reported the fact that I would not go away without accomplishing my purpose. So she must turn a stronger whiplash upon me.

I said nothing, refusing either to apologize or explain.

"Give me the necklace," she said, and held out her hand.

I wanted to defy her, but I could not when it came to this, and I fumbled with the clasp at the back of my neck, removed the fringe of jewels. "Perhaps you want the hatpin too," I said, and took it from the crown, took the flat lacy hat from my head.

She did not move in my direction and I was forced to go to her and give both moonstones and pin into her hand. But when she had taken them, she grasped my arm with her free hand and turned me toward the light, in order to examine my cheek with merciless blue-violet eyes.

"I think you will hardly run off to go on the stage like your aunt," she said. "But at least you've been blessed with my hands, so you can continue to earn a living at this ridiculous work of yours. Oh, I know about it—I've seen the pictures in the magazines! Disgraceful for a Gorham, but I suppose it's all you can do. Of course it would never have been necessary if your mother had accepted the money I sent her."

I had never known any money had been sent, and I was proud of my mother for refusing her help.

"Tomorrow morning you will return to wherever you belong," she concluded, "and I think you will not come here again."

I had never known anyone who could be so openly cruel, so lacking in human kindness. She left me both humiliated and astonished, and I could find no proper weapon to use against her. Nevertheless, I made a feeble attempt.

"Don't you feel anything at all?" I asked her despairingly. "Doesn't it trouble you that your daughter Blanche is dead?"

She did not so much as blink her thin white lashes. "As far as I am concerned, my youngest daughter died long ago when she chose of her own accord to leave this house. I have nothing left to feel as far as she is concerned."

I knew better than to remind her that I was Blanche's daughter and of her own and Diah's blood. She could not care less.

"Why did you come here after all these years and expect to find a welcome?" she demanded.

"I didn't come for a welcome," I said, and raised my own chin to match the tilt of hers. "I came here because my mother informed me of something before she died. She wanted me to tell her sister Arvilla the truth about certain things that happened in the past."

To my surprise her expression changed, and I saw that my grandmother had, after all, her own vulnerability. She put one hand to the cabochon ruby in the brooch that clasped the high collar of her gown, and I saw her fingers tighten upon it. Aunt Nina saw too, and she came near, watchful, ready to assist. My grandmother rejected her support with a look, and I took the opportunity to glance around for Wayne. He stood near his father's desk, continuing to hold himself apart from this family matter. I could laugh at myself for looking to him for help. I was the intruding stranger, of course, and I could expect nothing from his direction.

"From the time she was a small child," Grandmother said, "Blanche was a weaver of fabrications. She never spoke the truth if she could help it. Whatever she has told you is sure to be falsified. And I will not allow our peaceful lives to be disturbed at this late date by Blanche's make-believe."

I would not accept that. "I've known my mother for twenty-three years and I've never heard her tell a falsehood. She loved to make up stories—but I always knew they were stories. She was never a liar when it came to telling me *factual* things." That was true. She might sometimes evade— who didn't?—but she had not lied. And certainly not about anything as vital as her father's death.

Spots of color burned high in my grandmother's cheeks and the hand at the great cabochon ruby moved upward to her throat, as if she caught her breath in pain. Wayne dropped the papers on his desk and came toward her with a quick look of warning for me. I would not heed it. I had no sympathy for this tyrannical old woman.

"Mother told me exactly how Grandfather died on the stairs," I hurried on. "She saw the whole thing. It's true there was a quarrel between Arvilla and her father, and she did run after him up the attic stairs—but she was never responsible for his fall. He tried to stop her from whatever it was she meant to do and he lost his balance and fell. Mother tried to tell the truth afterwards—when everyone was blaming Aunt Arvilla. But no one would listen. Everyone wanted to blame Aunt Arvilla for her father's death because that was the easy thing to do."

Grandmother started to speak, and I hurried on before she could stop me.

"Aunt Arvilla collapsed afterwards and was in no state to comprehend anything. That was when Mother despaired and ran away. Not only because she wanted to marry my father, and you, Grandmother Julia, didn't want her to—because he was only a summer visitor and not New England born!—but also because she couldn't bear to live in the shadow of what was done to her sister. You know she came back years later, but her efforts then to tell the truth did no more good than they had in the beginning, thanks to you. I know all this. She told me just before she died. It's dreadful that Aunt Arvilla has had to live all her life under this terrible stigma—believing it herself!"

I saw by my grandmother's face that I was telling her nothing she had not heard before. She did not mean to accept my words now, any more than she had accepted them from others in the past. She *chose* to believe that her elder daughter was to blame for Diah's death—and she would never accept any other explanation. Nor was it likely that Aunt Fritzie herself would believe, even if I found an opportunity to tell her. The pattern had been set long ago, and nothing would change it now. This was a futile mission upon which my mother had sent me. I turned my back upon my grandmother and upon Wayne Martin, and moved toward the door. All I wanted now was to get out of these stifling stage garments and back into my own dress. I had no more purpose than that.

Grandmother Julia's words stopped me at the door. "What did your mother tell you about that quarrel? What did she tell you about the white dress?"

I turned back to her, puzzled. "She never mentioned a

white dress. She didn't tell me the reason for the quarrel between Grandfather Diah and Aunt Arvilla."

The tip of my grandmother's tongue came out to moisten lips that were no longer full and sensuous like those of the portrait.

"I think you are a liar, too," she said softly. "I think you are ready to make things up like your mother. But it doesn't matter because there is nothing for you here. No matter what you attempt—there is nothing for you. In the morning Elden Salway will take you to your plane. And that will be the end of this matter. Perhaps—if you go away quickly without causing any more trouble, I will send you a gift. A generous gift that will come to you every year and will make life easier for you, since you are unable to be a full-fledged model because of your face."

I had seldom found myself so angry. "Why should you want to bribe me to leave? No thank you—you can keep your gifts! I've never wanted anything from you but kindness for my mother. And I don't want anything now. If you care to know what I really think, I'll tell you! I'm sorry to be descended from Julia Gorham. I might have loved and appreciated Grandfather Diah, but I can feel nothing but shame that I am related to you."

I picked up the heavy train of my skirt and made as dramatic an exit into the hall as Fritzie Vernon could ever have made in this dress, and I did not look behind me to see my grandmother's probable outrage. Nor did I care what Nina Gorham thought—or Wayne Martin, who had stood by and let that dreadful woman slander her daughter and bait her granddaughter. I swished my way angrily up the stairs to the attic and was not in the least afraid that Grandfather Diah would mistake me for Fritzie and show himself on the stairs.

The upper floor was as chill as before, and Fritzie's candles burned low in pewter holders. My mauve-pink dress lay where I'd flung it across the open lid of the trunk and

I began an angry struggle with the hooks that ran from some inches below the waist all the way up the back of the silk costume. Those hooks that I could reach I managed to fumble open with unaccustomed fingers, but there was a whole row of the dreadful things in the center of my back, completely out of reach. I grew red-faced and furious with my efforts. Nor would the stitches give when I tried to rip the hooks open. This was no flimsy machine-made garment. How had women ever managed to dress and undress themselves in those days?

My unexpected rescuer was Kate Salway. She came running up the stairs at the peak of my humiliation, when it seemed that I must give up and seek help somewhere. She saw my red face and sensed the nearness of angry tears, for she was immediately soothing and kind.

"I've come just in time, haven't I? Your Aunt Fritzie sent me up. She remembered that you'd have trouble getting out of this dress. Here—let me help."

I offered my back and she finished the task quickly, efficiently, sympathetic toward the problem, but impersonal toward me. As I got out of the gown, I let my anger spill over.

"I've never seen so outrageous a person as my grandmother!" I cried. "What she did to poor Aunt Fritzie was dreadful. And so was the way the rest of you stood by and never lifted a finger to help."

Kate knelt on the dusty floor and began packing everything back into the trunk. "When you're dressed, you'd better return to your room, Miss Rice, and not come over to this side again."

I dropped the pink sheath over my head and ran the back zipper up far more easily than I had been able to cope with hooks and eyes. My anger seethed, and I further resented Kate's indirect rebuke.

"She behaves like an empress! And the rest of you—Aunt

Nina, Dr. Martin—even you!—all dance to whatever tune she whistles. I was sickened tonight, disgusted."

Kate looked up at me with her grave, wide-spaced gaze. "Then of course you'll want to leave as early as you can tomorrow morning. You won't try to see Miss Fritzie again and upset her further."

"Upset her!" I echoed. "Upset her, when all I've wanted was to help her understand that she isn't responsible for her father's death. I've brought her a gift—but that dreadful old woman downstairs won't let me deliver it!"

Kate bent to scoop up a handful of old programs, reached for a scrapbook of notices, packed them neatly into the trunk. "It isn't a wise gift at this late date. It can do her nothing but harm—just as your coming here has already harmed her."

"How?" I cried. *"How?"*

"Because you've started her trying to remember, trying to dredge up the past," Kate said.

"How can that do anything but good? There seems to be nothing wrong with her memory—or her wits. She only wilted when Grandmother spoke to her in that cruel way."

"Sometimes one has to seem cruel when a woman behaves like a child." Kate put both hands on the edge of the trunk and stood up to face me.

She was a gentle-seeming girl, with a core of determination, a quiet strength that I had sensed before. Her brown eyes were bright upon me, and not at all approving.

"How do you know that it's a good thing for Fritzie to remember?" she went on. "Your aunt has put up a barrier in her mind that shuts out all the things she couldn't cope with. Dr. Martin says this is what happens sometimes. She can remember beyond the barrier back into her childhood. She can remember quite happily her time on Broadway. But when it comes to Lanny Earle, she wavers. Tonight she was remembering too much. And when it comes to her father's death, she doesn't remember at all. She only repeats what others have told her. She doesn't know why she was at odds with him, or what happened that day on the stairs. Let her alone, Miss Rice. Sometimes I think I envy her the way she is. She's often really happy, you know, in a childlike way. Sometimes I wish I could shut out everything hurtful just as she has done. Memory can mean pain—or are you too young to know that?"

I was not too young. I knew. I thought of Kate's possible marriage to Gerald—marriage to a man with his handicap. And I thought in confusion of Greg turning away from my face in clear light. Yet—no matter what pain might do, or how deeply it could cut, I was still sure I would never willingly give up memory.

"Of course I know," I said. "Being alive means pain. A child learns that. But it means joy, too. Otherwise we're vegetables. Or animals."

She returned to her work on the floor, kneeling beside the trunk. "Perhaps my brother Elden's philosophy is wisest after all. The survival of the fittest. Elden lives close to nature and he sees weak plants give way to strong, and maimed animals destroyed by those that are whole."

I stared at her, finding it hard to believe that so gentle-seeming a person could repeat such a creed. "But we're men, not plants or animals! Compassion for people like Aunt Fritzie and Cousin Gerald—even for me—is what makes us—well, different—better perhaps."

"Does it?" she asked calmly. "How much compassion do you feel for your grandmother's tragedies?" She finished her task, rose to her feet and dusted off her hands and her skirt while I watched her.

"I suppose I'm not much better than the next fellow," I said. "But some people are able to feel compassion. I try to. And I should think Dr. Martin might, for all his brusqueness at times. That's what makes living bearable, isn't it?"

Kate smiled. "I suppose so. Are you ready to return to your room? I'll put out those candles. I must remember to fit up the attic with bulbs so Miss Fritzie won't burn the house down one of these days."

I did not want to hurry away and I picked up the heavy blue silk dress I had worn and looked inside at the waist lining. There was the embroidered blue rose Aunt Fritzie had mentioned. I held it out to Kate.

"What is all this talk about embroidered blue roses? Why is Aunt Fritzie looking for an old dress, and why do you suppose my grandmother asked if Mother had told me about such a dress?"

Something in Kate's face changed, as though she put up shutters against me. I wondered that I had ever thought candor would best suit Kate Salway. She could be an utterly secretive person, it seemed.

"These aren't questions you should ask me, Miss Rice," she said, retreating into her role of prim housekeeper, as she took the dress from me and returned it to the trunk, closing the lid.

I would not permit her retreat. "How can you bear to stay in this house and work for a monstrous old woman like Julia Gorham? How could you give up the satisfactions of nursing for something like this?"

"Perhaps I'm needed here," she said with quiet dignity, and went to the mantel and blew out the candles.

At once the shadows grew softer, their edges blurred by moonlight that came through the windows. I could not see her expression as she crossed the room, and she astonished me by clasping my wrist with her strong fingers.

"Just go away, Miss Rice. Go away and leave us to work out our lives in the way we think fit. We don't need a catalyst!"

The word Elden had said was my grandmother's— *catalyst*. But Elden was not of the same opinion. It was he who had felt that a shaking up by just such a catalyst as I would be good for them all.

When I tried to draw my hand away, her fingers tightened and she began to whisper, as if she feared the very shadows that might overhear her words.

"Now that your mother has frightened them with her letter about the white dress, you mustn't stay. It might even be dangerous for you to stay. Sometimes I'm like Fritzie in the way I can sense what's in the air, and I feel this strongly. Silverhill has never been good for you. Don't let it hurt you again."

She released my hand and slipped out of the room. Her full skirt seemed to leave its rustling sound behind long after I heard her steps retreat down the stairs. I was growing less sure now of Kate Salway's being anyone's pawn.

The attic had become a shadow-filled place and I lost no time in running along the hall to the front tower. On the other side the lighted hall was not marred by cobwebs and neglect, or haunted by the memory of a man who had died there long ago.

My room was as I had left it, yet though it seemed a quiet, innocuous place, I did not want to go to bed without knowing what else this floor might hold in its stretch of empty rooms.

A door opened at the rear of my bedroom and I went into it, switching on lights as I moved. There were, I found, three large rooms opening in a row before I came to the rear wall of the house, each room in turn giving onto the hall. Only my room was in use. The others were filled with odds and ends of discarded furniture, old screens, boxes, trunks—the usual accumulation of generations which had lived in one house. Yet these rooms were not in disorder —they were not abandoned and dusty, as the rooms on the other side seemed to be.

I picked my way through the last of the row and left it by way of a door into the rear of the hall. There a window opened upon the house. Below me stretched the roof of the gallery-corridor, and at either end of the gallery, to my left and right, rose the two-storied wings which the gallery connected. Lights burned on either hand, but I could not see the wings clearly without removing the screen and leaning out the window. At least the birches were contained here, beyond the picket fence that surrounded the garden, and I could look down, unimpeded, upon the great glass mound of the conservatory, rising like a blister from the garden's center. I could understand why Elden resented the conservatory, crouching as it did in the very midst of what he had created. I could not blame him for wanting its obstruction removed.

Beyond the garden I could see the crushed white gravel of the rear driveway, ending before what was apparently both garage and living quarters for Elden and his sister. At an upstairs window Elden lounged in an easy chair, a book in his hands, seemingly untouched by recent happenings in the house, except as his sister would bring them home to him. What would he be reading? I wondered. Thoreau, perhaps—or more likely the latest spy thriller?

It was the moon-silvered dome of the conservatory that continued to draw my attention, however, rising like a huge crystal ball which held, not my future, but the mystery of the past. Tomorrow, early, I might have to be aboard that plane for New York. There was nothing I could sensibly accomplish for my mother here. I had no wish to know my grandmother. I would return to New York and forget the Gorhams and Silverhill. There was just one thing I did not want to leave behind—and that was the misty piece of my childhood which still troubled me. Until that mist was dispelled and whatever had happened to me beneath the glass dome of the conservatory was clear in my mind, I would never be free of questioning.

As I had already discovered, no one here meant to tell me anything. There was hardly a person at Silverhill who

was not engaged in hiding some secret of his own. I could
feel concealment and secrecy all around me. Not only by
Gerald, but by the others too, living as they did under the
same spell of illusion as that cast by Diah's gallery.

I wanted no more of it. If I was to exorcise the past,
it must be through action of my own, since no one would
help me. Like Aunt Fritzie, I too had blocked off something
tragic and hurtful that had happened long ago, but since
my own memory was lost in childhood, it might be harder
to re-create. Tonight in the gallery with Gerald, when he
had pointed out the door to the conservatory, I had felt the
chill of recognition—a recognition bound in fear. If I went
into that place alone, with no one to see me, or set obstacles
before me, perhaps I could find again the small child who
had been so grievously hurt and scarred, perhaps I could
free her from old terror.

At least I must try.

But not tonight. I was not so brave as to dare that place
when only moonlight fell through the glass dome. Nor
could I turn on lights that would warn the household of my
presence. Tomorrow morning, however, as soon as dawn
touched the sky, as soon as the palest daylight reached the
glass, I would be down there. I would go quietly, so no one
would know, and I would give myself up to the warmth
of that sultry place and let submerged memory surface.
That it would be very warm, I knew—not only because any
hothouse is warm—but because this was a feeling I still
carried in my very bones, and in my flesh. It was part of
that long-ago terror. But whatever had frightened a child
should no longer frighten an adult. If Aunt Fritzie had
hurt me then, she would not hurt me now. Tonight she
and I had been drawn together as friends and the thought
of her no longer terrified me. It seemed ridiculous that
others should warn me against her.

I went back to my room and prepared for bed. But before
I got between the sheets I turned out the light and crept

into a deep dormer, knelt on the window seat so I could look out over the side lawn. One certainly had the illusion of birches coming closer to the windows after dark. Up here I could look out into their faintly rustling tops and follow the long white trunks to the ground. I could almost imagine that the trees moved as I watched them.

Or was it only imagining? Had I, as Gerald said, the "gift" to see? If I leaned closer would I hear the wailing of some long-ago Gorham child? But the movement was real among the trees. Someone in a dark dress stirred in the moon shadows and a pale face was suddenly raised to the night. Kate Salway stood there in the birch grove, her full green dress dark against white bark. As I watched, she seemed to slip down along the trunk of a tree until she was almost lost in shadow on the ground. Her knees were drawn up, her face pressed against them, so she was no more than a dark huddle. There was nothing to be heard except a rustling among the treetops and the din of an insect chorus. If Kate wept, she made no sound—yet somehow I knew she was crying her heart out down there.

I must not watch. I crept backward out of the dormer and went troubled to bed. At last I slept and wakened and slept again, dreaming uneasily while I waited for the dawn.

VI

Dawn mists were thick around the pond, blocking it from view, when my inner alarm wakened me. For a few moments I lay thinking of my mother, and of being alone in a house which should have welcomed me and had not. I thought of my grandmother's cold face as she had looked during that dreadful scene last night, and of her eyes that could still blaze with an amethyst fire.

I thought too of Wayne Martin. Not of the moment when he had withdrawn from us all during Grandmother

Julia's exhibition of tyranny, but as I had seen him earlier asleep in his chair, with his sleeping son in his arms. That was a memory to bring me comfort, but I did not want to know why. To feel such warmth toward a man I scarcely knew could mean more catastrophe. I would not have it. Awake he could be trusted no more than any other man. Like Gerald, I dared not think of love, of companionship, of marriage. I had told my cousin that his attitude was senseless, but now, in these dawn hours, I was no longer sure.

At any rate, I could not lie dreaming in bed. I knew what waited ahead of me and I got up and dressed hurriedly in a loose summer frock of pale yellow. Canary yellow! I did not know what the color would mean to me before the day was over.

Faint light touched misty lawns, and the eastern sky had begun to pale by the time I stole downstairs. The doors of Nina Gorham's rooms were ajar, but she did not stir as I went past. An old house is filled with creaking and my light steps would add no more sound than seemed usual. Below, at the door to the drawing room, I paused and looked in. The curtains had been flung open—by some earlier riser than I? Outdoors the silver trunks of the birches were touched with pale light, but no huddled girl wept among them. By day they stood back from the house and were only white birch trees.

I stayed for a moment to look up at the portraits of my grandfather Diah and his Julia, and saw that someone had turned on the hidden illumination that lighted them. Again, some earlier riser than I—or some wanderer in the night who suffered insomnia and came to look at the pictures? When he had married her, had Julia been anything like she was now? Had Diah suffered at her hands before he died, or had she only grown hard and unfeeling in the years that had passed over her since she had lost him?

But I was delaying, postponing. I must not waste time. I must reach the conservatory before anyone else was up.

The door to the gallery opened at a touch of my hand and I remembered the three steps down to the lower level. All was darker here than I expected, for this was the western side of the house and the sky still hung black as a velvet curtain, with mirrors and windows showing only shadowy reflection. Opposite where I stood something moved—and was still, then moved again. My heart leaped in my throat, until I saw that it was my own yellow-clad form seen in the mirror that covered the conservatory door. I crossed the gallery and put my hand to a knob set into glass, forced my fingers to turn the knob. The neck of a narrow, roofed passageway, completely dark and windowless, opened before me, leading to a second door. A door with a transparent panel of glass. When I pressed my face against it, I could see into the black tangle of a wild, scarcely-to-be-imagined growth. It was like looking through a window into a night-filled rain forest in which anything at all might hide to do me harm. My heart was a triphammer now.

Thankfully, far above the plant growth, where the glass arched high, I saw the palest tinting of light—a light that spread, even as I watched, swelling slowly toward the true radiance of dawn. In a little while all these plants would be lighted from above and I would dare to step into their midst. Until then, I could afford to wait. No one had made a sound about the house. No one was likely to be up at this hour.

Through the outer door I returned to the gallery, to find that faint light had begun to penetrate here. Chinese rugs were pale wheat color beneath my feet, and very soft, so that I made no sound as I moved to the glass case which Gerald had shown me last night. All I wanted was to distract myself, to take my mind from the ordeal I was not yet ready to face. Standing before the case I remembered that

Gerald had touched a switch to light up its interior and I reached beneath the cabinet, found the button.

At once the collection came to lustrous life, as it had done last night—but now my eyes sought only two places in the array. Yes, the necklace of moonstones and amethysts that I had worn last night was back in place, completing the parure of which it was the main item. But the hatpin with the crescent head of garnets was still missing, and uneasily I wondered why. Grandmother Julia had taken both, to be returned, presumably, to Gerald, who would put them back in the case. Had he held it out for some reason of his own? Or might Aunt Fritzie have given Kate the slip again last night and taken out the pin? I tested the lid with my fingers and found that it opened readily. The pin could easily have been taken away again.

By now the dawn was brightening, and the mirrors and windows about me were aglow with light. Not a strong enough light to fling shadows across the floor, but a gentle illumination that made the long gallery swim into blurred view, like something seen under water. I dared not wait any longer. This was the time to face my fears, defeat them, prove to myself that in spite of the tremors that ran along my nerves, I had only to walk into what was no more than an elaborate greenhouse, and find my way back into the past. Find my way as an adult who knew there was nothing there to frighten me.

At the same time, I must remember. I must try to remember every step of a way that had been taken long ago on some other, more dreadful occasion.

Once more I let myself into the passageway that led to the conservatory door, and I was sure that memory went with me, trembling through my very flesh, yet not awakening my mind except as I noted the approach of fear.

"Stop it!" I told myself, whispering aloud. "You aren't a four-year-old now!"

I opened the second door, thrust my way quickly through

and closed it behind me. Damp warmth and a long-forgotten odor struck me in the face so that my senses seemed to whirl into confusion. Yet I went on. I stepped onto a tile path that wound through thick plant growth and forced myself to look about me, forced my mind to an objectivity that denied my fearful senses.

An astonishing thing had been done in this place. Earth had been filled in deeply on each side of the terra cotta tiles that formed the narrow path I followed, and plants of every description were growing there—not in tubs and pots, but in deep, sloping banks of earth, held back at their lower edge by a guard rail of scalloped earthen tiles.

Deliberately, I delayed my entry into the heart of the conservatory, studying the plants as I went by, step by slow step. Near me was a sprawling growth with huge, dark green, leathery leaves. The next plant had clawlike fronds scraggly and uneven, twining a dead stalk. Farther on grew queer-looking leaves covered with tiny hairs that made them look like creeping insects, while the next plant was covered with what seemed to be tiny green blisters. I thought of Elden's remarks about "unhealthy growth." None of these plants were appealing—all had a nightmarish quality.

The moist, heavy warmth, the smell of this rank green world, was like a blanket, smothering me. The sky began to glow above the faraway bubble of glass overhead, bathing everything in a brightening green shimmer. Yet it was not the plants themselves which frightened me. They were only a background for something far more terrifying. I was aware now of a stir of sound that rose in volume as I listened—a chirping, a chattering and shrilling, that began to fill the air. It was the sound of birds wakening to the day—a sound, for me, that carried mindless terror.

In the humid warmth my skin felt clammy. It was only by concentrated effort that I kept my feet upon the path and followed the walk around a curve and into the heart of Grandfather Diah's conservatory. Here a large space opened beneath the center of a dome painted gold by the full light of dawn.

Here tropical fish darted about in a circular fishpond. More plants stood round it in pots and boxes, the wilder growth left behind. And everywhere—everywhere!—were cages of birds. They hung suspended from decorative supports, they rested on tables, on pedestals and stands, and from all directions came their chirping and shrilling and twittering—not the sounds of songbirds, but the sounds of fear, of anger.

Some area of my mind tried to save me, to chide me for ridiculous terror—but this was a terror of the blood, born of the long-ago fright of a child.

Something far overhead giggled shrilly in a near-human sound—a mad sound—and that was worst of all. I could not move. I stood in the midst of the angry scolding that gathered about me—the scolding of birds disturbed by an enemy. Then, quite suddenly, the thing that had giggled flew at me. It came down from its perch, flashing blue and gold wings past my face and swooped away.

I screamed then, screamed again and again. At once the uncaged bird swept back—straight at me, to land upon my shoulder and cling with talons that hurt my flesh. Its rounded beak darted at me and something hard and painful stabbed at my cheek. All the while I could hear myself screaming, unable to move, unable to stop. And while I screamed the birds fell suddenly silent—perhaps terrified into stillness by my sounds of fear.

It was young Chris who found me cowering upon my knees, while the blue-and-gold bird clung to my shoulder and made his repeated attacks. It was Chris who quickly took the bird upon his own wrist, and then pulled me up, thrust me in the direction of the gallery.

"Go back!" he said. "My father's just come home. He'll help you. Go back to the gallery!"

I stumbled along the walk, and found the door, flung my-

self through it. Wayne met me at the second door, drew me
into the quiet of the gallery where the sound of birds was
lost in the distance. Somehow the screaming that hung
about me had ceased, but I held to him sobbing in great
choked gulps in an effort to get my breath.

"You're all right now, Mallie." His voice soothed me, his
arms held me, protecting me from all unknown evil. "Stop
it, Mallie. You aren't hurt—you're only frightened. Stop it
now."

I knew I had been in his arms before, knew that he had
held me long ago and comforted me, ministered to my hurt.

"Her cheek's bleeding! The scar is bleeding!" That was
Aunt Nina's voice, speaking from beyond him, and I heard
the note of horror in her words.

Wayne propelled me to a chair, lowered me gently into it.

"Shall I get your bag, Wayne?" Aunt Nina cried. "You'll
need to give her something to stop her hysteria. You'll need
to treat that wound."

I would have put my hand in further fright to my cheek,
but Wayne held it away. His fingers touched my chin,
turned my head carefully.

"It's nothing but a scratch. It's not like the other time.
I've had as much from that macaw myself, and he's a
healthy enough bird. A little antiseptic will fix it up. In a
moment she'll stop crying on her own. But you can get my
bag, if you will, Nina."

She hurried off, her pink challis wrapper clutched about
her, her gray hair untidy in the early morning light. I was
recovering enough to be aware of detail now—of Wayne in
his shirtsleeves, his tie askew at the open throat of his shirt,
weariness staining the flesh beneath his eyes. I remembered
Chris's saying that he had just come home. The boy re-
joined us, barefooted and in pajamas, and I tried to smile at
him, to thank him for coming so quickly. He saw my attempt and his young eyes were as kind as his father's.

I was recovering fully now, and when another voice reached me I swallowed hard on a final sob and made no further sound aloud.

"Do you suppose she has killed any of the birds this time?" Grandmother Julia asked.

Wayne looked down the gallery to where my grandmother stood in the open door of her apartment. She still wore her long wine-colored gown and as we both stared at her, she came toward us with her firm step and regal carriage. She looked as neat as though she had been up for a long while—or perhaps had never gone to bed at all.

"That remark was uncalled for," Wayne told her wearily. "I can guess why Mallie was in there, but I hardly think she meant to injure any of Arvilla's birds."

Grandmother Julia seemed not to hear his words. She stood above me with such a look of rejection in her eyes that they seemed to carry repugnance at the very sight of me.

"Your mother was a fool," she said, "and I can see that you're a craven like her. Terrified of everything. Even of harmless birds. You'd better pull yourself together so you can make your plane this morning."

Wayne released me and rose to face her. For the moment, at least, I had a champion. "Mallie has had a serious shock. Perhaps it's our fault this has happened, but since it has, we owe her every kindness and consideration. She won't be on that plane. A later one, perhaps, when she has fully recovered. Right now, as soon as I've patched up her cheek, she's coming outside with me for a talk, well away from this house."

Once more color burned high in Grandmother Julia's cheeks. "I want a talk with you myself, young man. As soon as you're free, please come to my rooms."

She faltered painfully as she turned, but nevertheless thrust away the hand he reached toward her. I sensed the effort it cost her to walk firmly and steadily the length of the gallery and go up the few steps to her door. If she had not been so coldly inconsiderate, I might have admired her at that moment.

Aunt Nina returned to give Wayne his medical bag and she peered critically at my cheek. "It seems uncanny—history repeating itself like this."

Wayne was ministering to the scratch and I pulled away from the smart of the antiseptic, though not because it stung. "What history?" I cried. "What happened to me in there when I was a child that can still frighten me so badly now?"

"This is what we're going to talk about," Wayne said. "Steady now, while I put a patch of gauze on that spot. Just till the bleeding stops. Then we'll get out of here and have that talk. There's been enough hushing up of the past."

Grandmother Julia, her hand on the knob of her door, heard him and swung about. "We've hushed all that up for Arvilla's sake. You know that! We can't have her thrown back into old horrors. That's what matters most now."

"Is it?" Wayne said. "Isn't it time to think of what is good for Malinda Rice, who still has life ahead of her? And who happens to be your granddaughter?"

It renewed me to find the uninvolved man of last night gone, and a partisan in his place—a partisan on my side. I began to feel a good deal braver.

Aunt Nina made a choked sound at Wayne's words and cast a frightened look at Grandmother Julia. "I'd better go and see if all this screeching has wakened Gerald," she murmured and started in the direction of her son's rooms.

Before she reached his door, however, a tall woman in floating gray chiffon appeared in the doorway that led to the house, pausing for a moment on the steps, before she came down and sped toward me.

"What has happened, Mallie dear?" Aunt Fritzie cried. "What has hurt your cheek?"

I tried to tell her it was nothing, but she slipped around Wayne to drop to the rug beside me, touching me soothingly, comfortingly, as if I were a child.

"She's Blanche's little girl, you know," she said brightly to Wayne.

"I do know," Wayne said and fixed a bit of adhesive to my cheek. "Mallie went into the conservatory just now and that macaw of yours frightened her and pecked her cheek."

Aunt Fritzie patted me affectionately. "Oh, what a bad boy that Jimmy is! First hiding the necklace—and now this. But he doesn't know you, Mallie—that's all that's the matter. You should have let me take you in there. Jimmy is the only one of my birds I let go free. He loves living in among all the plants, and he knows us. He only means to be friendly."

I was aware of the silence of the others, of my grandmother poised before her door, and of Aunt Nina at the opposite end of the gallery. Neither had moved since Aunt Fritzie's appearance.

Grandmother found her tongue first. "Take Arvilla back to her room, Nina," she said, and Aunt Nina hurried obediently toward her sister-in-law.

Aunt Fritzie sidestepped her with accustomed skill, turning to Wayne. "Mallie is helping me to remember," she assured him. "I want her to stay here for a long while—stay until everything comes back to me. I know it's wrong for me to hide from the past. Sometimes you've told me that. After I met her last night I began to remember quite a few things clearly. Dr. Wayne dear, I'm going to get well—I know I am!"

Wayne put an arm about her, kissed her cheek. "That's wonderful, darling. This is what we've wanted for years. You work hard on that remembering."

"Remembering!" Grandmother Julia seemed to choke on the word. "When she couldn't even remember what she did with the moonstone necklace yesterday!"

Aunt Nina caught Fritzie by the arm and drew her firmly away. "That's enough excitement for now. Let's go back to your room, and I'll call Kate to give you your breakfast."

Aunt Fritzie was still ready to show something of the spark I had glimpsed in her last night. There was youthful defiance in the way she flung off Aunt Nina's hand. But when she would have spoken, Grandmother Julia settled the matter.

"Go with Nina at once," she told her daughter. "All this effort to remember can do you nothing but harm. If you're going to remember anything, perhaps you'd better recall that it was Wayne's father who said you'd be a lot happier if you were allowed to forget the past. I'm sure he was a wiser man than his son will ever be."

Her look seemed to challenge Wayne, to mock him, and he was suddenly very still. He faced my grandmother, held her eyes with his own so coldly that I had a sense of conflict between them that I did not understand. Then Wayne forced himself to relax and to speak without rancor.

"I can't quarrel with that," he said, "but a good many years have passed since Dad's time. Perhaps things have changed and his judgment might be different now."

Grandmother Julia turned back to her daughter without another word for Wayne, and Aunt Fritzie could not stand up to that look. She ran for the door and Nina Gorham went after her.

When they had gone, Wayne drew me to my feet and propelled me into the hallway as if he too hurried to escape my grandmother. We crossed the marble foyer and went through the front door. Outside the sun was pale behind a yellow mist, giving promise of a muggy day. Not until we reached the lawn did Wayne relax and smile at me, holding out his hand. I took it with a sense of repeating something done long ago—and felt curiously free. Together we raced down the long slope of grass toward a place where a dirt path left the drive and wandered away through the woods. I had not dreamed he could be like this and I felt released, unencumbered, unafraid. Nothing that dreadful old woman might do mattered, so long as Wayne was on my side.

When we reached the path we slowed our steps and followed its windings into the pine woods, and we still went hand in hand.

"I know a place where we can talk," he said. "Do you remember this path? Do you remember the way you used to tag after me sometimes when I went down to the boathouse? Do you remember the way you used to follow me around like a small puppy?"

He had thrown off his fatigue and there was an eagerness about him that delighted me. This was neither the serious young doctor, nor the worn, aloof, saddened man who had stood aside before Grandmother Julia's tyrannizing last night. He was a man of surprising changes and I liked this new eagerness, liked the way he put his questions, as if they were important. Something in me responded as eagerly, and with rising excitement. Wayne Martin was pushing me toward memory, but he was not letting me follow that road alone. He was coming with me back into time, so that I need not make the journey into old terrors by myself.

My conscious mind held no memory, but something in me recalled a strong hand about my own, and a strong presence that kept me from hurt and danger. Yes, of course we had walked like this before, and for me there was trust in the knowledge—and something more. The warmth of a child's long-ago love was stirring in me—but now I was a woman, and I knew it would not be the same.

I walked beside him with fresh courage, and he recognized acceptance in me. He knew I would go wherever he wanted to lead me.

VII

The path we followed had crossed a woodsy spit of land, and now it wound again in the direction of the pond. Occasionally I could glimpse water through the trees. I breathed as if I were hungry for the pine-scented air, and lifted my face to the dapple of misty yellow light that fell between well-spaced trees. The springy feel of pine needles in the thick carpet beneath my feet gave a lift to my step, and Wayne's step was quick and alive beside me. Overhead the treetops moved in a gentle whisper and when a breeze stirred them we could hear it coming from afar off. The only other sound in the world was that of a motorboat somewhere out on the water.

"No one but Chris comes this way anymore," Wayne said. "Except for his rowboat, the boathouse isn't used these days. You can see how the path is turning back to wilderness. I haven't been down here since last fall."

We no longer walked with clasped hands, but were somehow closer, with arm touching arm. He had flung off all the weariness that had marked him earlier, though dark shadows still smeared the flesh beneath his eyes.

"Did you get to bed at all last night?" I asked.

He smiled ruefully. "For a time. But babies come when they're ready to come. The hospital called me around one o'clock. There was trouble this time, but we made it."

I heard the satisfaction in his voice.

"You like being a country doctor," I said. My words were discovery, not question.

"I suppose I do. Though I became one mainly because it seemed necessary. Because I was badly needed."

Ahead of us the woods opened and I saw with sharp recognition a stone building on a slope above the pond. I knew this place. It meant something to me, I was sure.

"What about Aunt Fritzie?" I asked as we walked toward

the boathouse. "Is there no way to help her? Do you think your father was right when he said she should be allowed to forget?"

It seemed that we walked for a long time in silence, and when he spoke his words startled me.

"My father was nearly always wrong," he said quietly. "But perhaps he was right at the time about Fritzie. I don't know. I suppose this is the sort of question every man has to answer for himself. All I know is how I would choose if I had to pick between pain and loss of memory."

His remark about his father reminded me of the thing Elden had said about not many people having a good word for old Doc Martin. This seemed troubling ground and I moved away from it, agreeing that if I had a choice between forgetfulness and pain I would choose the latter.

"Do you think it's too late for Aunt Fritzie to make such a choice for herself?" I asked.

"It may be that we're going to find out," Wayne said, "whether your grandmother likes it or not. It seems that your meeting with Fritzie last night has stirred her up a good deal so that she's started thinking about the past."

We were close to the boathouse now and I saw that it was sturdily built of fieldstone collected from Gorham land. It offered a partly enclosed picnic place on the level from which we approached. There was a single large, stone-floored room with a huge fireplace at one end. When we walked up the few steps and into the big room, I went at once to a wide window that opened over the water. On the pond side there were two levels, with a shelter for boats beneath the main room. From the shore a small dock extended into the water, its boards brown and splintery with age. Around its pilings water washed in and out with a sucking sound, and out on the pond the frisking motorboat cut the calm surface, leaving the frothing of its wake behind. The low sun glowed sulphur yellow through thin mist and the day was already growing warm.

Wayne leaned upon the window ledge beside me. "I suppose not very much stays with us at the age of four," he said. "Or at least it goes where we can't easily reach it. I keep waiting for you to recognize something. You used to love to go fishing with me, and I must have had more patience than most boys my age to take along a little girl. You were always very good and you never scared away the fish."

"I knew this building as soon as I saw it," I said. "Perhaps I'm remembering more than I know. I keep recognizing with my emotions, if not with my mind. That's the way I feel about you. You helped me that other time in the conservatory, didn't you? Will you tell me about it now?"

"That's why I've brought you here," he said. "It's better told in a place that has no connection with unhappy times. You loved to come here, Mallie. So let's sit down and talk."

There was a picnic table and benches in the center of the big room, and before the blackened, empty fireplace stood a rustic wooden bench made of logs that had been split and peeled. He led me to it and sat down beside me. I was trying hard to hold my calm, happy feeling of being relaxed and without concern, but the very knowledge of a door about to open made me stiff with apprehension. His doctor's eye—or perhaps it was only the eye of a man who was considerate— noted the fact and he took my hand again and held it between both of his.

I managed to smile at him. How had I ever thought Wayne Martin a harsh, unreachable man? There was nothing but kindness in him now, and perhaps the trace of an old affection. This was what loving was like, I thought in wonder—this complete trust, this warm flood of outgoing emotion. I had a curious longing to do something for him because of all that he was doing for me. But there was nothing I could offer except the tightening clasp of my fingers about his.

He began to talk and after that I thought of nothing but listening. He did not tell me the story baldly, but painted a word picture for me of something that I could see and experience. He wanted me to understand, I realized—not only with my mind, but with my feelings as well.

When my mother brought me as a small child to Silverhill, the conservatory had been a forbidden place to me. Aunt Arvilla was far from well, and her birds and plants were her one consolation and her whole concern. Not even Gerald Gorham was allowed among them—though he could be fully trusted among his grandfather's treasures.

Just once was I allowed to go through the conservatory, when my mother was with me, and Aunt Arvilla was there to show us about. Ever since she had come for her visit, Mother had been prevented from being alone with her sister. But this time she slipped away to the conservatory with her, unnoticed, and brought me along. Aunt Arvilla had been nervous lest I touch or damage something—or frighten her birds. The place had apparently fascinated me. It was like something out of a storybook, with eerie green vegetation that had a creeping life of its own, and the treasure of all those darling birds in the heart of an enchanted forest.

When and how I got in by myself later, no one knew. Children are clever at catching the moment when their elders are preoccupied and they can slip away unobserved. What happened had been more or less reconstructed by questioning me afterwards. I had apparently made one main mistake. I thought Aunt Arvilla was elsewhere and that I would have the whole magic place to myself. Somehow I was brave enough to follow the path alone through all those reaching, creeping green creatures that were called plants, and get to the fishpond and the bird cages in the center.

Apparently, more than anything else, I wanted to open one of the ornate cages and take a cuddly little yellow bird into my small hands. A feathery bird must have seemed a wonderful thing for a child to hold. I managed to pull a stool below the cage of my choice in order to climb upon it. Beside the stool stood a table with a round top and pedestal foot, and upon that was set a cut glass vase of roses from the garden.

It was possible that I knocked the table as I climbed upon the stool, for I admitted later to breaking the vase. It must have tipped over on the table, breaking the top jaggedly from the stem, spilling out flowers and water. This, I recognized, would bring punishment if discovered, and I must hurry in my purpose.

I scrambled onto the stool and stood on tiptoe to release the catch of the cage, undoubtedly frightening the two birds within. One of them flew out at once and escaped me, but the other must have cowered on its perch, for I was able to reach into the cage with my two hands and take the small thing into my grasp, bringing it out to hold close to my face. I had never hurt anything as a child, and perhaps it would never have been hurt at all, if it had not been for Aunt Arvilla.

All the while she had been in another part of the conservatory, off on one of the paths that rayed out from the fishpond. The birds of course raised an outcry over the small marauder in their midst and she came hurrying back to see what was wrong. Her first intent was probably no more than to rescue the canary from my ignorant, child's hands, but she flew at me like one of her swooping birds, frightening me so that I tried to pull away. When she snatched for the bird, I fell sideways to escape her attack and crashed down upon the small table. Everything went over with me, including the sharp broken spear of the vase stem. It was that which pierced my cheek as I fell upon it on the tiled floor.

What happened next, Wayne said, would always be lost in confusion. Certainly I began to scream. Certainly Aunt Arvilla was still thinking only of the bird, still clasped in my hands, crushed and smothered out of its fragile life as I fell. By that time I was more terrified of her than of anything else. I managed to evade her clutching hands and fled screaming from the conservatory. I ran from the house by the first door that offered itself—and out upon the side lawn. But my legs were not long enough to outdistance a pursuing adult, and I tried to hide among the birch trees.

Aunt Arvilla caught up with me as I cowered there, crouching on the ground with the little dead bird still clasped in my hands. The boy, Wayne, was the first to reach me there. He held Arvilla away until the others came. He opened my fright-stiffened fingers and took the canary from them. By that time I was feeling the pain of my wound, aware of blood streaming down my face, and it was Wayne who soothed and calmed me and staunched the flow. Mother went completely to pieces, sure that I was bleeding to death. While Aunt Nina struggled with Arvilla, Grand-mother Julia summoned Elden's father to drive me to the hospital. Again it was Wayne who went with me and held me in his lap all the way there.

All that long time ago this had happened to me. Now, in the boathouse, I stared into the empty fireplace and lived the whole experience over again. Wayne remembered the part about the hospital very well.

"I suppose I was already imagining myself a doctor," he told me. "Because I'd visited the hospital a good many times with my father, they let me come into the operating room. They let me stay with you while the stitches were taken, and afterwards. By that time your grandmother had sent Nina into town by taxi—and Elden's father drove us all home. Your mother was the really ill one afterwards and had to be nursed for a week or so. As soon as she recovered, you both went back to New York. I never saw you again until I came upon you yesterday beside your mother's grave."

I sat very still, staring at my hands where they lay in the lap of my yellow dress. Once they had been a child's hands, holding a tiny canary, crushing it unwittingly to death. But that was long ago and far away—and only the scar on my cheek remained as evidence of what had happened. Even

Aunt Fritzie had forgotten that day, forgotten her long-ago anger.

She had been furiously angry, Wayne said. "We had to watch you after we brought you home, and keep you away from her. She had some twisted notion of revenge in her mind—and she was in a much worse state then, mentally, than she is now. This is why your grandmother doesn't want her to bring everything back. She's afraid of what may happen. I'm not sure I agree. Much of the time these days Fritzie is perfectly sensible. She knows who you are, and she seems to be developing a liking for you. If the bird incident returns to her mind, she may be perfectly able to shake it off. But at that time she couldn't. She used to go out to that grove of birch trees repeatedly and look for you there."

I stared at him, suddenly chilled.

"She kept telling us you were hiding there in your blood-stained white dress. She called you a witch child and said you were planning to kill her other birds. It was a long while before she stopped hunting for you. Even now she sometimes thinks she sees a child among those trees."

So the wailing ghost child that haunted the birches was only Mallie Rice! The thought was faintly unsettling. What would I do if *I* saw that child? I moved closer to Wayne and he released my hand to put an arm about me.

"You're shivering," he said. "But there are happier memories. During the remaining days you spent at Silverhill you devoted yourself to me. You followed me around and even proposed to me a few times. I think I promised to marry you when you grew up. You were in a good deal of pain at first with your cheek, and I was afraid it was going to leave a bad scar. I worried about you and grew very fond of you. Somehow you were my responsibility, and after your mother took you away I wrote you letters. I must have mailed you three before she mailed them back to me and asked me not to write anymore. I suppose she was right. She wanted you to get over what had happened and not go on being reminded of it."

Somehow this breaking up of a friendship seemed more hurtful than all the rest.

"She was wrong!" I cried in quick denial. "I should have been allowed your letters. They might have helped me. But Mother didn't want to be reminded of what had happened herself. As a result I grew up with a feeling of terror that came whenever I was near caged birds. And I had a sense of guilt and shame about the scar. She would never tell me why I felt as I did. She never let me understand so I could grow out of it. That's why the fear has stayed with me all these years—to burst out crazily this morning. If I'd known —if I'd understood—"

"Hush," he said and held me close to his shoulder. "Don't blame her too much. We're none of us wise enough to know how best to deal with this sort of thing."

"At least you've told me the truth," I said. "There's been too much concealment, too much covering up. Not only by my mother, but by everyone at Silverhill. You can feel it, can't you?"

He let me go, nodding a bit distantly. "I'm a part of it. But perhaps there's something in every life that needs to stay hidden."

I dared a question. "Do you mean because of your father? Did you mean what you said to me back in the woods?"

"That doesn't bear talking about," he told me brusquely. "Anyway, you can understand now why it's better for you to leave Silverhill. If Fritzie instead of recovering should remember and lapse into her old feeling about you, that might mean real disaster. There's nothing you can do for her at this time, I should think."

I shook my head stubbornly. "Perhaps not. But I want to stay long enough to walk into that conservatory and behave in a normal fashion. I suppose it's like flying after a crash.

I have to go back into that place and cure myself of silly
fright over the chirping of a bird. Even today I might have
seen it through if I hadn't been demoralized by that macaw."
I fingered the square of gauze on my cheek and pulled it off.
There was no need for it now. "I've got to go back!" I added
doggedly.

He left the bench and walked up and down before the
fireplace—a tall man who usually moved with reassuring
purpose—though there seemed indecision in him now.

"I see your point—but I'm still not sure—" He paused before me and there was remembered tenderness for a hurt
child in his eyes. "I suppose I still feel that you're my responsibility. I can't forget—"

I jumped to my feet and faced him. "Look at me! I'm
not a wounded child. Don't mix me up with that other
Mallie."

He did look at me then, quite gravely, and he was so
close that I could have touched my cheek to the early morning roughness that was beginning to shade his chin.

"I'm not likely to forget," he said. "The difference of
years between us has shrunk. Just the same, I can't forget
that you've grown from a little girl I remember with affection."

"I don't think I've ever forgotten you, either," I told him,
as grave as he, and a little tremulous now. "I never realized
before how much I can remember with my feelings."

There was a moment of stillness between us in which I
was aware of my own racing heart and quickening breath.
Not altogether gently he pulled me into his arms and I felt
their hunger as they came about me. For an instant I thought
unwillingly of "Ann, beloved." But she had belonged to another life.

He kissed my mouth and then touched the mark upon my
cheek with his lips, tenderly. When he let me go his eyes
were shining—though I think there were tears in my own—
and the last trace of weariness had lifted from his face.

"That's for a beginning," he said. "Don't go away again, Mallie. Leave Silverhill, but stay for a while in Shelby—so we can learn about each other. We've wasted a lot of time we need to make up for."

When we left the boathouse we no longer held hands in our earlier companionable way. Events had moved swiftly and there was a restraint upon us. We were strangers who had come together unexpectedly, and who must now move apart in order to see beyond the flare of our own emotions. Something important, something that must not be rushed at and spoiled might lie ahead. All this I knew instinctively—and was content to move slowly.

Later I was to remember this unhurried willingness to wait. I was to wonder if it would not have been better to snatch at the moment before it was lost to me forever. But at the time I felt safe enough, and quite able to let Wayne go out of my sight, foolishly certain that he would return, feeling toward me just as he did now.

When we reached the foot of the steps, I paused. "There's something I want to do," I said.

He nodded, understanding. I watched as he went into the house, knowing very well how much I was going to love him. I was no longer so foolishly young as to believe that the warm rush of feeling which possessed me was all there would be to love. The time was right for both of us, but first I must make my peace with the past.

My thoughts were pleasant ones as I walked toward the grove of white birches. Last night Kate Salway had crouched here weeping. It was a place of tears. Through the passing of time the white trees seemed to have attracted the terrified, the sad, the lost. But I was no longer any of these things.

I stood in the shadow of their upflung branches and touched powdery white bark with my fingers—bark the Indians had liked because it peeled so easily. At the foot of which tree had a small child cowered? Where had I knelt on this earth and held a dead bird in my hands? A bird as yellow as the dress I now wore. There was no horror for me in the knowledge but only pity for a frightened child—and for poor Aunt Fritzie who had hurt me so badly without intending what she had done, or understanding that she had done it. Was it to free me of all this that Mother had wanted me to return to Silverhill?

I doubted that. There were still too many unanswered questions for me to believe it was as simple as that. I left the grove and walked to the side door of the house.

In the kitchen Mrs. Simpson, the cook—a burly woman with iron-gray hair and a matching expression—looked as though she might fling a frying pan at anyone who crossed her.

"Have you seen Kate Salway, Miss?" she barked the moment I came through the door. "It's her job to help me get breakfast on the table. We're half an hour late now, with not a sign of her. And the coffee ruined, the bacon burned! That idiot girl from town doesn't get here until ten."

I told her I had not seen Kate, and left her to her grumbling. From the hall I went down the steps into the gallery and was just in time to see Elden come through the door of the conservatory holding a long hatpin with a crescent head of garnets in his hands.

When he saw me staring, he waved it at me, as though he felt it necessary to explain. "It was in there among the birds. A fine place for it! I don't know where she'll hide things next." He looked at me searchingly. "You all right? Recovered from your hysterics? I could hear you screeching clear over in our place." Apparently, like everyone else, he knew what had happened.

"I'm fine," I told him cheerfully.

He continued to stare, as though something about me puzzled him. "That's evident. You look more than fine. You look like the sun coming up to wipe out a rainy day."

He saw more than I wanted him to.

"Dr. Martin has just told me what happened here when I

was little," I said. "Now I know how I got this scar. Now I can lay all my ghosts."

He studied the point of the hatpin, grimacing. "Interesting, if true. How do you plan to do that?"

I started past him across the gallery. "I'm going in there again. I'm going in where the birds are and listen to them. Since I understand what happened to me, I don't need to be afraid of unknown terrors anymore."

"Better not," he said. "Not right now. Your Aunt Fritzie's in there and she's in a state. She says one of her birds is dead and she's got to find it. She was poking around with this hatpin and I took it away from her. You know where it belongs?"

His words alarmed me. Did this mean Aunt Fritzie had reverted—gone back in her memory to another time?

"Over there," I said, and pointed toward the display case, but before he reached it Gerald came through the door from the main house and saw what Elden held.

"What are you doing with that?" he demanded. "Give it to me!"

Elden handed it to him silently, attempting no explanation to Gerald.

My cousin went at once to replace the hatpin in the case, his back to both of us. I saw Elden's face, saw the dark flush that swept up to his sandy hair before he wheeled and went through a door that led into the garden. I took another tentative step toward the conservatory, unwilling to postpone the defeat of my last fears, but before I reached the mirrored door, Grandmother Julia came through it, and I drew back, startled.

She passed me as though I were invisible and went toward her grandson, a tall figure in her red gown, her white hair smoothly combed, her chin held high, so that the looseness of skin beneath was somewhat controlled.

"Good morning, Gerald," she said. "I hope our hysterical disturbance a while ago didn't upset you."

He answered her dryly. "I'm not that easily upset, Gran. Kate told me what happened, and I see that Cousin Malinda has fully recovered."

If Grandmother Julia heard my name, she paid no attention. "So you've been talking to Kate this morning? I want to see you both in my rooms after breakfast. I mean to call Dr. Worth today and make the date for the wedding final. There's never been a wedding held in this part of the house, and I want it here. So you and Kate—"

"Kate and I are not going to be married, Gran dear," Gerald said evenly. "You might as well get this notion out of your head. I've asked her—because you wanted me to—and she's refused me. So that settles it, don't you think?"

Grandmother stood on the opposite side of the jewelry display, her hands reaching out as though to warm themselves at the fire of the stones. On one finger I saw the red shine of a great ruby centered among tiny pearls.

"Nonsense!" she said. "Kate refused you because she knew you expected refusal. You did it clumsily, I'm sure."

Gerald reached across the case to take his grandmother's hand, and before she knew what he intended, he drew the ring from her thin finger and held it out to me.

"Come here, Malinda. This is the ring I wanted to see on your hand. Come and try it on."

I did not move. His action seemed outrageous under the circumstances, yet Grandmother Julia did not appear to be angry. For the first time she seemed to notice my presence.

"Well?" she challenged me. "Are you afraid to put on my ring? Are you afraid it will look ridiculous on your hand?"

More than anything else, I wanted to walk out of the gallery and leave them both—yet I did not quite dare. I needed to be angry to face her down, and now, with the thought of Wayne coloring everything, I could not be angry with anyone. Still in my separate dream, I went to Gerald and let him slip the ring onto a finger of my right hand. It was much too large and ornate for my taste. They both studied my hand and the ring upon it with incongruous attention—as critical as though I had been in the studio posing for a camera.

"No flair," Grandmother Julia pronounced. "She's too accustomed to wearing cheap trash. Anyone who goes into hysterics because a macaw lights on her shoulder could never carry off a ring like that. I shall give it to Kate on the day she marries you, Gerald."

I took off the ring and set it upon the glass. What this byplay meant I had no idea. Perhaps it was only part of the continuous duel that went on between the two of them. There seemed to be affection for Gerald on my grandmother's part, but I had no real knowledge of how he felt about her. He looked petulant now, like a spoiled child who refuses discipline.

"If you keep up this insistence on my marrying Kate," he said, "Elden will take her away and you'll lose them both. Perhaps you can force me into marriage, but you can't force Kate. The sooner you see that, the better for us all."

Calmly Grandmother picked up the ring. To my surprise she did not put it back on her finger, but held it out to me.

"Keep it," she said. "I want you to have it."

I could only blink at her in astonishment.

For the first time her fine, blue-violet eyes seemed to rest on me without antagonism. "Not bribery," she said, and her mouth seemed to wear the same secretly amused smile as the young lips of the portrait. "A reward. Because I heard what you told Elden just now about going back into the conservatory. That makes up a little for the way you behaved. I should hate to think a granddaughter of mine was a craven. When you go in again and come out without screeching, the ring is yours."

Now I could be thoroughly angry. "When I go in I'll go

for myself. I'm not here for either bribery or rewards. Perhaps that's something you aren't able to understand."

She nodded at me, almost as if in satisfaction, while Gerald watched us, puzzled, yet alert.

"You're not like Blanche, are you?" she said. "You're far more like me, whether you accept that fact or not. I believe you're telling the truth and that you really don't know what your mother wrote me in her letter. Since you don't, you can do no damage, and you may stay here for a few days. That is, if you can prove you've got more gumption and courage than you've shown this morning."

"Thank you," I said stiffly, though at that moment I did not mean to stay. Once Aunt Fritzie was out of the conservatory, so that I could go in there alone, I would perform my last test. After that, I would move to Shelby. In town I could see Wayne when he had time for me, and I would get a job of some sort to keep me going. If I returned to New York, it would be to dispose of the apartment and pack my things. But no matter what I did, Silverhill and Grandmother Julia would see me no more. There was nothing I could do for Aunt Fritzie. It was probably best if she stayed in her own dream world, happy with her plants and her birds. I no longer wanted to disturb her in order to satisfy a promise I had made my mother. The mystery of my own childhood disaster had been answered and a period of my life was about to close—a new one to open.

Feeling strong and brave and cheerful about the future, I left the ring where it lay upon the case and walked away from them both. With no sense of foreboding, I went into the house and climbed the two flights of stairs to my room. The morning had brightened a little, and though the sun still burned behind a haze, the yellow glare had grown stronger, hotter.

The glow of it came through my dormer windows, a patch of light falling upon the open sheets of my unmade bed. It gleamed yellow upon the pillow that still bore the imprint of my head. I stood quite still, staring. The spot of light on my pillow had nothing to do with the yellow glare that pressed against the windows. It was a separate yellow entity in itself. I bent above the pillow and looked at the canary that lay upon it. Its small feet were spread limply against the pillow case, its tiny eyes were glazed, and on its breast there was a speckling of red.

This was the horror of the conservatory—and worse. Only my hands pressed over my mouth held back the scream that wanted to come. The mischievous acts of a confused mind could be borne, perhaps smiled over sadly. But this was madness with a cruel intent.

After the first frozen moments of horror, I took my hands from my mouth, knowing that I would not scream this time. There was no terror for me in the pitiful thing that lay on my pillow, but only in the question of who had put it there. Who wanted to frighten me as much as that? It could be any one of them. This was a question which must be answered at once.

VIII

Without touching the small yellow thing on the pillow, my hands seemed to remember the softness of feathers about a tiny form of flesh and bone and blood—feathers that covered something that had been warm and alive, and would now be growing cold. A small thing which had been able to fly and sing, and now was nothing I could understand. The mystery of death. My mother; this canary.

I could not bear to pick it up without covering it first, so I found tissues in my dresser and laid them gently around the little bird. The canary seemed to weigh nothing in my fingers, yet there was a difference between live weight and dead. How easy it would be for a child to squeeze her hands together and crush away such fragile life. But this bird had not died by being crushed.

I went into the hall carrying the small burden. I would take it at once to Wayne. No one had fastened the tower doors against me and I went through to the other side of the house. The rooms of the attic floor were empty and quiet this morning, and the hall, as always, was dark and piercingly chill. No light burned above the stairs and I went down carefully past the blue roses of the wallpaper —those little ghost faces that had once frightened my mother.

On Wayne's floor the tower doors stood wide to let in warmth and light, and the doors of his living room were open as well. I looked in and found no one there. From the rear of the hall came the slam of a refrigerator door, the clatter of dishes, and I followed the sounds to the kitchen at the rear.

Chris sat at a table, pouring himself a glass of milk. Egg stains and toast crumbs on his plate told me he was finishing breakfast alone.

"Your father?" I asked.

He was a wise little boy—older than his years—and he regarded me with grave interest. "Something has scared you again, hasn't it? But Dad's asleep now. Do we have to wake him up?"

I remembered Wayne's weariness when he had spoken of the struggle at the hospital, and gave up my first purpose. "No, of course we mustn't waken him," I said.

Chris came around the table and looked at the tissue-wrapped thing I held in my hands. "You can show me, if you want. I don't think I'll be scared."

At that moment I trusted young Chris Martin more than I did anyone else in the house except his father. I turned back the paper and showed him the small yellow body. He cried out in dismay and took the bird from me. Clearly he had handled dead birds before and the fact of death did not frighten him. He was sorry, but he was realistic, as a child can be.

"It's Picadilly!" he told me sadly. "I can tell by the brown feathering at the tip of his wings. He never was pure yellow. He's been sick lately. We knew he was going to die. Where did you find him?"

"Someone put him on a pillow up in my room," I said. "I don't think he died of being sick."

Chris shook his head in bewilderment. "What a funny thing for anyone to do—putting it on your pillow. It sounds like Aunt Fritzie—except that she'd never hurt one of her birds."

"If—if someone else hurt it," I said, "—do you suppose Aunt Fritzie might still put it there for me to find?"

He thought this over, the grave look of his father upon him, his fawn's eyelashes long upon his cheeks.

"I suppose she might," he said. "But I thought she liked you. This morning she was worried about you—she wanted to help."

"Then who—?" I began, and stopped. I had no right to ask Chris Martin to sit in judgment on his elders. Whatever was going on here was no matter for a child.

"I suppose we'd better not try to guess," he said. "Let's take this downstairs and show Elden. He'll have to bury it anyway—he always buries Fritzie's birds when they die."

Again I admired a realist's approach. "I'll wait while you finish your milk," I said, knowing that I wanted his company on this errand. He knew more about birds than I, and more about the people in this house, as well.

He drank his milk halfway down the glass, then stored the remainder frugally in the refrigerator and came into the hall with me. No one was about on Aunt Fritzie's floor, and Chris led the way to the door that opened into the gallery. We went down into an empty room. Gerald and Grandmother were gone, and the door to the conservatory remained closed. Chris knew the maze of mirrors, windows and doors better than I, and he walked at once to the door that led into the garden, opening it for me.

At another time I would have been delighted by the old-fashioned beauty of Elden's garden, with its flagstones winding around the obstruction of the conservatory, its blooms crowding the walk. As it was, Chris ran ahead of me carrying the bird, and I hurried after him, with no time for the garden.

Near hollyhocks that grew against the picket fence, Elden stood talking to Aunt Nina. She had taken time to dress for the day in charcoal-gray cotton, and once more looked trimly, neatly herself. I had a quick incongruous vision of her as a young girl on a tennis court, beating a topflight player—though she still looked as though she might be quick and light on her feet. Elden, as usual, wore his brown corduroys, and there were earth smudges and the stains of plant juices on his hands. Looking at them, I thought of what his sister had told me of his feeling about the maimed. Would a sick bird be readily sacrificed if he had some secret purpose? But I could think of no reason why Elden should want to frighten me.

As Chris and I reached them, they both glanced around and Chris held the bird up on its nest of tissue for Elden to see.

"Somebody put this on a pillow in Mallie's room," he said. "What do you think happened to it, Elden?"

Aunt Nina uttered a soft cry of distress. "Oh, no! Not another trick!"

Elden betrayed nothing of what he thought or felt. He turned the bird gently about, and with one forefinger he parted the feathers on its breast where the speckling of red had stained them. His face was expressionless and his sandy brows drew down so that they hid the look of his deepset eyes.

"So that's what she wanted the hatpin for," he said at last.

Chris stared in astonishment, but I would not be quiet. "You can't mean that Aunt Fritzie would do such a horrible thing to one of her own birds just to—to frighten me?"

Aunt Nina looked a little sick. "We never know what she will do. Or when it may be something more serious than the death of a bird. Mother Julia will have to hear about this."

"Yes, she'll have to hear," Elden said.

He looked across the garden toward the conservatory. A dragonfly hovered near a rosebush and bees were already at their early-morning work. The quiet of the garden lay all about us and now I let my eyes wander over old-fashioned blooms—phlox, forget-me-nots, a border of blue anemone. The sweetness of mingling scents was everywhere and the scene was one of peace, not horror. Yet Elden's face was dark and far from peaceful. He held a dead bird in his hands, and his eyes saw only Grandfather Diah's conservatory.

"Maybe it's time for that thing to come down," he said. "What Fritzie is raising in there isn't normal growth. She feeds those plants into deformed monstrosities. And the birds are a neurotic lot. Feathered things belong outdoors, not in cages. You can't tell me any different, no matter what they're bred to. Cage 'em and they go wrong in their silly brains. The way she's gone wrong in hers."

He was saying too much and as always he made me uneasy. While he might not care whether I remained at Silverhill or not, he held a very real grudge against Aunt Fritzie. I turned my eyes toward the blank windows of the house, and caught a flicker of movement in Gerald's wing—as though a lifted curtain had been dropped in place. Obviously we were being observed from that direction. I shifted my gaze quickly to Grandmother Julia's wing, but I saw no movement of the curtains there, and no one stood watching at a window.

Aunt Nina paid no attention to Elden's words about the

conservatory. "Bring—that," she said, nodding toward the canary. "We'll take it to Mother Julia at once. It's past breakfast time, but she can delay a little longer. I can't think what's got into Kate this morning. Where is she, Elden?"

"Maybe she's cleared out," he said, still glowering at the hated bubble of glass. "I keep expecting her to. Her bed was slept in last night, but she was gone early this morning when I got up."

Aunt Nina shook her head. "That's wishful thinking, Elden, and you know it. She hides herself now and then, but she won't go away. It will take something more drastic than wishing to keep Julia Gorham from marrying your sister to my son."

She seemed to consider him thoughtfully, and Elden gave her look for look.

"Maybe it will, at that," he said.

They seemed to have forgotten both me and the attentively listening small boy at my side. Each was observing the other as though a reluctant alliance had been made. Neither, obviously, wanted this marriage, and I was sure that each must resent the other's reasons for opposing it, even though they found themselves joined in a common cause. Grandmother Julia was not going to have an easy time in putting across her plans. But none of this concerned me. All I wanted was to know who had been so desperately bent on frightening me. And why.

Before I could break in upon their mutual concentration, a frantic interruption stopped me. I heard Aunt Fritzie's voice as she rounded a turn in the path.

"It's that child again!" she wailed as she came toward us. "That dreadful child! I know she's taken one of my birds. 'Dilly is dead—I know he is.'"

We turned to stare as she swooped down upon us. She had not yet dressed for the day and her chiffon ruffles made her look like a predatory gray falcon as she flew toward us.

Aunt Nina moved in alarm, as if to shield the bird from her view, but Elden made no attempt at concealment. He held up his hand with the dead bird resting upon the palm. Aunt Fritzie saw it and gasped. She took the small thing into her hand and cradled it against her cheek, moaning softly in grief which quickly gave way to anger.

"Where is the child?" she demanded of us. "Where have you hidden her?"

Aunt Nina's lips pursed in distaste, but she looked a little frightened as she flung me a glance. "There isn't any child, Arvilla," she said.

"Of course there's a child!" Aunt Fritzie looked suddenly at me. "I know she's been here. She was down among the birches last night. Didn't you hear her crying? She must have got into the conservatory again. And if I catch her—"

She stepped close to me, searching my face with her deeply blue eyes, while I stood my ground with difficulty. A shivering had begun again somewhere inside me. I must not think of a small child reaching for a fluttering bird, or of a grown woman swooping in fury.

"I've seen you before," she said. "I know I've seen you before."

Elden ignored Aunt Nina's warning look. "She's the child you're looking for. She's that child grown up. But it's not Mallie who did this, as you know very well. It was you who went into the conservatory. I asked what you wanted the hatpin for. I asked you why you'd hidden it among the plants—remember? Now do you see what you've done?"

It was a merciless attack. Chris made a sound of indignation, but Elden appeared to be enjoying himself. His pale-blue eyes were wide open, with no glowering now, no lowered brows as he challenged her to remember what I could not believe she had done. Already Aunt Fritzie's lips were trembling in response, her face crumpling into lines of shock and pain. I could not stand by in silence and endure what was happening. Aunt Fritzie was my first reason for being here and she sadly needed a champion.

"Don't tell her such things!" I cried angrily. "She wouldn't hurt one of her own birds. Someone else has done this."

He flung me a look that told me to mind my own business. "Look among the feathers on the breast," he ordered Aunt Fritzie. "It's only a little wound—a wound pierced by some sharp instrument. Now are you beginning to remember?"

She opened her hands and let the bird fall to the path as though the touch of it had become suddenly repugnant. "Did I really do that? Oh, Elden—I can't remember! I can't remember anything about what happened after I got up this morning."

I hated him for what he was doing to her. "Of course you can remember, Aunt Fritzie dear." I took her convulsively clasped hands into mine. "Just this morning you were telling me how much you had begun to remember. You promised Dr. Wayne you were going to get well."

She pulled her hands away and turned helplessly to Aunt Nina, rejecting me as a stranger. Her gaze seemed unfocused and there was a blurred slackness about her mouth.

Aunt Nina drew her away, not unkindly, and Aunt Fritzie went with her, unresisting, with no real awareness of what had happened. Apparently she had even forgotten the bird.

The moment she was out of hearing I turned upon Elden. "How could you do a thing like that? How could you be so cruel?"

"Cruel?" he said. "What do you know about real cruelty?"

He sounded so assured that for the first time my blind belief in Aunt Fritzie wavered. What did I know about her, actually?

Elden picked up the bird from the path and examined it again. There was dust on the yellow feathers and he brushed it away almost tenderly.

"I'll take this to Mrs. Julia," he said brusquely. "No use waiting any longer. Do you want to come? So you can check on my sadistic tendencies?"

I shook my head, and he gave me a wry look with no liking in it and went off toward the house. When he had gone I stared blankly about me, almost as Aunt Fritzie had done. Shock and confusion—and a sickness over what had happened—mingled to shake any convictions I might have. I had forgotten Chris was still there until he touched my arm.

"Elden shouldn't have said what he did," he told me. "Aunt Fritzie wouldn't have hurt 'Dilly—no matter whether she remembers or not."

"But then why was he so sure?" I demanded. "Why did he behave like that?"

Chris nodded toward the conservatory. "He's got a thing about that place. He hates Aunt Fritzie's plants and he thinks it's wrong to keep birds caged the way she does. Besides, Dad says he's awfully mad about something Mrs. Julia wants that he can't stop—so he does mean things to let off steam. Anyway, I'll watch for a chance to talk to Aunt Fritzie. Sometimes I can get her to feel better when other people have upset her. She knows I'm her friend."

I gave him a quick hug of affection and he did not resist me. Whether Aunt Fritzie could be trusted as he seemed to trust her, I was no longer sure, but she still needed more than a small boy on her side. Abandoning her would be my one regret when I left Silverhill.

Chris was still watching me, a certain eagerness upon him, as though he had been waiting to tell me something.

"I know where Kate is," he said. "I know where she goes when she wants to get away. But I can't tell anyone. I promised her I wouldn't tell."

I stared at him and saw the betraying turn of his head, the brief flick of his eyes toward the attic on Aunt Fritzie's side of the house. He was not a foolish little boy. He had not made that betraying gesture by chance. Nor had he actually broken his promise to Kate Salway. I had a sudden wish to see him carefree and playing with children his own age, instead of concerning himself with the ingrown problems that belonged to Silverhill.

"I'm going back to my room now," I said gently. "Do you mind if I come inside with you?"

His smile was relieved as we went into the house together, and I knew that some of his concern was for Kate Salway. We climbed the stairs to the second floor and found his father in the doorway, waiting for us.

There was a moment of uncertainty as we met again. We were still two strangers who must look at each other from a distance, questioning. Then he smiled and everything was right with me. I had not dreamed him. Nothing had changed since I had gone down to the boathouse with Wayne Martin, to find my life turned completely around —turned in a direction of hope and happiness.

I smiled at him as openly. "Tell your father about the bird," I said to Chris, and continued up the stairs to the attic floor.

Very soon I would be gone from Silverhill. The cruel trick someone had played with a dead bird placed on my pillow had not been necessary to get me to leave, but there were still troubling matters I hated to turn my back upon. Perhaps Kate might help with Aunt Fritzie—providing her own problems were not too all-engulfing.

I did not go through the tower to my own side when I reached the third floor, but wandered in among the trunks and boxes that Aunt Fritzie had been unpacking last night. By morning light the cobwebs and dust, the evident neglect, were more obvious than ever. Where Aunt Fritzie had walked about, or knelt before a trunk, there were smudges and trails in the dust. Otherwise it was undisturbed. I opened an adjoining door to the rear and looked into the next room. Here nothing had been touched for a long time. No tracks marked the dusty floor, or interrupted the surface of dilapidated furniture that had been stored here. Neither Grandmother Julia nor Aunt Nina had come up here in years. The fact that they had not, indicated an association with pain that must keep them both away.

I closed the door and continued along the hall. Here it was too dim to see very much and I found my way cautiously to the last door at the rear. It opened softly at my touch and there was nothing to be seen but an empty room —with another door to what must be a smaller room at the very back corner of the house. Here, at least, the floor had been swept, and there were no telltale tracks in the dust. Perhaps it had been swept for that very reason.

When I pulled the last door open I found it blocked by a huge old-fashioned wardrobe of dark mahogany set just inside. Yet in the instant of my opening the door I caught a glimmer of light beyond. Light that was extinguished with an immediate click.

"Kate?" I called softly. "Kate—it's only Mallie Rice. Will you let me in?"

The light came on again and I saw that there was space enough at one side for me to slip past the big wardrobe. Kate Salway stood facing me, leaning against a three-legged table that had its fourth corner held up by books piled upon a chair. She wore a short blue nylon negligee over her slip, and her aqua uniform hung on a wall hook.

After one glance at her white, tear-stained face, I looked at the room instead. The light came from a lamp with a cracked parchment shade, set upon the table. Behind her an army cot held a pillow and light blanket, and there was a chair and a bureau with a cracked mirror—nothing else.

"I thought this might be a good place for getting away

from everyone," I said. "But can't they see your light from the driveway?"

She relaxed from her frozen pose and brushed her brown hair back from her face with a tired gesture. "Not in the daytime. There's a dark shade at night, and the eaves and that big elm tree in the corner of the garden shadow the window—so I can leave it open for air. Why did you come looking for me?"

The small room was warm, in spite of the open window, and I pulled the single straight chair over to the opening and sat down so she would know she could not be rid of me easily. From where I sat I could look directly out upon the second-story roof over Gerald's wing, with the gallery roof a story below, connecting the two wings. But it was not the architecture that interested me—I was marking time while I sought for words.

"Perhaps I came up here because I wanted an escape myself," I told her. "Anyway, I wanted to talk to you before I go away for good."

"Sometimes I can't stand it downstairs!" She dropped onto the cot and clasped her hands about her knees, bent her head over them.

"I can see that," I said. "I've been here just one night and I've had all I can take. I'm going to leave as soon after breakfast as someone will drive me to Shelby. Why don't you come with me?"

There was sudden alarm in her that I did not understand. "You're leaving today, Miss Rice?"

I nodded. "I'm going to follow your advice. And please call me Mallie."

She leaned toward me intently. "Perhaps it wasn't good advice. Perhaps I've had more time to think about it."

"What made you change your mind?" I asked her bluntly.

But Kate's troubled thoughts had turned back to her own problems and she did not answer that. "They tear at me so," she whispered. "They pull me in different directions. Elden and Mrs. Nina and your grandmother."

"And my Cousin Gerald?" I asked.

Her brown eyes clouded with pain. "Not Gerald. So long as everything stays safe for him, he'll do what his grandmother wants, even though he doesn't want it."

I leaned toward her. "You don't have to marry him! Come to Shelby with me and we'll get a room together. We'll get jobs and make a new life for ourselves."

The idea had come to me suddenly and I felt elated over the plan. I liked Kate, and we could help each other.

She looked at me as though I had taken leave of my wits. "Leave Silverhill?" she said.

I jumped up and moved impatiently about the small room until she reached out to catch my hand and pull me down upon the cot beside her.

"Hush! Don't walk about or they'll hear you downstairs. Though Chris already knows I'm up here. And probably Dr. Wayne knows too, though he won't give me away. I have to have a hideout, or I'll go mad."

"You don't make any sense to me," I said. "I can see why you don't want to marry a man like Gerald. I can see—"

"I don't mind his arm," she broke in defensively. "I've known him all my life and I'm used to it."

"I didn't mean that! It's just that I think he's completely selfish and self-centered. It's what the arm has done to him that matters, so that even if he is a brilliant scholar, and very rich—he'd make a dreadful husband. No girl in her right mind would want him."

"*I* would," Kate said.

I stared at her. The little room was very quiet. Beyond the open window the elm branches stood breathlessly still in the somnolent yellow glare, hiding the garden, and I heard, far away, a rumble of thunder. The girl beside me began to cry softly into an already sodden handkerchief.

"I've loved him since I was a little girl," she wept. "I used to make up stories about growing up to marry him. I used to pretend he was the Frog Prince and that my love was going to transform him. I hated it when he went away to school and met other girls and took them out. He always had money to spend and he must have had a sort of fascination for the girls he went around with. Oh, he wasn't always a recluse! Though it never got serious because he was always paying them back. For his arm, I mean. He would never put himself to the test of marriage. He would never let himself get really involved."

"Yet he might marry you?" I said.

"Because I don't matter!" Kate cried. "He's used to me and he knows how I feel. He knows I won't hurt him, though he won't mind hurting me. He's perfectly willing to use me if that's the only way there is to get what he wants. What he wants, of course, is his grandmother's money, this house, everything in it. Then he can live here on his own terms and be a sort of private museum curator for the rest of his life. His grandmother is saying, 'No marriage, no money.' Gerald doesn't like that, and he's trying to hold out against her. Of course if he marries and still has no children, he'll at least have tried. Or no one can prove he hasn't. Except perhaps me!"

I listened to her in growing dismay. "Come with me to Shelby. Let him go!"

"I'll never let him go." Her voice was low, almost a whisper, and I sensed again the core of stubborn conviction in Kate Salway that nothing would ever shake. "I want to marry him, of course. But not because his grandmother is forcing marriage on him. He'd have to want it himself—because he loved me. I won't have him any other way—so I won't have him. There'll be no marrying between us!"

"Gerald and love?" I echoed. Little as I knew my cousin, I already doubted that he could love anyone but himself.

She answered me simply enough. "He needs me more than he knows. I make him comfortable. I've often typed his articles and answered letters for him, helped with his research and cataloguing. I'm not just a housekeeper here, you know."

"Then let him find out that he needs you. If you come away with me—"

She broke in impatiently. "You can't leave now. You're my only hope. You've got to stay at Silverhill for a while longer."

Her contradictions exasperated me. "But you said I must leave. You told me that the first time we were alone."

"That's when I was trying to think of you." She raised her head and looked at me so grimly that I wondered why I had ever thought her a gentle girl. "Now I'm thinking of me, and of Gerald. Though of course he wouldn't believe that if he knew. You're the only chance there'll ever be for us to escape. Help me, Mallie—help us both!"

"How can I possibly help anyone?" I demanded.

"I can't explain. I'm not even sure what's best for Gerald. I swing back and forth without making up my mind. All I know for sure is that you've become the center of everything for them all. I think Mrs. Julia already recognizes this, and she'll find a way to use you if she can. It's been a shock for her to have you turn up here after that letter of your mother's. But if she changes toward you, then you'd better watch out."

There had been a faint indication of such change this morning in the matter of my grandmother's ruby ring, I remembered uneasily. But where this led I had no idea, and I could not accept such unfounded hints. I wanted time to know Wayne Martin away from Silverhill; time to let what had begun between us grow into what it might become. Remaining in this house would do nothing toward that.

"I can't stay," I told her flatly. "I've finally discovered what I want of life. And I mean to have it. If I remain here, Silverhill will spoil everything. I've had enough of death and white birches and secrecy!"

Resolutely Kate wiped her tears away and stood up. "I'm dreaming, of course. Not for anything would Mrs. Julia see her treasures go into anyone's hands but Gerald's. I think she'd see you dead before she'd turn more than a small amount of money over to you. There's no hope there."

"There certainly isn't," I said dryly. "That's hardly what I want, or hope for. But now I'd better forget about fortunes and go down to breakfast, before they start searching for us both. Perhaps I won't see you again, so I'll say goodby, Kate."

I had moved toward the narrow space beside the wardrobe when she stopped me. "Wait, Mallie. Please!"

I paused unwillingly. With every passing moment the longing for escape was growing in me. All I wanted was to put it into effect as soon as I could. Aunt Fritzie's sad problems, or no, I had to get away. My own life had begun to count for me more than it ever had in the past.

"I could hear the voices clear up here," Kate said. "What happened in the garden this morning?"

I told her of my finding the dead bird, and what had followed when Chris and I had taken it downstairs. Before I finished, she was staring at me with dark shock in her eyes.

"Then it's begun," she said. "Oh, I knew it would have to sooner or later. Don't trust any of them, Mallie. The bird is only the beginning. I don't know what they'll do to poor Fritzie, now that she's beginning to remember."

I knew one person I could trust, I thought warmly. "I'll be moving into Shelby, so it doesn't matter whether I trust them or not. At least I can trust Wayne Martin."

She looked aghast. "Oh, no! He'll turn against you fast enough if Mrs. Julia twists his arm. After all, it was his father—no, don't think of trusting any of them."

I could hardly credit such words about Wayne. Already

I knew him better than that. I knew he would not change toward me.

"Who do you mean by *they?*" I asked.

"Your grandmother, of course. And your Aunt Nina, who is afraid of her. Wayne Martin. Gerald and my brother Elden, who have fought since they were children."

"Why? Why do your brother and Gerald hate each other?"

"Elden says it's because Gerald always resented his having two arms. But it goes deeper than that. Elden has always hated anything that goes against nature. He can't abide sick people. So he holds Gerald's arm against him —and Gerald knows it. Both of them were born away from the house and came to it as babies, yet they both feel as though Silverhill belongs to them. Gerald cares about everything that's inside, and Elden cares about the outside —the garden, the trees, the land. I was born right here and I can't care about any of it. It could burn down, for all of me, and I'd never shed a tear."

"Didn't Uncle Henry and Aunt Nina always live at Silverhill?"

"They lived here all right, but at the time Mrs. Nina was carrying Gerald, your Aunt Fritzie was brought home from New York, and everything was in a turmoil. Mrs. Nina couldn't stand the quarrels and your grandmother's tempers, to say nothing of Fritzie going to pieces. She went away to Vermont to stay at a sister's house and have her baby in peace. Little good it did her, considering his arm. Henry Gorham brought them both home and Gerald hasn't left the place since. Now he likes to forget that he was born anywhere else. He has a blood feeling for the place that almost frightens me. Elden came here when he was a year old, but he has the same feeling for the land."

"Do you think one of them—the bird, I mean—?"

Kate slipped out of her gown and took her uniform from its hanger. She did not look at me.

"I don't know. I don't even want to know. It's too horrible. But I can tell you this—Fritzie will be blamed."

I had heard all I wanted to. I let myself out through the space beside the wardrobe and returned to the hall. The chill quality of stale, dead air, the mustiness of disuse seemed stronger than ever. I fled from blue roses and went through the tower to my own side.

This time I did not stop in my room, but hurried toward the stairs. On the way something caught my eye and I bent to pick up a fluff of yellow—a canary feather. As I went down I held my hand over the banister and let the feather float free. I did not want to think of the touch of feathers in my hand.

Aunt Nina's rooms were empty as I passed her doors. Downstairs there was no one in the drawing room and the lights above the two portraits had been extinguished. I followed the sound of voices into the dining room beyond.

This morning Grandmother Julia sat at the head of the table, with Gerald down its length at the opposite end. Aunt Nina had not yet taken her place, but Elden Salway was there, standing near Grandmother's chair. They were speaking together, but there was an immediate silence when I walked into the room. All three stared at me, and the warning echo of Kate's words stirred at the back of my mind. But I must not worry. I had only one purpose from now on. I would sit at the table and eat a meal in this house for the last time. After breakfast I would pack my suitcase and long before noon I would be gone. Surely not one of them would want to stop me. There was nothing I could do against any or all of them when it came to Aunt Fritzie.

Gerald rose to pull out the chair at my place, and Grandmother Julia turned back to Elden, continuing her conversation.

"Of course it can't go on," she said. "We've all been under this strain for years, and it's time it stopped. Still—

I have a responsibility to my daughter. My husband's favorite child."

Gerald set down his coffee cup as though the hot liquid had burned him and waited impatiently while Mrs. Simpson came to find out what I would have for breakfast. When she had gone he spoke to his grandmother.

"You've been sentimental about Aunt Fritzie for too long a time, Gran."

The vitality that still burned in Julia Gorham challenged him down the length of the table, though she did not speak at once, and her very silence seemed deadly.

She looked different this morning, since she had changed from the long wine-colored gown that suited her so well, and wore a dress of beige pongee that was short in the skirt, and rolled softly open at her aging throat. She held her head as proudly as ever, and her hair was like the hair of the portrait, for all that it was no longer dark. She wore no jewelry except for tiny jade earrings and her wedding rings. The ruby was gone from her hand.

When she had let her silence tell upon all of us, she went on. "No matter what Arvilla has done, your grandfather loved her, Gerald. *I* can never forgive her, but for that very reason I must treat her fairly."

"While the rest of us suffer her tricks!" Gerald was still impatient. "All things considered, Mallie has come through a nasty experience this morning. I'd have expected her to go shrieking through the house after finding that bird, but even though she didn't, we can't have this sort of thing repeated."

Grandmother chose to hear only part of what he said. "Malinda is going into the conservatory this morning and lay all those old ghosts for good. Aren't you, Malinda?"

I shook my head. "I don't need to now. All that is behind me. When I picked up that bird and brought it downstairs I knew I needn't be afraid anymore. Right after breakfast I'd like to pack my things and go into Shelby. Do you suppose Elden can take me?"

Elden stood beside my grandmother's chair, listening, watching, saying nothing.

"I don't blame you for clearing out," Gerald said. "You must be scared to death of us by now. You've made a wise decision."

My grandmother spoke as though she settled the matter, her voice firm and clear. "It's not her decision to make," she said. "It is entirely mine."

Mrs. Simpson brought my toast and coffee, and Aunt Nina rushed in, hurried as always, and let her son seat her at the table. I hardly saw the food set before me, or noticed Aunt Nina because I was staring in astonishment at my grandmother. For the others, it was Aunt Nina who was now the center of attention.

"Arvilla is resting—finally," she told Grandmother. "Chris let Wayne know what happened and he came down to see her. She doesn't remember anything—she's in the worst state I've ever seen her. Malinda's coming has done her nothing but harm. She has begun to remember what happened that other time—but only in bits and pieces. Wayne gave her a sedative and she'll be all right now. Kate came in just before I left and she's with her."

"Kate is over her sulking, then?" Gerald said.

Elden made the sound that reminded me of a growl, and Grandmother Julia spoke to him quickly. "Please find Dr. Martin, Elden, and ask him to be sure to see me before he leaves for the hospital this morning. We'll talk about the conservatory and what to do about Arvilla's birds another time. After all, my husband built that conservatory and—"

Gerald grimaced. "And nothing Grandfather Diah built must ever be touched! Not even if the whole place falls down around our ears, or is destroyed by Arvilla's tricks! If she takes anything from the jewelry collection again—"

His mother reached across the table and touched his hand. "Don't, dear. This is a hard decision for your grandmother to make. She isn't as young as you are, and we mustn't—"

Elden left, with a last brooding look for Gerald, and Grandmother broke in upon Aunt Nina. "I'm quite able to make hard decisions when I have to. I mean to talk to Wayne Martin about this today. We'll have to find a suitable place to send Arvilla. It's obvious that she needs constant attention and that we can't keep her here any longer."

Aunt Nina sighed softly, and I knew she sighed with relief. Gerald touched a finger to his temple in salute to his grandmother.

"Bravo, Gran. This had to come sooner or later. And it's better to do it before Fritzie's condition gets any more serious."

I found it difficult to speak for the shock I felt. Grandmother's earlier remark about my staying here had already astonished me, and now that I understood what they planned for Aunt Fritzie, I fumbled with words that were more blurted than careful.

"You can't believe this about the bird—that Aunt Fritzie would have harmed it! Surely you won't railroad her into some institution, when her whole life is here. She's happy with her plants and birds. What would she have to live for if you sent her away?"

"What does she have if she stays here?" Gerald said.

I paid no attention to him. I knew who ruled Silverhill and I kept my eyes upon Grandmother Julia. She was regarding me thoughtfully, as though my words had given her pause, perhaps half persuaded her—though I could hardly believe that possible. She did not answer me, however, but spoke again to Gerald.

"I've called Dr. Worth," she said. "I've told him the wedding will be in two weeks."

Aunt Nina put her hand on Gerald's arm, but he shook it off.

"Then you must call him back and revoke your plans," Gerald said. "Kate doesn't want me. Mother doesn't care for your choice of a wife for me, and Elden would probably shoot me rather than see me marry his sister. Besides, while you don't trouble yourself to think of me—I prefer to remain a bachelor."

"You'll change your mind, of course," Grandmother said evenly, unmoved by his outburst.

"Why should I?" Gerald demanded. "Do you mean to disinherit me and leave everything to Mallie?" He was sure of himself, almost arrogant.

Grandmother considered him for a moment and I recognized the secret smile of the portrait on her mouth. "I might, at that," she said. "How would you like that, Malinda?"

I pushed away my barely touched breakfast. "I wouldn't like it at all! There isn't anything in the world that would make me accept such an arrangement. I would never be trapped by this house the way it seems to have trapped the rest of you."

Aunt Nina made a sound of disbelief, while Gerald studied me warily. Perhaps they both thought my disavowals a way of gaining Grandmother's trust in my lack of cupidity. She did not believe me either.

"I dislike your display of bad manners," she told me—as though the entire scene at the table had not been such a display. "One of the things that concerns me about you, Malinda, is your emotionalism, your excitability. You are too much like your Aunt Arvilla."

I further proved my excitability at once. "Oh, no, I'm not like Aunt Fritzie! I'm much more like you. I won't go to pieces and have a breakdown the way poor Aunt Fritzie has done. And I won't be used for your purposes against Gerald, or Fritzie, or anyone else. I'm going to Shelby and I'm going to live my own life."

"Then you'll have to walk there," Grandmother said. "Or hitch a ride on the highway. By my orders no one here will drive you in. If you're the bright girl I believe you are, you'll spend the rest of the day quietly thinking things over. When you've come to your senses, we'll have a talk."

I knew my face was scarlet, my anger boiling toward explosion, and I'd had enough of the frustration of trying to talk to this woman. I had never had to deal with anyone like Julia Gorham and I was a novice at her sort of warfare.

My chair rocked as I left the table. I ignored Aunt Nina's astonishment and Gerald's amusement as I ran into the hall and burst through the door to the gallery. I wanted to find Wayne Martin and tell him what they were scheming. I wanted to warn him so that he would be ready when my grandmother told him her plan. Only Wayne could keep her from sending Aunt Fritzie away. It was Wayne I must see.

IX

At the instant when I stepped into the gallery, Wayne came through the door from the other half of the house and we met in a near collision. He laughed at the sight of my angry face, swung me in a circle, kissed me resoundingly, and headed for the door through which I had just come.

"Wayne!" I called. "Please—I have to talk to you!"

He waved a hand at me. "I can see your grandmother's upset you again. But we'll talk about it this evening. I'm late for my appointments now, and your grandmother may make me later if she's in that sort of mood."

Before I could say another word he had gone through the door to the house. My rage left me abruptly. How could I remain angry with Grandmother Julia when she mattered so little, and Wayne mattered so hugely that he filled my whole horizon? He had surprised me again by his sudden action, and I crossed dreamily to the other side of the house, lost in reliving that wild whirl, feeling the gay tenderness of his kiss. Never had I thought that Mallie Rice would turn out to be so foolishly sentimental. But I liked her this way. There was no longer any need to be on guard.

Now, however, I must go upstairs and pack in order to be ready as soon as I could find someone who would take me to Shelby. I would say goodby to Aunt Fritzie, and then work out some means of escape. My one regret over leaving Silverhill concerned her. In a sense I was abandoning Aunt Fritzie to those who wanted to dispose of her as though she were of no more consequence than one of her own plants. If it had not been for Wayne, my leaving her would have been more difficult. But Wayne Martin was the one person who would stand up to Grandmother Julia. I knew with all my heart that he would never permit this treatment of Arvilla Gorham.

I was thinking of these things, trying to reassure myself, as I went through the door and walked along the lower hall on Fritzie's side. I passed the empty kitchen first, then the small dining room next to it. What had once been a rear parlor had been turned into a bedroom, and I paused in the doorway, looking first at the woman who lay on the bed, and then at Kate Salway, bending over her. Neither of them saw me and I had a moment to glance about the room in some surprise, learning still more about Aunt Fritzie from the furnishings she had gathered about her.

It was a bright, gay room, with windows that opened upon a lawn so wide it held away any encroachment by the forest trees on this side. Only an oak tree stood near the window, and while one could see all the gray birches that rimmed the forest, they grew well away from the house. The green of outdoors was echoed in wallpaper on which a vine-like plant wove itself about the room, imitating the luxuriant life of a huge philodendron on the windowsill.

The carpet was deeply piled and of a paler green, while the curtains were a complementary yellow. There were no dark antiques here, no family treasures. The furniture was cheerfully, inexpensively maple, and the bed upon which Aunt Fritzie lay was a modern fourposter with machine-wrought pineapples trimming its posts. Only the fireplace with its golden chestnut mantel, and its inset of tiles that was typically old New Hampshire, belonged to the past.

Kate put a finger to her lips as she came toward me. "Don't disturb her, poor thing. She's had a dreadful time."

"Let me stay with her for a while," I offered. "I know you have things to do."

She looked rather dreadful herself, though she had obviously bathed her eyes in cold water and brightened her mouth with fresh lipstick.

"You needn't stay long," she whispered. "She's nearly asleep. Did you tell your grandmother you want to leave?"

"I told her. She said no, and I said yes. So that's the way it stands. I'll get away as quickly as I can."

Kate nodded, but I think she was not convinced. She was accustomed to being ruled by Julia Gorham, as I was not.

When she had gone I walked to the bed and stood looking down at Aunt Fritzie. She had put off her 1920 ruffles and dressed for the morning in a wildly printed green and yellow shift. It lay shapelessly about her, clearly chosen to match the room with its twining leaves. I wondered if she had embroidered a blue rose on some hidden seam of the dress.

Her lashes fluttered against her cheeks as I looked down at her, and I noted an endearing touch of vanity—they had been darkened with mascara. Oddly enough, the sight sent a pang through me because it meant that in spite of everything, Aunt Fritzie had never quite given up. There was a young person trapped in her aging body, and perhaps a little bewildered by the way the years swept by with their outward changes, leaving a young woman imprisoned there.

When she opened her eyes wide and looked at me, I drew a chair close to the bed and sat beside her. "It's Mallie, Aunt Fritzie. If you like, I'll stay with you till you fall asleep."

There was nothing in the least sleepy about the look she gave me out of eyes that still seemed marvelously blue.

"Good!" she said, and wriggled herself upright on the bed. "Though you'll wait a long time before I fall asleep. I've been wanting a chance to talk with you when the rest of the clan wasn't around."

She sounded perfectly lucid—as she had with me last night. Apparently the sedative had not yet begun its work. She seemed to read my thoughts, for she held her hand out to me and opened her fingers. Upon her palm lay two white tablets.

"Such a job of swallowing I did!" she said. "It was a good thing Wayne and Kate were so busy discussing my distraught state, or they would have noticed that I only swallowed water."

She reached toward a glass on the bed table and dropped the tablets into it. Then she plumped up the pillow and sat up against the head of the bed, her expression rueful. I found myself thinking in surprise that there was nothing childishly mischievous about her action—it was more like the ruse of a woman who had to fight for whatever freedom she could attain.

"Why didn't you tell them you didn't play the cruel trick with the canary?" I asked.

She looked at me with her clear-eyed gaze. "Thank you, Mallie dear," she said with dignity. "I knew you would believe me. But it would have done no good to deny anything with the others. Don't you suppose I've found out that the only way they want me to be is foolishly helpless and forgetful?"

She was all too clearly in possession of her senses, and a feeling of horror rose in me. Horror laced with despair. If Fritzie's supposedly demented state had been thrust upon her from outside, if she had been kept a prisoner by the illusions of others—this was a more dreadful injustice than I had imagined.

Again she seemed sensitive enough to guess the trend of my thinking. "Don't look so shocked, Mallie dear. They're not entirely wrong, you know. Some days I have my spells of anger—and I really don't know what I've done afterwards. I know perfectly well that something goes wrong with the wheels in my brain now and then. But when I try to be truly reasonable and sensible, they dismiss everything I say. They won't listen to me with their minds. Except for Chris and Dr. Wayne. Dr. Wayne is my friend. Yet I know I can't count on him because of Mother. In the long run he's her friend first. Because of his father, and all she did for him, as well as all she has done for Wayne himself. But that belongs to the time I'd better not try to remember. The time of the white dress I was making, with the blue roses embroidered on it."

Her thin hands, that had once been the pretty plump hands of Fritzie Vernon, had begun to clasp and unclasp in her lap. I leaned forward to kiss her cheek, and felt the soft crumpled texture of her skin beneath my lips.

"I'm glad I've found you out," I said.

She smiled at me tremulously. "Of course I know the danger I'm always faced with. When I try to speak the truth —the way I did last night about the necklace and the hatpin —they put what I say down to my—my nuttiness. As they have poor little 'Dilly's death. And some of the time they're not wrong. I know I lost my temper and tried to hurt you when you were only a child, and I didn't understand what you'd done. So how can I trust myself? Yet I know I didn't hurt that bird today. It has been sick and Chris has been doctoring it. I would never have put it on your pillow to frighten you. You believe that, don't you, dear?"

"Of course I believe it!" I wondered at the sinking of my own heart, the feeling of despair that deepened in me.

"Just the same, I knew I'd better put on an act with them —an act of not knowing what I was doing. Otherwise, they'd be at me again. If I fall apart, they come running and bring Dr. Wayne, and they pamper and soothe me. And they're pleased with me, because I take the blame for something one of them has done. Only—there's a further danger. The real danger."

"What danger?" I asked, though I was beginning to understand very well.

"For years there's been talk of putting me into an institution, Mallie. They want to hide me away with other mad old women who can't behave themselves properly in what seems to me a very mad outside world. They pretend to think I'm dangerous, and they fuss and talk and push at my mother to have her send me away. Dr. Wayne won't allow it. And Mother, at least, has a conscience. So nothing happens. But sometimes I'm terribly afraid. Mallie—I like it here. It's the only home I know. They let me fix up this room just the way I wanted it, so it's bright and cheerful and green. And Mother won't let Elden tear down the conservatory and take away my birds and plants. Sometimes I think he's the one who is a little mad. But I can understand how he feels, and sympathize with him. It's because of his sister Kate and Gerald. That drives him half out of his mind at times. But at least I think about him—while he doesn't think about me. Not as a person."

I held her hand tightly and sat very still beside her. Tears burned behind my eyes and I did not want to shed them. I wanted to stay free—free to go and find my own life that had suddenly become so important to me. And of course I could, still. Because of Wayne. Because Wayne would never give in to my grandmother.

After a little while Aunt Fritzie turned her hand in mine
almost apologetically and drew it away. "You're hurting
me, dear. You mustn't look so worried. I've really done
very well for myself, and I haven't been unhappy. I know
I've lived a make-believe life, when once I wanted the
world—I wanted everything to be real. Even suffering is
real, you know, but they've taken that away from me, too.
Mallie, I wish I could have seen my sister Blanche before
she died. I know there was something she wanted to tell me
when she came here that other time, but no one would leave
me alone with her long enough, and she was never as en-
terprising as you are. She never flew in their faces except
for that one time when she was young and surprised everyone by running away and marrying your father. But I wish
I knew now what it was she wanted to tell me."

"I can tell you what it was," I said. "I came here because
she never gave up wanting you to know. It's about that
time on the attic stairs when Grandfather Diah fell to his
death. Afterwards everyone blamed you because of some
quarrel you'd had with him. But you weren't to blame.
Mother saw what happened. He had a temper too, and he
tried to shake you, to take something away from you. You
only caught at him to save yourself, and he lost his balance
and fell. It was no one's fault but his, and Mother hated
the way you were made to suffer for his death."

Aunt Fritzie closed her eyes and leaned her head back
against the head of the bed, her face drawn with pain.
After a while she looked at me again with that blue, candid
gaze that could seem like the gaze of a young girl.

"Thank you for telling me, dear. But I'm afraid it comes
too late to matter very much. Indeed, I'm not sure it matters
at all. Perhaps Blanche was trying to salve her own conscience. But whether I struck him there on the stairs, or
even pushed him and caused him to fall—none of that is
the point. I was still to blame, though I can't remember
exactly why. Mallie, I don't think I want to remember. I'm

too old for young suffering now. I can hardly remember Lanny Earle, or why he seemed so wonderful to me. I tried to recapture something last night through you, but I've lost all that, and it doesn't matter anymore. Let's not trouble old graves, Mallie. What's important to me now is my everyday life. I'm really quite busy and happy, in spite of the upsets that happen now and then. All I ask is to have this left to me as long as I live. Now that you've come, I feel a little safer. You're young and brave and you don't know us well enough to be afraid."

But I was beginning to be afraid, I thought. Oh, I was beginning to be!

"What about last night?" I said. "You were afraid on the stairs."

Her smile was still young. "Playacting! That was fun, since you look so much the way I used to. I don't mind dipping back into the past in ways like that. Often I entertain myself by looking at old stage photos and playbills, and reading my own notices. When they let me have them. Mostly I'm forbidden the attic, and I hadn't been up there for years until you came."

"And Grandfather Diah?" I urged. "On the stairs?"

Her smile did not change. "I like to keep them off balance. I think they half believe he returns to the attic. That way they leave all its dust and neglect—and treasures!—to me. Only Kate comes up there to hide away in her little room at the back. We have a secret between us over that. You needn't worry about the stairs, Mallie dear. There's only one place around Silverhill that's haunted. That's outdoors, where the birches grow close to the house on the other side. That's where the child hides and cries. Whenever the moon is right, the child is there. I've seen the flicker of a white dress a good many times, and I've heard the crying."

This time I could smile in response. "Now you're playacting again, aren't you, Aunt Fritzie? I know all about that child. That's where I ran away and tried to hide from you when I was small—with the dead canary in my hands."

Her eyes had a distant look that troubled me. The lucidity had lost itself in mistiness, as though she wandered away from me.

"I think the rest of them have seen the child too, and heard it crying," she went on. "They always get upset and change the subject when I mention what I've seen. Except for Gerald, who never really believes."

"Now you're disappointing me," I said. "I've had a rather poignant feeling over that grove being haunted by the ghost of myself as a little girl."

"I'm sorry," she said calmly. "I don't want to disappoint you, but you're not the child who hides there. One of these nights I'm going to catch hold of that white dress—and when I do, then I'll have all the answers. I'll know all the things they don't want me to remember."

She moved so easily and swiftly from a state of clear-thinking sanity that I would vouch for against any detractor, to a state that was strangely eerie and unbalanced, and I was no longer at ease with her. There was no telling, really, what her true mental state might be. It was perfectly possible that those who knew her better than I were well aware of these changes, and of the dangers that might lie hidden beneath them. It was even possible that at times she might do things that she could not account for later—or would perhaps completely forget. She herself had admitted this.

On the other hand—an institution, with its impersonal white uniforms, its case-accustomed nurses, and jargon-talking doctors who were too busy—perhaps through no fault of their own—ever to attempt what might be a real cure, if such a cure was possible . . . oh, no, I couldn't bear to see Aunt Fritzie sentenced to spend the rest of her life in a place like that. I had come here to say goodby to her, and now I could not. Not yet. Not until I had talked to Wayne and made sure that he would take a stand against Julia Gorham.

I left my chair and moved about the room, trying to please her by praising the wallpaper and the color of the rug, admiring the lusty health of the philodendron, which had obviously responded to Aunt Fritzie's green and loving thumb. At the mantel I paused, my eye caught by an unusual piece of sculpture that rested upon it.

It was done in terra cotta—the head of a woman, cunningly, cleverly wrought. I saw at once whom it represented and turned it toward the light. Someone had created a near-caricature of Grandmother Julia. The bone structure of the head was hers, but here the deep-set eyes were sunk far into their sockets, like the empty eyes of a death's head. The nose was my grandmother's proud nose, but the nostrils flared a little too proudly. The smile was very nearly the smile of the portrait, but the lips were too thin, too cruel, and their corners lost themselves in the folds of old age. The head was partly the portrait, partly my grandmother as she was now—and partly something else, something frighteningly tormented.

Aunt Fritzie startled me by speaking at my elbow. She had rolled herself off the bed and come to stand beside me, the green and yellow of her dress making her look a little like one of her own luxuriantly blooming plants.

"Good, isn't it?" she said.

I nodded. "It's remarkable. And uncanny. Whoever modeled it doesn't like Grandmother Julia very well, I'd say."

"That's what she claims!" Aunt Fritzie laughed with faintly malicious enjoyment. "She ordered the head to be broken up after she saw it. She doesn't know I brought it here, because she hardly ever comes to this room. I like it. It gives me courage whenever I get to thinking about how I was never half the woman my mother was."

"But who made the head?" I asked. "Whoever did this has tremendous talent."

She nodded vigorously. "He has talent all right. It was Gerald, of course."

"Gerald? With one hand?" I bent to examine the fine lines of the modeling, the careful, detailed work.

"Of course it was Gerald. He can do marvelous things with his one hand. But he's somehow ashamed of the way he has to work and he doesn't show what he sculpts."

I touched the mark on my cheek in something like shame. No handicap was any more important than a man or woman made it. If I had learned nothing else by coming to Silverhill, I had learned that.

"I'm going to tell him how good I think he is," I said. "If he has done other things, I'd like to see them. How proud I'd be if I had a talent—"

Aunt Fritzie reached past me and turned the terra-cotta head to the wall so its haunted eye sockets no longer watched us. "No, Mallie dear. I understand about the need to be let alone, because I have it myself. It's too late for him now. He has grown twisted inside. That's where the worst twisting lies—not in his arm. If he would marry Kate, she might save him. But she, poor girl, won't have him on his terms."

"I know," I said. "I like Kate. I had a talk with her this afternoon."

To my surprise, Aunt Fritzie leaned toward me and returned the kiss I had given her a little while before. "You're a nice child—and kind. Thank you for coming to see me, dear. I feel much better with you in the house. I hope you'll stay a long while. You care about other people. I can see that."

Her words added to my growing sense of guilt. I felt both humble and ashamed. Had I ever cared enough about others in the past? Or had I suffered with such self-centeredness over a mark on my face that it took precedence over all real feeling for others? Was I any better than Gerald unless I caught myself up short?

She left me, to open a bureau drawer, and from it she took a small brass key. This she fitted to a flat mahogany box on top of the bureau. When she had opened the lid she drew out several glossy photographs and held them out to me.

"I want you to have one," she invited. "Take your pick."

There were three poses of Fritzie Vernon, and they might have been pictures of me, except that she had been a real beauty. In one she wore the gown with the lace bertha and flouncing train that I had put on so awkwardly last night. The same flat-crowned, lace-covered hat sat gracefully upon her pompadour, and she stood with her hands resting on the handle of a furled parasol. In the second picture she wore another costume from her play—an evening dress that left her beautiful young shoulders bare, with the fringe necklace of moonstones and amethysts adding a touch of elegance about her throat. The gown was fitted to show off her tiny waist and rounded hips before it fell away in folds of lace and silk that brushed the floor.

The third picture was more roguish. She was not in costume, but dressed as herself in the Twenties. Her straight pleated skirt came just above her knees and she had bobbed her fair hair and wore it in a straight cut, with a bandeau across the bangs. One hand twirled a long string of beads, and her great wide eyes flirted with the camera.

Aunt Fritzie was watching me. "Lanny liked me in costume," she said. "After I met him I let my hair grow again. Which one do you like best?"

"This," I said, touched and pleased that she would give me one of her precious pictures. I chose the one in which she was wearing the gown I had put on last night. "Will you autograph it for me?"

The request delighted her and she found a pen and

wrote, "To Mallie with love, from Fritzie Vernon," in a backhand scrawl across one corner.

"I'll always treasure this," I assured her.

She smiled at me. "I feel much better now. I do believe I'll lie down and see if I can nap. But without any pills. I hardly caught a wink last night for being excited, and I'm really worn out over what happened to poor 'Dilly. Of course he would have died in a day or two anyway. He was a very sick bird. But he needn't have died that way. He must have been dreadfully frightened. His poor little heart—but I mustn't think of that."

She ran to the bed in her stocking feet and lay down upon it. There was no need to sit with her while she fell asleep.

The rest of the house was silent as I retraced my way down the hall and returned to the gallery. I left Fritzie's photograph there for the moment and found the door to the garden. Outside I followed the path I had come along so frantically earlier that morning. This time I went through the gate in the white picket fence and out upon the drive in time to see Wayne backing out his car.

I called to him and ran to the driver's side, put my hands on the ledge of the open window. "Did Grandmother tell you?" I cried. "Did she tell you that she means to put Aunt Fritzie away in some place for mental patients?"

He turned his head and looked directly at me. I saw his face and it looked like death.

"I can't talk to you now," he said.

I had never felt so frightened. "But did she tell you?" I pleaded.

"She told me a good deal," he said. "Let me go, please, Mallie. I still have my patients to think of."

"But Aunt Fritzie!" I wailed. "What are you going to do to stop Grandmother Julia?"

"I won't try to stop her," he told me grimly. "Perhaps an institution, or a private nursing home is the best place for Arvilla. This sort of thing can't go on, you know. The bird and all the rest."

I pounded on the window ledge with both fists. "You can't be so cruel! You can't be like the rest of them! Not you!"

"Don't be too sure about what is cruel and what isn't," he said. "Don't be sure of anything."

Not since yesterday at the cemetery had I glimpsed the unyielding quality that could come over him. Quiet marble —cold marble!—without any leavening of mercy beneath the hard surface? I took my hands away and stepped back as he swung the wheel and went off down the drive, making the turn toward the pond.

I could not believe what had happened. I ran around the side of the house, ran part way across the lawn until a clump of trees blocked my way. I stood among them and watched his car turn again on the edge of the pond and swing back to follow the road that wound through the stand of Norway pines my great-grandfather had planted. Even after the car had vanished from sight I did not move, but stood listening to the fading sounds it made—that noisy, uncared-for car of Dr. Martin's, grumbling along toward the distant highway.

When the sounds had faded out completely, I looked about me, dazed and uncertain. For the first time I saw that the thundery yellow of the morning had lifted and that Mt. Abenaki stood out clear and blue-green against a sky that had changed to a normal blue. But the mountain did nothing for my spirits now. Something dreadful and life-crushing had happened that I could not understand. Wayne Martin was going to let Aunt Fritzie be taken away from all that she lived for—and he had completely rejected me besides.

The trees I stood among were the white birches, though I had not recognized them until now. They whispered gently over my head and I had the curious feeling that I did not dare to hear what they might tell me. What was

real, and what only imagined? Once a child who had knelt
here crying had been, for her small self, all of reality. Now
that child with her bleeding cheek existed only in memory,
as did the Fritzie Vernon of long ago. And I, the young
woman who stood here in the aching, frightening present
—soon I too would be only memory.

Yet now I could not run away. If I did, the Fritzie of
the present would have no champion at all—no one to oppose my grandmother.

Slowly I walked out into the sunshine and down across
the lawn toward the beginning of the narrow woods path
that Wayne and I had followed this morning. As I neared
the pond I saw a rowboat out on its surface, with a single
fisherman sitting patiently with his pole extended over the
water. The fisherman was Chris Martin.

Determinedly I set off through the woods in the direction
of the boathouse. After a little while I began to run across
the brown, springy turf of pine needles. I passed a clump
of dead trees with their scraggly dry branches intertwined,
and went on through living woods. Here and there ferns
grew thickly in shaded spots, and once when I paused to
make sure of my way, a tiny tree toad looked directly at
me from a nearby twig. For an instant we seemed to stare
into each other's startled eyes—then he was gone and I
went on. There was no joy to my running—it was only
flight.

The boathouse was the only haven I could run to. Ahead
of me I could see the water again, with the gray stone building ahead, and I hurried. Not until I reached the open side
of the building and looked in, did I realize that someone
was there ahead of me. No one was in view, but at the far
end a huge trapdoor stood open in the floor, with steps
leading down to the boatroom underneath. Two people
were there talking, and I caught Elden's voice first, then
Nina Gorham's.

X

"I'll get a man out from town to clear out all this junk," Elden said. "The wood is rotted from neglect and everything leaks. The only boat that's been kept in shape is Chris's rowboat, because he takes care of it himself. He wants an outboard for it now, and later he'll be wanting a real boat."

Aunt Nina answered him absently, and I could hear them moving about down there. I looked for a place where I could wait until they were gone and I might have the boathouse to myself. But unless I went outside there seemed no hiding place. I moved toward the trapdoor to let them know I was there.

"We can stop worrying now," Elden went on. "My sister and your son can be safe from each other. There'll be no wedding."

"Of course there will be none," Aunt Nina answered tartly. "Gerald has taken a stand against his grandmother —and eventually she'll come around to seeing things his way."

"You think so?" Elden's laugh was unpleasant. "Have you forgotten how fast Mrs. Julia can take off in a new direction when the notion hits her? Can't you see the way she's heading now?"

"I don't know what you're talking about," Aunt Nina said, but there was doubt in her tone.

I would not have stopped listening for anything, and I took a step closer to the open trapdoor.

"What Mrs. Julia wants is a continuing line to leave everything to—as you know well enough," Elden said. "Until she saw young Mallie I doubt she had any notion of changing her mind. But now you can see the way she's heading. She'll more likely get a great grandchild through this girl than through your son Gerald. I think she's made her switch by now, so you can breathe easy, and so can I."

I heard Aunt Nina's choked gasp. "Mother Julia would never do that. Silverhill means everything to Gerald—everything!"

"And I wish I'd had his chances with it!" Elden said roughly. "A lot of good he's done with it. It would be a waste to throw it all away on Gerald Gorham, and she's beginning to see that."

"You—you forget yourself!" Aunt Nina cried.

Elden laughed again, and I could hear him clambering over old boats and pieces of lumber. Moments later he came out by some lower exit and made off through the trees at a good clip, never looking back.

Aunt Nina climbed the stairs and came through the opening to the trapdoor. Her face was tense with anger and she did not see me until I spoke her name. Then she put a hand to her mouth and stared at me in something like horror.

"I heard what Elden said," I hurried to tell her. "And I don't believe a word of it. But it wouldn't matter even if Grandmother got such an idea into her head. I keep telling everyone that I don't want Silverhill or anything in it. You needn't think of me as competition for Gerald."

There was strain in every line of her face and I could tell that she did not believe a word of my disavowal. She spoke earnestly, as though she must somehow convince me of what I already knew.

"Silverhill is Gerald's lifework. I don't know what he would do if someone tried to take it from him. When he is angry—" She seemed to shiver at the thought of Gerald's anger and did not go on.

There was nothing I could say which would change her blind conviction, and when I too was silent she tried another course, turning about desperately in her effort to persuade me.

"You said you wanted to leave, Malinda. If you like, I'll

take you into town. I can drive the Bentley, and we can go as soon as you're ready."

I wished that I could give her this assurance, at least, but since lunchtime everything had changed.

"I can't go away and see this awful thing done to Aunt Fritzie," I told her. "How can you be so considerate of your son, and not see that Aunt Fritzie can suffer too?"

A tinge of angry pink came into her face. "I? Think of her! When all our misfortunes stem from Arvilla Gorham? When it was her fault that Gerald was born as he was! She was to blame for that because of what she did with her willfulness, her tantrums, her wild ways. I had to get away to have him born at all. I've never seen anything like the way she behaved when she came back to Silverhill. She was a madwoman. For a while she had to be locked in to keep her from running off."

"Locked in?" I broke in on her words indignantly. "What a dreadful thing to do! Why couldn't Grandmother let her make her own life and go out to California to marry her Lanny Earle?"

"Marry *him?* What nonsense! Don't be sentimental, Malinda. Do you think Father Diah didn't have the fellow thoroughly investigated? He already had a wife. He couldn't have married Arvilla, even if he'd wanted to—which was doubtful. But she would have run off to him nevertheless and made a horrible scandal. Mother Julia would never stand for that. And Father Diah felt if they could just keep Arvilla home until she got over her infatuation, everything would improve. But her notorious movie actor was killed in an auto crash, and when she found it out—we tried to keep it from her—she was worse than ever. I couldn't endure what was going on. I had to get away. Old Dr. Martin —Wayne's father—said a baby could be marked in the first months after its conception. He always believed that emotional stress could have a damaging effect upon a pregnant woman, so that almost anything might happen to the baby."

I listened to her miserably. No matter what poor Fritzie had done, or how she had behaved during that tragic time, so that Nina felt Gerald had been marked by her own emotional upset, it was all over, lost in the past. Nothing could change what had happened, and nothing could be more unjust than to hold the past against Fritzie now. She was not the same woman today as the one who had behaved so wildly and broken-heartedly, any more than I was the child who had unwittingly crushed a bird to death. The past had built her, as it had built me, but we were an evolvement and not the same beings.

Yet I could see how Nina Gorham must feel. However foolish her notion might be, Nina clearly believed it—and she had the everyday reminder of Gerald's arm to keep her anguish and resentment against Fritzie alive.

Her words rushed on again, as soon as she had drawn breath. "Even as a baby Gerald almost died because of Arvilla. Henry brought me home with Gerald when he was only a month or two old—which was much too soon. We were here when that awful thing happened that was more of Arvilla's doing—her father's death. That was when she should have been put away where she could injure no one else. She was jealous of me because I was married and had a baby, and she kept stealing Gerald out of his crib and running away with him—the way child-hungry spinsters sometimes do. Once she even brought him down here and tried to take him out on the pond in a boat. She might have drowned him if Mother Julia hadn't caught her. It was an awful, awful time. You can have no idea—you're too far away from it. But Mother Julia remembers, and so do I. No, we can't bear much love for Arvilla. We've done our best —but it's not good enough. We can't endure anymore, now that she's begun to play hateful tricks on Gerald again, and steal things from him. It's beginning all over again—and it's too much."

I heard her out with a growing sense of shock, yet of pity too—for them all. Nevertheless, most of my pity was for Aunt Fritzie now. The others had lost perspective. Probably they could not see her as she was in the present, and as I, unencumbered by the past, could view her. I could not walk out on her now. Especially I could not abandon her after Wayne Martin's abdication from what ought to be his responsibility to protect and help her.

I walked to a window that looked out over the water. Wind rippled the blue surface and small waves lapped over the pebbled beach below. The young fisherman had begun to row toward the shore.

I spoke over my shoulder to Aunt Nina. "A little while ago Aunt Fritzie showed me a piece of Gerald's sculpture. He does remarkable work."

His mother shook her head sorrowfully. "He might have done." She came to stand beside me at the window. "What he creates is always spoiled because everything he does takes a cruel turn. He hurts others with every piece he creates. Now he keeps his work from me, from us all. Except for the few things he shows his grandmother. She was angry about the head he did of her, but she enjoys it when he ridicules someone else. He wasn't always like this. I can remember him as a little boy."

She leaned upon the window ledge, watching Chris as he neared the shore.

"Gerald and I used to go rowing when he wasn't much older than Chris Martin. We'd sit side by side on the board seat and I would put an arm about him so that we felt almost like one person. Then we would row together, with me managing the right oar and he the left. There were so many things we used to do together in those days. His father was too often impatient with him. Henry was never an imaginative man and he thought sports were the only thing to develop a boy. Sports, for Gerald! So my son was closer to me than he ever was to his father."

I ventured a question. "Why don't you want him to marry Kate Salway? Isn't a wife like Kate what he needs more than anything else?"

She looked at me with real horror in her eyes. "That dreadful girl! You don't know her the way I do. The sly things she does—she and that awful brother of hers! If I had my way—"

"My grandmother thinks she's quite suitable," I said.

Aunt Nina tilted her chin. "Perhaps it's time that you realize how little sensitivity your grandmother has where others are concerned. She has never been a woman to understand or trouble about anyone else's feelings. Aside from the fact that Kate Salway is far from good enough for my son, I would never want to see him submitted to the intimacies of marriage. At least I can imagine his sufferings, if she cannot. I held him in my arms as a baby. I took care of him as a little boy. I know all the ugliness that he hides from the world."

She turned from me with a certain pitiful dignity and walked abruptly from the boathouse—a woman who would always delude herself first of all. No girl would ever be good enough for Nina Gorham's son to marry because she herself could not cut the cord of silver that still held her to him. It was a wonder that Gerald Gorham had not slashed through the knot himself long before this.

I looked out the window again, and saw that Chris had reached the shore and tied up his boat at a wooden piling of the dock. He waved to me as he crossed the pebbled beach and disappeared from view in the lower room of the boathouse. A moment later he came up through the trapdoor, closing it carefully after him.

"I saw you, so I came in," he said. "The fish aren't biting anyway."

This morning he wore a faded blue shirt and rolled-up

blue jeans. His cowlick was awry and he seemed to have garnered still more freckles across his nose. He stood with his bare feet sturdily apart, studying me with that thoughtful air that belied his years.

"Is Kate all right now?" he asked.

"I think so," I told him. "We had a good visit."

"And you didn't tell her that I—?"

"There was nothing to tell." An idea came to me and I suggested it to him. "Will you take me into Aunt Fritzie's conservatory, Chris? Will you go in with me and tell me about some of her plants and birds. Then I can be sure I'll never be frightened of that place again."

He nodded, pleased. "Sure I will. I help her with them sometimes, you know. Do you want to go now?"

The time seemed right, since all I could do was fill in the hours until Wayne came home, or my grandmother sent for me. All of a sudden time had turned leisurely, the minutes moving at tortoise pace because there was so much I could not work out alone. It was troubling to be helpless, to be unable to speed matters to some sort of solution. I had no knowledge then of how soon the minutes would run away with me, hurtling themselves to meet events I would always want to forget. I did not guess what appalling memory had begun to stir in Fritzie's mind to prompt her to disastrous action.

Chris and I left the boathouse together and we walked through the pine trees to the winding woods road. We moved at no great speed because Chris had a habit of making darting forays to right and left in order to investigate everything that caught his eye, from the bark on a tree to a hole in the earth. In some respects life at Silverhill was obviously a fine thing for any small boy. But he was too solitary, with no summertime company of his own age.

When our pathway met the drive and we crossed it to take a shortcut across Silverhill's sloping lawn, I found the house shining like platinum in the morning sun, its central tower and tall windows far less watchful and ominous than they seemed at night. It was not the house I feared, but the people in it, and the almost insoluble problems that still lay ahead. When she was ready my grandmother would see me and I must somehow be strong enough to deal with her and to stand up for Aunt Fritzie. How that was to be managed, I could not see. And there was still Wayne. I had been able to find no time to be alone in the boathouse and renew myself in remembrance of what had happened there this morning. There had been a shocking change in him since that gay moment when he had whirled me around and kissed me as we met by chance in the gallery. The unyielding man who had turned away from me in the car had not been the same man I had met in the gallery.

As we went up the sloping lawn together, Chris began to talk, and I put aside my troubling thoughts to listen.

"I wish I could have seen Silverhill years ago when the birches were growing a long way off from the house, over near the edge of the woods," he said.

I threw him a quick look and found his young face serious. "That clump of birches?" I said. "Growing near the woods? How is that possible?"

"Uncle Gerald says they grew there when he was a little boy," Chris informed me. "He says they walk about at night and sometimes they forget where they belong, so they move a little closer and a little closer to the house all the time. He says they've watched us for so long that they've forgotten they're really trees. They think they're people. What they'd like is to move right into the drawing room and wrap themselves around us. That's what he says."

I laughed in relief. For a moment he had startled me. "You like such stories, don't you, Chris?"

"Sure!" He grinned at me. "It's fun to be scared. Sometimes. Uncle Gerald has lots of stories like that. Kate doesn't like it when he starts making up all that stuff—but I think it's fun. So long as I'm someplace safe, so I'm sure none of those things can happen. Just the same, I've sneaked outdoors at night a couple of times to see if I could catch the trees moving."

"And have you ever?"

We had reached the front drive and crossed it, and Chris led me over the grass toward the stand of white birches. They were tall, beautiful, straight-trunked trees, unlike the crooked gray ones that grew in the woods, yet the entire grove seemed to have a windswept air of leaning toward the house.

Chris stood with his arms folded, his wide eyes fixed upon the trees as he considered my question. "I'm not sure. Sometimes I think they really do move. But then again, it might only be the wind. They aren't close enough yet to touch the house, but I think they try to when the wind blows. Uncle Gerald says that when they finally thrash themselves against our windows, the old way of things will be over for Silverhill. Once the birches can touch the house, they'll take it for themselves. So I always watch out for wind storms. Maybe there'll be one tonight."

I shivered in sudden dread.

He smiled at me kindly. "You needn't be afraid. I'll be around if thunder weather comes back. I think it's just moved around to the other side of the mountain for now. You can see the yellow haze off that way, and sometimes there's a rumble."

"I'll count on you," I said.

He laughed, pleased with such dependence. "Come along!" he cried and began to run.

We ran together around the house, through the gate in the white fence and along the walk toward the gallery. In a corner of the garden Elden knelt, digging in the earth with a trowel, and Chris came to a halt beside him.

"You've buried 'Dilly, haven't you?" he said.

Elden scowled. "At least sick birds are good for some-thing—good for feeding the flowers."

I did not like the way he looked and I was glad enough to follow as Chris hurried up the back steps. From the gal-lery he went at once into the conservatory, opening the two doors, one after the other, leading me into a midmorning glare of light and heat. The place could steam by day, I discovered. No wonder Aunt Fritzie often felt cold else-where. Bright sunshine lighted the entire dome and the birds were singing cheerfully in an orchestrated chorus. Green plants steamed, unnaturally motionless with no wind allowed to stir their leaves and set them rustling. The plants were like gluttons, I thought, constantly feeding their own fat growth, with never a chance to wave their fronds in a breeze.

I did not like it here. I was uneasy, yet there was no longer the old senseless terror.

Chris called the macaw down and introduced him to me properly. "Jimmy's a sort of watchdog for the place, you know. That's why Aunt Fritzie lets him stay loose. If there's trouble, or if any of the other birds need help, Jimmy starts yelling and lets us know. He's really scary when he gets ex-cited and wants to call for help. Sometimes he yells 'Bloody murder!' and it's pretty awful. But now he's acquainted with you and he won't attack you the way he did this morn-ing. Look, I'll show you."

Chris set Jimmy on my shoulder—where I did not want him—soothing him gently.

"Bloody murder!" the bird shrieked in my ear, and I must have leaped a foot. Chris was a hard master, however, and he would not let me off. He calmed the macaw until it told him, "Good-boy-Chris, good-boy-Chris!"—and after that Jimmy rode with me peacefully, whether I enjoyed it or not.

The three of us went through the entire conservatory. I managed to pretend that the perspiration that beaded my forehead was due only to the steamy atmosphere. Sometimes the macaw rubbed his beak against my ear, or cleaned it off on my shoulder after Chris offered him something to eat, and I steeled myself to endurance. The experience was, I supposed, therapeutic. Knowing why I was afraid had helped me to come a long way since this morning.

All that I did now was a mere marking of time anyway. I must see Wayne, I must talk to him. That was what mattered most.

I marked time further by lunching with Aunt Fritzie and Chris on her side of the house, and I found her wide awake after her nap, and as lucid as she had been with me earlier. Only once did she mention the past.

"I've almost got it," she whispered to me when Chris went out to the kitchen to make himself another sandwich. "Everything is coming back clearly, though still with patches missing. It hurts me to remember, but just the same I think it will be good for me. I can't force it—it must come by itself. If I can remember everything, then there won't be any question of sending me away somewhere, will there, Mallie?"

"Of course not!" I answered her with a confidence I could not feel. It was Aunt Fritzie's remembering that seemed to threaten those who lived at Silverhill. More and more, it seemed to me that the effort with the bird had been made with a double purpose—to frighten me away from the house, and to convince Grandmother Julia that her older daughter was altogether mad. But why did someone fear her remembering? Was it because there was more to Diah's death on the stairs than my mother had realized?

Chris returned with a large conglomerate sandwich, and nothing more was said of personal matters for the rest of the meal.

Through the remainder of the day the clocks of Silverhill ticked away minute by slow minute—and I waited. Waited to see Wayne Martin again. Waited to be summoned by my grandmother. By dinnertime neither had come about.

Only Chris's prophecy concerning the return of thunder weather was borne out. The sky grew dark early and curtains were pulled against the peering birches. Now and then a rumble of thunder reached us from beyond the mountain, and above its darkening crest the sky occasionally flashed with lightning. At the dinner table candle flames dipped and grew smoky in gusts that blew through open windows and stirred the curtains.

The girl who came out from town to help about the house left ahead of time, and we dined a half hour early, with Kate helping between table and kitchen.

When I entered the dining room I found that Grandmother Julia had appeared for dinner. Once more she wore her long, dark-red gown, and there were ruby earrings in her ears and the ruby ring was conspicuous upon her right hand. The left, as always, wore Diah's diamonds. She was as calmly elegant and as coolly self-possessed as though the day had not beset her with difficulties. She had, in fact, the air of a woman who had surmounted all adversity, and that in itself made me increasingly uneasy.

No sooner were we seated at the table than Elden Salway came in from outdoors. Grandmother had apparently sent for him, and he had washed the earth stains from his hands, and slicked back his sandy hair with a wet comb so that he looked a little more presentable than usual.

"Elden's here, Mrs. Julia," Kate said, coming in just ahead of him, carrying a tray that held cups of cold consommé.

Elden came to the head of the table and stood at Grandmother's elbow, looking around boldly at each of us in turn. Gerald and Aunt Nina resented him, I knew, but Grandmother never seemed to mind his New England bluntness.

"I want you to watch for Dr. Martin's car, Elden," she said. "I want to know the moment he appears. He was angry when he left, and he may try to slip past my door without coming in. You're to tell him I want to see him at once, please."

"I'll tell him," Elden said with more relish than I cared for. If anything, he seemed to feed on family conflicts.

When he turned to go, Grandmother stopped him. "Wait, if you please. And you, too, Kate. Set those cups on the sideboard and listen to me. I want you both to hear what I have to say." For an instant she permitted her fine blue-violet eyes to rest upon me, then her gaze moved away. "Wayne phoned me this afternoon to say that he has made a temporary arrangement for Arvilla in Shelby. There is a home that will take her there, until she can be transferred to some more suitable place. She must, of course, have proper medical care and I will see to that. Wayne will drive her to town day after tomorrow."

Startled silence met her words. I was too aghast to speak, too stricken at Wayne's final betrayal of Aunt Fritzie. I think no one there had believed that Grandmother Julia would act with such dispatch. Kate uttered a sound of distress that she immediately stifled, and Aunt Nina fidgeted with a spoon, nodding her approval. Gerald, however, was already shaking his head.

"Day after tomorrow may not be soon enough," he said. "If Fritzie senses what is going to happen, goodness knows what she's likely to do."

"I think we can handle that," Grandmother said. "All right, Elden—"

"What about the birds?" he put in.

"For the time being you and Chris can undoubtedly take care of them," Grandmother said. "No—you needn't argue. I'm not going to do anything about them at once. I know how you feel about the conservatory, but first I want to see how this new arrangement works out for Arvilla. After all, I'm not entirely without a heart."

"I think you are!" I cried, and the sound of my voice surprised us all. I went on recklessly. "I think you're doing a dreadfully cruel thing! I don't see how Wayne Martin can go along with it. There's nothing wrong with Aunt Fritzie that a little kindness and consideration won't cure or help."

Gerald laughed unpleasantly and Elden snickered. Only Kate's expression told me she was on my side—on Aunt Fritzie's side—though clearly she would say nothing.

"You have been with us for two days, Malinda, and you seem to know all about us," Grandmother said. "Please continue."

I could feel myself flushing, but I had to plead for Fritzie, who could not plead for herself.

"No matter what any of you think, I don't believe she killed that canary, or put it on my pillow. I don't know which one of you did that vicious thing, but it wasn't Aunt Fritzie!"

The room was quiet again in a queer, breathless way. They were all staring at me as though it was I who was demented, I who had gone stark, raving mad. I stumbled on.

"She's begun to remember the past quite clearly. She told me so at lunch. Maybe that's just the trouble. Perhaps you don't want to give her enough time—to remember."

Someone—I don't know who—drew a deep breath and then released it. I looked only at my grandmother, who surprised me by smiling as if in kind sympathy—when I knew there was no sympathy in her.

"Interesting that you should feel this way," she said. "Enormously interesting."

Her words left me with a greater feeling of alarm than if she had scolded, or dismissed me from the room. She was planning something—and when Julia Gorham made secret plans someone else was likely to come out on the losing end.

I was not kept in the dark for long.

"Your attitude is interesting," she continued, "because I have decided to change my will. I am an old woman and

I must face the fact that Gerald will probably never take a wife and the line of inheritance for Silverhill will end with him. On the other hand, Malinda, you will undoubtedly marry and have children. Through you the line will go on and all that Diah and I have built will continue to your descendants."

Aunt Nina made a faint choking sound. Gerald said nothing, though he had gone white.

"This is absurd—" I began, but Grandmother Julia broke in at once, looking about at the others as if she thoroughly enjoyed their consternation.

"You will have nothing to say about the matter, Malinda. I will see to certain restrictions in the will's wording so that you will be unable to dispose of anything carelessly, whatever your whim."

"But I don't want all this!" I protested. "I won't have—"

"You *will* have," said Grandmother Julia. "And of course we all know you will come to your senses when you've had time to think matters over. In the next few days everything will be arranged to my satisfaction. That is, unless Gerald chooses to reconsider what I've asked of him."

Elden watched in malicious pleasure, while tears shone in Kate Salway's eyes. Not one of the four—not even Grandmother herself—believed in my unwillingness to be her heir. Yet at that moment Gerald surprised me. He met her challenge with a bitter smile, though all color had left his face.

"I suppose you know what you are doing," he said. "Nevertheless, with no reflection on Kate, I won't go down this road under your duress, no matter what you do. But I'll give you fair warning that I'll try to stop you if I can."

For almost the first time I found something to admire in my cousin. I even found myself wondering if he might not have more strength of character in him than we knew. A strength that had never been tested, never had a chance to show itself.

Grandmother gave him a startled look. "How will you stop me?" she began—but at that moment Aunt Fritzie came abruptly through the door from the hall, making as dramatic an entrance as any she could have made on a stage.

She pushed her way past Kate, past Elden, and went to stand beside her mother. She was still dressed in the flowered green and yellow shift that gave her a resemblance to one of her own lush plants. Yet in spite of its gaudy colors and inappropriate length, she carried herself with an air of real and tragic dignity. She was utterly filled with her own purpose, unaware of the anxious moment into which she had blundered.

"I can remember everything!" she announced to her mother. "I know why I made the little white dress and embroidered blue roses all over it for luck. It was a baby dress. It was a dress for *my* baby—the one you took away from me!"

No one at the table moved except Grandmother Julia. She reached for a crystal glass and sipped the wine it held. When she spoke her voice was as calm as though Aunt Fritzie had mentioned the thunder that rumbled outside.

"If you can remember everything that well, Arvilla, then you must try to remember the rest. The baby died, you know. That's why it was taken away from you. Can you remember that?"

So Aunt Fritzie had spoken the truth! This was the cruel root of all her suffering. Kate took a step toward her, but she paid no attention. She pointed a finger at her mother and the gesture was accusing.

"I knew you'd try to tell me the baby died! I knew you'd say that. But I remember that I found him in his crib—a little boy!—and he was alive. You thought I was too ill to get out of bed, but I got up and hunted until I found him and held him in my arms. He was Lanny's child and mine. I knew you'd try to take him from me, so I meant to run off and hide until I could get away from Silverhill. I carried him outdoors but I wasn't strong enough. I got only as far as the birch trees at the side of the house. Father caught me and brought me back—and I never saw the baby again. Sometimes I can hear him crying out there even now. It was because of the baby that Father and I quarreled later, when I was able to be out of bed. I followed him up to the attic one day to show him the dress I'd made, to prove that I knew the baby was alive. I didn't mean what happened on the stairs. And Mallie says I didn't push him. Blanche was there—she knew. If I can find the white dress, I'll show it to you—"

"We've heard enough of this!" Grandmother Julia's self-possession was cracking a little. "Kate, take Miss Arvilla to her room at once."

Before Kate could move, Aunt Fritzie stepped swiftly to the other side of the table, out of reach.

"Don't you understand?" she cried. "I *know* about my baby! I held him in my arms only that one time, but I know he lived and that you took him away from me."

Grandmother Julia put her hand to her throat as if she had difficulty breathing. "No," she said, "—no!"

For once it was Aunt Fritzie who commanded us, held our horrified attention.

"Babies grow up," she went on. "My son would be in his forties now. And since I am Father's oldest child, he should be the one to inherit Silverhill and everything in it. *My* son—not Nina's son, Gerald. Somewhere there's a real heir—and I want to know where he is. I want to find my son!"

Grandmother Julia's calm had broken. I saw the tightening of her lips as she winced in pain. Her words faltered as she spoke to her daughter.

"I'm sorry that you've remembered this, Arvilla. We've tried to spare you the hurt of remembrance all this time. After your illness, your breakdown, you forgot everything connected with the baby. It was better for you that way. Even if your son had grown to manhood, he would be illegitimate, you know. He would scarcely stand in line to inherit his grandfather's fortune, which now belongs to me. You must go back to your room and rest. The baby died a long time ago. You must forget it. Kate, if you please—"

As Grandmother Julia spoke, the brief spark died out of her daughter. She seemed to wilt before our eyes and she began to weep softly with her hands to her face. Kate slipped a consoling arm about her, led her gently from the room.

I glanced at Gerald to see how he was taking this talk of another heir, and found him staring at his plate. It came to me with sudden insight that he was not really concerned. All his attention was still turned inward upon his own problem, his own interests.

"Gerald—" Grandmother began brokenly, and could not go on.

He roused himself by an effort and looked at her coldly down the length of the table. He would find a way to punish her now, I thought—not because of Aunt Fritzie's child, but because she meant to change her will in my favor.

"I've heard the rumors, of course," he said, "though I never knew whether to believe them. Now suppose you tell me the truth. Is there a grown son of Arvilla's? Have you kept track of him?"

Aunt Nina put a quick hand on her son's arm. "Darling, you needn't worry. Every possible care was taken. The child—"

"So you know too?" he said, and drew his arm away.

Grandmother Julia frowned at her daughter-in-law and Aunt Nina subsided at once. "Very well," she said to her grandson, "I will tell you the truth. The child lived. I know where he is. But the facts of his birth have never been revealed to him and he has no idea of his identity. Nor will he ever know, if I can prevent it. His knowing would serve nothing now. Does that satisfy you?"

Elden made a slight movement at her elbow and she

seemed to remember that he was there and looked up at him, recovering herself a little.

"You understand that what you've seen and heard here today is to go no further?" she said to him. "I want no gossip started up again in Shelby. Whether there is a child of Arvilla's, legitimate or otherwise, carries no weight, since Silverhill will pass to the next heir in my will. You are to tell your sister exactly what I am telling you, so she will understand. There is to be no discussion of our affairs away from the house."

Even Elden could be abashed when Grandmother put on her autocratic manner and there was no mockery in him now. If Elden Salway respected anyone, he respected Julia Gorham, even though he sometimes rebelled against her rule. There would be no gossip as far as he was concerned.

When he had gone from the room Gerald flicked a look my way and spoke again to his grandmother. "How will you assure yourself that the heiress-apparent does no talking?"

For an instant I thought Julia Gorham's proud façade would crack entirely, and that she would plead with her grandson. She did not. Instead, she rose from the table, outwardly herself—even to the smile of the portrait, faint, secret, disturbing.

"I have my own plans for silencing Malinda," she said. "Now, if you'll excuse me, I will finish dinner in my own rooms. This has been an upsetting day and I need to be alone."

Gerald rose as she moved toward the door and for the first time I saw her stumble. At once Aunt Nina sprang up and went to help her from the room.

When they had gone, Gerald brought himself and me a cup of consommé from the buffet and we ate in moody silence, avoiding each other's eyes. Mrs. Simpson brought in our dinner grumpily and set it on the table. I did not know what I ate—or if I ate. My thoughts were all for poor Aunt Fritzie and the unhappy past, for Wayne and his be-

trayal. Gerald's thoughts, I suspected, were entirely concerned with his patrimony, and in that I had no interest.

When the silence grew heavy, Gerald raised his wine
glass and toasted me grimly. "To your coming good fortune, Cousin!"

I looked at him then. "My good fortune will be to get
away from this house as soon as I can. I'll stay as long as
there's a chance of putting up a fight for Aunt Fritzie, and
no longer. That Grandmother should plan to send her away
is wickedly wrong. All the more so if there was a baby.
When I think of what she must have suffered at her mother's
hands—!"

"And how will you stop Grandmother Julia?" he challenged me.

"Through Wayne Martin," I told him with certainty.
There had to be an explanation of Wayne's behavior—there
had to be!

Gerald grimaced. "If the stories I've heard carry any
weight, it was Wayne's father who attended Fritzie when
the child was born—and must have connived in whatever
skullduggery went on. Which gives Gran a nice lever to hold
over Wayne's head."

I hated Gerald then. "Wayne's not like that! He'd never
be blackmailed or bribed. He'll be on Aunt Fritzie's side in
the long run. I know he will!"

Gerald whistled softly. "So that's the way the wind blows!
You work fast, Cousin. I can see why Gran is already hoping for a grandchild. Perhaps there'll be a wedding held in
the gallery, after all. You must send me an invitation, when
the day is set."

I could only stare at him angrily.

"Nevertheless," he went on, "I think Wayne will do exactly as Grandmother Julia says. After all, he has her to
thank for keeping his drunken father from going to prison
for malpractice years ago. We all know what sainted Old
Doc was like. Gran and Wayne's grandmother were de-

voted friends when they were young, and old Julia never let her friend's son down, no matter how he behaved. She's responsible for Wayne's education as well, and she's given him a home. But Gran is the sort who never hesitates to extract blood for any debt that's owed her. Not if she can profit by it. In what you call the long run—Wayne will do exactly as she says."

I heard him out, sickened. I no longer knew who could be believed. Kate had said I could trust no one—not even Wayne. I pushed my chair back from the table and stumbled to my feet. Gerald was up at once, barring my way to the door.

"Just one thing, Cousin—if I were you, I wouldn't count on coming into that inheritance Gran has promised you."

"I don't want—" I began, and knew by his face that I could not talk to him, or make him believe. He was wholly lost behind the blinders he wore. I could almost feel sorry for Gerald Gorham, in spite of my disgust, because his mind was as badly twisted as his body. Events would surely prove him wrong about Wayne. As for the inheritance, my grandmother could not force it upon me without my cooperation—and that I would never give. The very thought of touching anything that belonged to Silverhill appalled me. But Gerald's myopic view would never permit him to understand this.

When he saw that I would say nothing more, he dropped the arm with which he barred my way. At once I fled from the room and through the gallery to the other side of the house.

I wanted only to see Aunt Fritzie. I wanted to put my arms about her and comfort her. I wanted to promise her my loyalty and support for as long as she needed them. I would even promise her to help find her son, if that was what she wanted.

Perhaps we would manage to comfort each other.

XI

The hall was unlighted, Aunt Fritzie's door closed. Kate Salway sat in the shadows outside it, a reluctant jailer.

"Kate," I said, my voice as soft as Gerald's, "what can we do? How can we keep her from being sent away? I can't believe that Wayne Martin will help Gran in this."

Kate looked up at me, troubled and uncertain. "Perhaps he's right, Mallie. Perhaps this is the best thing to do under the circumstances. Everything is too difficult for her here."

"Difficult!" I repeated. "After what she has suffered! At least Grandmother can't hold me to silence. If I can find out where the child was taken, where he is now, then I think Aunt Fritzie has the right to know and be reunited with her son."

Kate caught my hand so tightly that I winced. "No, Mallie—no! Let well enough alone. Don't try to find out or you'll wish you hadn't. You'll stir up a hornet's nest."

Deliberately I pulled away and walked to a wall switch. When I had turned on the hall light I went back to her and looked closely into her face. For a moment she tried to endure my searching eyes. Then she bent her head and covered her face with her hands.

"You know something, don't you?" I said. "You've known about the child all along. Perhaps you even know where he is? Who told you? How do you know?"

I was the stronger of the two at that moment and I had no mercy for her state of misery. When she did not answer I took her by one shoulder and shook her hard.

"Tell me!" I ordered. "Tell me at once!"—and disliked hearing the sound of my grandmother's tones in my own voice.

Kate took her hands from before her face and stood up to plead with me. "No, Mallie. Your grandmother is right.

This is something that mustn't be disclosed because of the harm it could do."

"You make no sense," I told her impatiently. "How do you know any of this?"

She made a helpless gesture with both hands. "I read your mother's letter. For Gerald's sake, I had to know what was in it. I managed to get my hands on it before Mrs. Julia burned it. Blanche put down all the truth. She told your grandmother she was going to tell you everything, and that she would send you here to right the wrongs that had been done her sister Arvilla. Mrs. Julia was in a fury until she made sure that your mother had died before she told you that old story. The little you knew didn't matter, so you weren't dangerous to them after all. But I know the rest. I've known it ever since you came."

I could better understand Kate's behavior toward me now —her doubts about me when we first met, her reluctance to respond to my own efforts to be friendly. But she had not told me enough.

"I want to know all of it," I said. "Mother meant for me to know, in order to help Aunt Fritzie."

"Your mother was wrong. The truth won't help her now."

She closed her lips tightly upon her own words and sat down in the chair, her hands folded in her lap, resisting me with that quiet core of strength that could defeat any force that set itself against her. There were times when Kate would bend like a reed and seem ready to blow away before the first adverse wind. But always in the end she found enough heart to take a stand and do whatever had to be done. I knew quite well that I would get nothing more from her now.

"May I see Aunt Fritzie?" I asked.

She hesitated for so long that I thought she might refuse me. Then she rose and opened Fritzie's door softly, to let me look inside. I could only stare in shocked silence at what I saw.

Aunt Fritzie sat upon the floor beside an old chest from which she had taken most of the contents. She held a wad of something in her arms, rocking back and forth, crooning over it. The voice that had once sung *Zobelia* so gaily was murmuring a heartbroken lullaby.

Kate closed the door softly. "Let her be. She's found the baby dress. She says it was in with other old things of hers all the time—only she didn't really know what she was looking for. After a while I'll get it away from her."

My throat felt choked with tears. "Why must you? Why can't you leave her that at least?"

Kate answered me simply. "Because a dress is no substitute for a baby. And there is no baby."

"Somewhere—" I began.

"Don't be sentimental!" she cried as Aunt Nina had done. "Mrs. Julia is right. Somewhere there's a grown man who will not thank you for telling him who he is, and who may very well resent what has been done to him."

"How do you know that's right?" I cried. "How do you really know? There's been too much hiding of the truth. Perhaps nothing can heal until it comes out into the open and all the lies are cleared away."

She looked at me strangely, but I turned my back on her and walked in the direction of the front door. She was after me at once, catching me by the arm.

"There's one thing more, Mallie—please!"

I waited, yielding nothing.

"Don't let Elden know anything of what I've told you. If he thought I knew something that he doesn't he would make me tell. And he must never know—never! I couldn't bear to see the power it would give him. Elden loves power and he's always hated Gerald. He could make his life miserable in a hundred small ways."

I listened to her blankly, my astonishment growing. She had not told me the truth outright, but she was throwing herself upon my mercy. I could begin to understand just a little, and the possibilities alarmed me.

"At least I won't tell Elden anything now," I assured her.

She returned to her post before Aunt Fritzie's door and I went into the front foyer where the bracket lamps had been lighted. The black and white marble was cold beneath my feet. In his corner Mortimer once more stood restored, lance in hand, and armor brightly shining. I let myself through to the other side of the house and looked into the parlor. No one was there and I found a shadowy corner down the length of the room and sat in a wing chair.

Elden! I thought. Elden, who had been brought here, supposedly by his parents, when he was only a year old, and who had grown up almost a Gorham himself. Elden, who was devoted to his sister Kate—who might not even be his sister. Bit by bit everything was falling into place. Illegitimacy no longer carried the stigma it once had, and I doubted that Elden himself would consider it a handicap. Of course Grandmother could will her fortune wherever she chose, but wills could be challenged—and I suspected that Elden, once he knew, would be a challenger. He would wreck Gerald if he could. He might even try to remove him from Silverhill. Under such circumstances, I could see why Kate was terrified, why she, like Grandmother, wanted the secret kept. The thought of how Elden would feel if he discovered that Aunt Fritzie was his mother made me shiver.

Now, indeed, I could not talk. I would be forced to keep Kate's secret, my grandmother's secret, and let the old deceptions continue. If only Elden himself was not on the verge of dangerous discovery. I remembered all too well the look on his face as he had listened in the dining room.

It was the whispering sound of Grandmother Julia's gown that returned me to the present. She came into the room and stood full in the lamplight, facing Diah's portrait on the wall above the mantel. Her hands were clasped, her shoulders rounded, and her usually proud neck permitted her head to droop forward in an old woman's stoop.

"It has gone badly." She spoke to the picture. "All of it has gone badly."

I left my chair and she heard me, responding with a lift of her chin, a straightening of her shoulders. Rubies winked in her ears as they had done when she was young in the picture, but the face she turned toward me was an aging mockery of the portrait that hung beside Diah's.

She must have seen my eyes move from her to the painting, for she gave me a remote smile. "The portrait must be taken down. Diah has remained the same, but I haven't. I am no longer the woman who posed for that picture."

I thought of her words—that everything had gone badly. Surely the fault was hers.

"Isn't there still a way to mend what has happened?" I asked.

She moved to a sofa with her usual graceful walk, seated herself and gestured toward the space beside her. She seemed confident again and in command. The stoop had vanished.

"There is a great deal to be done in the present, Malinda. Come and sit beside me. I can waste no more time, and you must help me."

I sat uneasily on the sofa's edge, ready for flight. "If you meant what you said about changing your will—" I began.

She shook her head. "Of course I didn't. Sometimes, since you've been here, I've almost wished that what I proposed was possible. But the thing I value most is that you can't be bought. I was mistaken when I thought you came here out of greed for whatever I might do for you. You don't need me—and I'm proud of you for that. But now I need you."

I stared at her, both astonished and tremendously relieved. She smiled at my expression and I saw more warmth in her face than I had ever glimpsed before. With a quick movement she drew the ruby ring from her finger and placed it in my hand.

"There—it's yours. To remember me by. It is the only thing I will ever give you—and it is given freely, whether you help me or not. Nevertheless, I hope you will help."

The ring slipped onto the fourth finger of my right hand and I looked at it, more moved than I cared to admit, and unable to speak.

"I meant every word I said at dinner tonight," she went on. "Perhaps I am an old-fashioned woman, but in a world that has changed too fast for me, I want a continuing line that will go on living in this house, caring for the things Diah and I have brought here. I want this one thing to remain. But museums are cold, impersonal places. I would like to see this house open again, with parties and dancing, children running about. Once it was like that. And it might be possible again, even with Gerald, if only he would marry Kate. He lives in a mirror—a mirror in which he sees a distorted image. Kate would smash the glass and teach him what reality is like, if only he would give her the chance."

I heard her out gravely, but I could not believe in the fulfillment of such a hope. I had the feeling that Gerald had removed himself from reality for too long a time. He would only hurt Kate if he married her.

"There must be a marriage," Grandmother said. "There must be children. You can help me to force Gerald's hand, to force Kate's."

"What of Aunt Nina?" I asked dryly.

Grandmother Julia shrugged. "She will do what is best for Gerald, and she will do as I say. As soon as they believe that I really mean to change my will and leave everything to you as my heir, they'll all come around. Will you help me, Malinda? Will you play this role for me? It will take only a few days, I think. Perhaps no more than today, since they are already frightened. Between us we will make a partnership that can't be beaten."

I left the sofa and went to a side window. I parted the curtains and looked out at a blowing world where the moon sailed between jagged clouds, and white birches bent in the wind, reaching toward the house.

"I'm not good at role-playing," I said over my shoulder. "Don't you think there's been too much of that already? Ever since Aunt Fritzie—?"

She interrupted me. "This is the last role I'll ask anyone to play. There'll be no more need for pretense after that."

I closed the curtains and turned back to her. "I wonder if that's true. Your secrets are coming out on all sides, you know. Not only because Aunt Fritzie is remembering, but because of Kate, and because of me."

She stiffened as I sat down beside her. "What do you mean?"

"Kate read that letter my mother wrote before you destroyed it. So she knows the whole story. And now I know it too."

I could only admire the way Julia Gorham could rally anew after every blow that was dealt her. Once more her lively, adventurous, scheming mind was ready to snatch up the changed situation and take off with it, never faltering in her final objective.

"Then you understand that Gerald must be protected at all costs," she said. "Silverhill must be left safely in his hands and the truth must never be revealed. He would hate us all if he knew the fraud we've perpetrated."

And what of Elden? I wondered. How would he feel if he knew of the fraud? How would he behave? But my grandmother seldom considered the victims of her schemes, being too thoroughly blinded by her own ends to worry about who might suffer from her means. At least Elden could look out for himself, while there was one of her victims who could not.

"And Aunt Fritzie?" I said. "What of Aunt Fritzie, who still has a right to a son?"

She could scarcely have looked more shocked. Long ago she must have discarded her daughter as an individual, and that I should go out of my way to think of Fritzie now was something my grandmother could only dismiss as nonsense.

"Wayne will see that Arvilla is properly cared for," she said. "This must be accomplished all the more quickly now, before she can tell everything she remembers. Or thinks she remembers."

"But why?" I demanded. "Why must you hurry? Aunt Fritzie doesn't know what was done with her baby, and I don't think anyone will inform her—unless it's me. But when it comes to Wayne—I can't believe that he will be as heartless as you claim. As soon as he comes home I shall tell him—"

"There will be nothing to tell," Grandmother Julia said. "I have already told him everything. He has hardly been in the dark about his reprobate of a father—though he has never known the whole story as it concerns Arvilla. Now he understands how Doc Martin helped when Arvilla came home pregnant and something had to be done. After all, his father owed me everything—I'd even spent the money for good lawyers to keep him out of prison—and he did what I asked when it came to Arvilla."

I slipped the ring from my finger and held it out to her. I could not bear the feeling of it on my finger. She would not take it and I dropped it to the sofa cushion beside her.

"So you've decided?" she said arrogantly.

A revulsion toward her, even toward Wayne—toward everything about Silverhill—seemed to choke me so that I could not speak.

"Very well," she said. "Then perhaps bribery will be necessary after all. If I agree to keep Arvilla here, will you help me then? If I call off Wayne's plan and let her stay here among her birds and her plants, will you help me to force Gerald's hand?"

"I think you are monstrous!" I cried. "I think you deserve all the trouble you've brought upon yourself. The only pity is that you've harmed so many other lives as well as your own. I think Grandfather Diah would not have been proud of you."

She leaned forward suddenly, clasping her arms about herself, and I heard her smothered gasp. This was another act, I thought—another ruse to bend me to her will, and I watched her unmoved.

"Why couldn't you let everything alone?" I said. "Why couldn't you stop meddling and let matters take their course? With Gerald and Kate; even with Aunt Fritzie! I saw her just now and she broke my heart. She was rocking herself and crooning a lullaby."

The woman beside me forced her body erect. "I know," she said. "I've seen her too. She has crossed the borderline completely. If I should let her stay, I would have to bring in a nurse to watch her, to take care of her day and night. But I will even do that—if you will help me, Malinda."

"And if I won't?"

"Then I'll act alone. I'll go through enough of the motions to convince them of my purpose. I have in my favor the fact that no one has believed for a moment your claims that you want none of this for yourself."

"I suppose you bribed Wayne too, with this matter of Aunt Fritzie?"

She seemed to have recovered from whatever spasm had seized her, whether sham or otherwise. "I tried to. I threatened to make public all that his father had done if he did not help me to put Arvilla away."

"And that's why he agreed?" I asked, sickened.

"He agreed. But not because of anything I said. So you needn't look like that. Oh, I can tell how you feel about him. And you're right to feel that way. I'd like you to think he gave in to my bribery because that would give me a stronger position with you. But he didn't. Wayne is a man. He's a man like Diah was in his younger years, before he began to let me bully him. So now it's up to you. Arvilla will be put into an institution as soon as it can be arranged, unless you are willing to help me."

"Why couldn't you have waited?" I cried again. "Why couldn't you give everyone more time?"

She closed her eyes and I saw thin white lashes fringe her cheeks—where the lashes of the portrait were dark and thick and long. How cruel age could be unless some quality of character shone through the body's deterioration. As I watched her critically and with no generosity of my own, I saw two tears form at the corners of her eyes and roll down her cheeks. She brushed them away impatiently.

"I have no time to wait," she said. "A few months. Perhaps a year. Barely time to see my first great grandchild born, if I am lucky. Wayne knows. He understands what drives me."

This time she had shocked me anew. This one thing I had not guessed, though there had been occasional signs. "I—I didn't know—" I faltered, and might have touched her hand, had she not snatched it away.

"No! On this I will not use bribery. I'm not afraid of pain, and I'm not afraid of death. If you help me, it will be for other reasons—and not because you are suddenly sorry for an old woman who is dying."

Thunder broke close to Silverhill with a sharp clap, and Grandmother rose quickly to her feet. I think she was anxious to get away from me by now.

"It's going to storm. I must see about windows. And you must have a chance to think over what I've said."

She started toward the door and then came to an abrupt stop as Elden appeared from the hall. His brows were beetling in their characteristic way so that his eyes were almost hidden.

"How long have you been standing there listening?" Grandmother demanded.

He gave her his grimace of a smile and did not answer directly. "Miss Fritzie's taken herself off someplace. She sent Kate on an errand to the kitchen, and then skipped out of her bedroom. I went to look for her upstairs in Doc's rooms, but she wasn't there. Chris says he heard the front door and thinks she's gone outside. Kate's out looking for her now."

"Then go and help her!" Grandmother snapped. "It's going to storm and she must not be out in the woods."

Elden hurried off and I heard the front door bang after him, giving evidence of his spleen.

Grandmother turned back to me. "He was there—listening. He does that, you know. Did we say anything—?"

"I don't think so. Nothing he doesn't already know."

She held out a hand to me. "Come here, Malinda. Everything is in the open between us now, isn't it? Your coming here was a good thing. You're like me in some respects, but you're even more yourself. Arvilla went to pieces when she had to meet trouble. I soured. I think you will do neither. There's a good deal of Diah in you—and that will see you through."

For the first time I wanted to put my arms about her, but I did not dare and I knew she would resist any such softening. She left me with a swish of her red gown, hurrying back to her apartment to close the windows.

I stopped long enough to close those in the drawing room, and then went out through the front door and stood at the top of the steps. The countryside was blowing past in a dance of torn leaves, and on swirls of dust from dirt roads. Lightning flashed, but the storm was still not immediately upon us.

I must help in the search for Aunt Fritzie, I thought, and ran down the steps and let the wind carry me around to the side of the house. There I came to a startled halt, bracing myself.

Wayne had come home. He stood on the side lawn watching a vivid lightning display that flashed and crackled about the rocky head of the mountain. He could not have heard me above the noise of thunder and wind, but something made him turn and look in my direction. I knew at once that a vast distance lay between us. This was what my grandmother had done. But I could not leave it that way, and I walked toward him, resisting the wind. He watched me warily and did not speak until I was close.

"Your grandmother says she means to change her will and leave everything to you. I suppose she has told you this by now?"

So she had presented Wayne with that lie as well! There was no truth in her. But I must not let myself be angry. Not with Wayne, nor with my grandmother. In spite of what she had done, in spite of the way he looked at me from a cold distance, I must somehow be gentle and loving and as honest as I knew how to be. I must understand that it was his own pain and all the hurtful knowledge Grandmother had placed in his hands that stood between us and held us apart. These things had nothing to do with Wayne and me, really. They had only to do with a past that must be thoroughly exposed—and then forgotten.

"Grandmother Julia is bluffing," I told him. "Nothing she said makes any difference to me. Silverhill will go to Gerald, not to anyone else. I only want to help Aunt Fritzie in whatever way is best for her. And I have to trust you for that."

He took a step toward me. "Julia told you—everything? About my father. About Fritzie's baby?"

I nodded. "Some of that. What she didn't tell me, I learned from Kate. Wayne—why have you stayed here under such circumstances? Why did you come back after your wife died?"

His eyes were grave upon my face. "I've a debt to pay. Things to make up for because of my father, things to clear away for Chris's sake. And for the last two years Julia has needed me. She's dying, you know. I've done what I could, and I've helped to keep an eye on Fritzie."

"Yet you're sending Aunt Fritzie away?"

"For her own good. Perhaps even for her own safety. Once your grandmother told me the whole story, I knew she mustn't stay under this roof."

"Mustn't stay—?" I began, and suddenly remembered. "Wayne, she's missing now! She got out of her room and ran away. Elden and Kate have been looking for her."

The look in his eyes warned me that the danger was real.

"I'll go up to the attic," he said at once. "There's Kate's little room up there. You look downstairs—everywhere. She must be found quickly."

His alarm infected me. I had never thought of Fritzie being in any real danger—or dangerous. In fact, I did not understand why this should be so. All that she knew had come to light. That is, all except the truth about Elden, and that she couldn't know. Elden! I thought. Elden, who would not want Fritzie for his mother.

Wayne and I raced toward the front door together, just as lightning flashed close and there was a tremendous clap of thunder. Even as Wayne pulled open the door all the lights in the house flickered, brightened—and went out. Inside we faced a dark hall, dark stairs. At once Wayne started up the flight, calling over the rail to me on the way.

"You'll find candles in the drawer in the hall table. And there's a brass holder there. Go look for Fritzie!"

I fumbled my way along the hall, bumped into the table and managed to pull open a drawer that stuck. My hurrying fingers touched wax and I drew out a long candle, then sought for the holder and thrust the candle into it. The failure of electricity was not uncommon at Silverhill and there were matches in the drawer as well. I struck one, held it to the wick. The stiff white tuft was new, and it resisted the match so that it seemed minutes before the flame caught, wavering in the draughty hall.

The storm had broken in full fury. Between thunderclaps I could hear the beating rain. Noise seemed to clatter and boom throughout the house. Somewhere on the floor above I glimpsed a flicker of light and knew that Wayne too had found a candle.

With the light in my hand and the shadows jumping, I walked toward the gallery. I did not believe that Aunt Fritzie was outside. Some inner conviction that had its source in sympathy and understanding told me where she would be. Beset by trouble she would run to the conservatory.

XII

I opened the door and went down the gallery steps into the hall of mirrors, into a world of confusion. A hundred candles—a thousand candles!—bloomed through the long room, repeating themselves in mirrors and windows, marching without end in myriad rows that receded to the infinite. There were as many repetitions of my yellow dress and of the long gown of my grandmother, glowing red in the depths of mirrors. Yet I could not tell at once where she stood.

Lightning flashed and every candle dimmed in the livid blue glare. At once the gallery leaped to life with all its cabinets and cases and ornaments multiplied, confused with a thousand glimpses of the garden outside. All registered on my startled sight for the fraction of a second—and then vanished, replaced by darkness and multiple golden candle flames. The unreal flickering danced on every hand and showed me nothing clearly. I stood lost in bewilderment, touched by fear.

"Put out your candle, Malinda!" Grandmother's words were a command. I saw her extinguish her own light. She was a thousand women in red gowns disappearing in an instant as a flame was blown out. I blew out my light at once.

Yet with two candles put out, a third still burned on a

small table, reflecting itself endlessly in every glass surface. It seemed to me that somewhere in the dark gallery a dim figure moved and it was not my grandmother. In all the mirrors there was shadowy movement and I cried out in warning to Grandmother Julia.

She turned and I caught again the red gleam of her gown. But darkness moved too and suddenly became a thousand lifted hands, white among the shadows. Before my horrified eyes a thousand brass candlesticks were raised as one weapon—not to light, but to strike down. I cried out again in warning, but thunder crashed deafeningly, booming over my cry, while lightning slashed nearby. The brilliance blinded me. As I blinked it was gone, and for a moment I could see nothing anywhere. If there had been the thud of a blow, if my grandmother had cried out, the thunderclap had covered all sound.

I must go to her at once. I must somehow find my way through this noisy confusion. But I no longer knew where to look for the real, or where the sham. What was actual and what was reflection? I had no idea in which direction to turn. The sense of nightmare was terrifying. All about me was the beauty—and the evil!—of the gallery.

"Grandmother!" I cried again, and stepped out blindly. I was already lost. My knee struck a taboret and it fell on its side, tumbling everything it held to the rug at my feet. At once a moving shadow stepped between me and that distant candle flame—the real flame. The smell of danger was the sulphur smell of the storm and fear ran liquid in my veins.

I dared not risk crying out again. I must reach Grandmother Julia, but I must not stumble blindly into the same weapon which had struck her down. I flung my own candle-holder away from me and heard it crash against breaking glass, hoping the sound would lead the shadowy attacker astray. But when I moved again my toe struck a fallen cannister on the carpet and set it ringing. For an instant I knew someone was very close to me. I heard a suddenly indrawn breath. Outstretched fingers brushed my cheek. Instinctively I dropped to my knees, crawling blindly away over the rug until I struck my shoulder against a wall.

I must find Grandmother Julia—yet I knew now that it was I who was being hunted. I was unable to tell the path of real escape from that of make-believe. On all sides there were doors and windows—and all the mirrors that threw them back at me. I managed to pull myself desperately to my feet and felt cold glass at my back.

Glass—always more glass! This cursed hall of mirrors! Running in blind panic I turned toward what I hoped was free passage, but my temple struck instead the icy, diamond-hard surface—glass! I was stunned by the impact, and fear rose like a soundless scream in my throat. Then as I fumbled desperately, I felt a knob beneath my groping fingers. This was a door as well as a mirror. The only way I could help my grandmother was to escape the danger that hunted me. Before the next flash of lightning came I turned the knob and let myself through the door, closed it as softly as I could behind me.

I had reached the dark passageway to the conservatory and I fled along it, flung myself upon the inner door, knowing pursuit would soon be upon me and that no cry of mine could be heard above the thunder. As the second door opened, moist heat and the familiar rank green smell enveloped me. There were no mirrors here, but only honest glass panes flashing with lightning overhead. Now I could find a hiding place among the plants.

Something screeched a curdling cry of "Bloody murder!" close at hand, but even that could not stop me. Something flew past my face with a flutter of tiny wings. Not the macaw, but a small bird, somehow free. I had no time to wonder how it had escaped its cage. The great dome lighted my way with repeated flashes and I fled along the path. It was almost like being outdoors, though the rain and the wind could not touch me, for all their clatter.

Now I heard the other sounds—the strange, wild sounds of frightened birds, penetrated by the shrill alarm of the macaw, screeching his warning cry. I recognized the difference from the other time. These were not angry birds, disturbed by my intrusion. They were birds caught up in a terror as great as my own. Not until I reached the place where everything centered, and stood beside the small fishpond, did I realize what was happening.

The birds were loose! Not one or two—but all of them. On every hand cage doors stood open, as I could see when lightning flashed. Except for a few which cowered on their perches, too frightened to emerge, all about me canaries and parakeets and finches and the rest darted about in the continuous flashes of light, a hundred birds crying out in a frenzy of fear. Fear of their very freedom in an untested world.

The birds were loose, but it was not the birds which frightened me. It was the mind behind their loosing. The mind behind that hand with the raised candlestick.

As suddenly as the storm had broken, thunder rolled away and lightning receded into the distance, leaving darkness behind. The birds ceased their mad darting, unable to see, but they continued to fill the air with their cries of fright. They were calling for the help I dared not call for—if only someone would hear.

I knew I must find my way to a hiding place. The pursuit of me was not yet finished. In the dark I could not be sure where the edge of the fishpond began and I felt my way a step at a time until my foot found the rim.

When electricity returned it was with appalling suddenness. All the lights of the conservatory came on, and in the wild green world about me the birds stirred into flight again in an effort to escape unknown danger. I did not welcome the glare of light, but at least it showed me the way. Following the curve of the fishpond, I tried to put as much space as possible between me and the door to the gallery. Not until

I reached the far side of the pond did I pause to look back —and saw her.

She stood where she had come out of the jungle growth from the direction of the gallery, and she was staring—not at me, but all about her at the soaring, swooping birds. There was a look of exhilaration on her face, and in one hand she clutched the small white garment I had seen her crooning over.

"I've done what Elden wanted!" she cried. "I've freed them all! I've opened all the doors of all the cages!"

Grandmother was right. Fritzie had crossed the border-line. Step by step, I began to move backward toward an opening path, but she saw the movement at once.

"Don't go," she said more quietly. "Stay with me, Mallie. Stay right there till I come."

I dared not mention Grandmother Julia, but I tried to delay her with words. "Why did you let the birds out of their cages?"

She smiled almost reasonably and edged toward me around the pond. "Because I don't need them anymore. I can let them go now. They were only a substitute, really. Mallie, I have a baby."

"No," I said. "That was a long time ago, Aunt Fritzie. There's no baby now."

Her smile did not waver. "Oh, I know that. *She* took him away from me. My mother. I'll never forgive her for that— never! He's grown up now, of course, but he's still my son."

Somehow I had to keep her talking so that she would not remember what she had come here to do, would not remember that I had been with her back there in the gallery.

"How will you find him?" I asked. "How will you know where he is?"

"I already know," she told me, and held up the baby dress. "Because of this, I know. Poor little thing! To be taken away from his mother who would have loved him more than anyone else possibly could."

A voice called from the direction of the gallery, and for the first time I drew a free breath. Help was coming. I need not stand here much longer trying to hold her away from me with words.

"Arvilla! Arvilla, where are you?" Aunt Nina came rushing along the path, her face a mask of alarm, of fright.

Fritzie turned to look, and then hurried around the path in my direction. At once Aunt Nina cried out to me.

"Don't let her near you! She's utterly mad. She has killed her mother. The lights came on and I found Mother Julia lying there. I've called Wayne, but it's too late. Mother Julia's already dead. Watch out, Malinda—she's dangerous!"

I was already backing away, but Fritzie forgot me and whirled in Aunt Nina's direction, waving the white dress.

"Yes—I am dangerous. To you! I've remembered everything. I know the truth about what you all did to me. The secret won't be kept any longer. It was you who killed my poor sick little bird—so I would be blamed, and Mallie would be too frightened to stay. It was you who wanted to send me away, wanted Mallie to leave. I know all about you now!"

There was a moment of sudden stillness. Even the birds stopped their screeching—perhaps at the familiar sound of Fritzie's voice. The heavy heat was like a sopping weight pressing me down, making it hard to breathe. We stood in silence, the three of us, but it was Aunt Fritzie I watched in new bewilderment. I saw the change that had come over her. She was no longer wildly exhilarated. If she had been on some emotional binge, it had quieted, just as the birds were quieting. The look that was often too young and guileless had gone from her face. In its place she wore a new dignity, an air of quiet courage.

Nina moved swiftly. She ran around the edge of the pond and flung herself at Fritzie. She tore the white dress from her hands and threw it into the fishpond. In her frock of charcoal gray she was like a shadow granted a life of its own

—the same shadow that had moved in desperate violence, a thousand times repeated, in the gallery. Like Fritzie I knew the enemy now. When she reached to snatch up a glass vase from a table, I stepped quickly between her and Aunt Fritzie.

She came at me with sudden exultance, as if she welcomed the change in opponents. She raised the vase and I caught at her arm. As the blow descended it grazed my shoulder, deflected. I wrenched the glass from her grasp and heard it shatter on the brick. As another vase had shattered long ago! For an instant I faltered. Her wiry arms came about me at once, her hands reached for my throat and Aunt Fritzie began to shriek for Wayne at the top of her voice.

Somewhere running footsteps sounded, and a moment later he was there, pulling Nina away from me, pinioning her arms. I stepped back breathing hard. After the first moment she ceased to struggle. She let herself go limp in Wayne's hands and turned her head to look up at her captor almost docilely.

"It doesn't really matter," she said. "Gerald is safe now. Julia is dead. She'll never change her will and leave everything to Malinda. I've owed her this for a long time. Let me go, Wayne. What happens to me doesn't matter."

He did not try to hold her. She pulled away from his hands and turned in the direction of the gallery—an oddly eager little woman, who moved as though she still had something important left to do.

I could not let her go like that. "Wayne—it was Nina who struck Grandmother down."

"I know," he said flatly. "But there's nowhere left for her to go—is there?"

Aunt Fritzie was paying no attention to us. She knelt beside the fishpond and reached into it for the little dress, pulled it out and began to wring it free from water.

Wayne came to me, touched me gently. "Did she hurt you?"

I shook my head. I was beginning to tremble in the old way, but I did not want him to see.

Aunt Fritzie held out the dress to me. "Look, dear. I made it for him when he was a baby. I'm afraid it's going to be a terrible shock to him to know that I'm his mother. But he must know now. Don't you think so, dear?"

I took the baby dress from her because it gave me something to do with my hands, and smoothed it out. It had been made with a curious distinguishing pattern. One sleeve was of normal length. The other was hardly more than a cap.

"But—but this is a dress you must have made for Gerald," I said.

She nodded at me. "Yes—for my son, Gerald. Now I must find him and show it to him. I must tell him the truth."

I gasped and turned to Wayne, saw that he already knew.

"Must you?" Wayne asked gravely.

I could only look from one to the other in blank astonishment.

Fritzie smiled with new assurance. "Of course I must. Secrecy has been the trouble all along—the hiding and the trickery! It must come to an end. Even if he hates me, it has to end."

She walked past us around the fishpond and there was nothing for Wayne and me to do but go after her. On the far side she paused to look back at empty cages, at all the birds perched among her plants.

"You'll have to go back inside in a little while, my dears," she said. "You'll feel better then. You aren't wild birds, you know. But don't fret. I'll see you safe. I owe you that."

She reached the gallery door just ahead of us and we went through into mirrored golden lamplight. Amid the richness of Diah's gallery Grandmother Julia lay, a spread covering her face and her red gown. I saw the heavy brass candlestick from Spain lying on the carpet, and I shivered.

Had Diah bought that candlestick one long-ago day in Seville?

Gerald stood nearby looking down at his grandmother, with Kate Salway just behind him, his expression one of disbelief.

As we entered the gallery, Elden came through from the main house, and I stared at him with new eyes. Elden was only Elden after all, and had never been anyone else.

"I've done the phoning, Doc," he told Wayne. "They'll be driving out from Shelby right away."

Wayne thanked him, but Aunt Fritzie saw no one but Gerald. She would have moved toward him at once, but Wayne put a hand on her arm.

"Wait," he said, and spoke to Elden. "Can you go after Mrs. Nina?"

Elden seemed to understand his special meaning. He did not ask what direction she might have taken, but went back into the house at once. We stood silent until the sound of the front door released us. Only then did Wayne let go of Aunt Fritzie's arm. She went toward Gerald with the little white dress in her hands, still dripping water from the pond.

"Gerald," she said—eager, yet at the same time a little frightened. "Gerald—I—I have something I must tell you."

Kate stepped closer to Gerald and he turned to her, made a slight gesture of questioning—a man still dazed and unable to speak. Kate answered for him.

"I've already told him," she said to Fritzie. "Mallie made me see that he had to know the truth."

Aunt Fritzie waited, searching his face hungrily, yet asking nothing of him. If Gerald should hurt her now, I couldn't bear it, I thought, and longed to do something to stop him from speaking, from turning the cruel lash of his tongue upon her.

At his silence Aunt Fritzie burst nervously into words. "I—I want to tell you about your father when there's time.

He was never like they said, Gerald. They never knew him
—and I did. I want to tell you everything!"

For the first time Gerald looked directly into her eyes and
I saw in his face something I had never seen before. Gerald
Gorham was ashamed. He met Fritzie's look—so tentative,
yet so ready to offer love—and he remembered all he had
done to her and was ashamed.

"Yes," he said quietly, "you must tell me all you can. This
will take some getting used to. You'll have to help me in
that."

Aunt Fritzie's hands clasped and unclasped. "We'll help
each other. I'm not Nina's sort of mother, you know. I've
had very little practice at mothering. And I—I never was a
tennis player."

Gerald very nearly smiled. A curious look passed between them. Not the look of a mother and a son—but perhaps the look of two strangers meeting, of a man and a
woman who appraised each other and might learn mutual
understanding and respect.

Kate broke the silence. "What about Elden?" she asked
Wayne. "I know why you sent him away. And I think you
were right. Must my brother know?"

I remembered her fear of having Elden learn the truth.
A fear that had misled me, taken me down a wrong road—
all because she was terrified over how Elden would use
such knowledge to torment Gerald about his illegitimacy
and the fact that the Gorham name did not belong to him
on his father's side.

"I've only postponed the matter," Wayne said. "What
happens now is up to Gerald. And you."

"He needn't know," Kate said hastily to Gerald. "I'll never
tell him and—"

Gerald's moment of shame had given way to something
else. Almost visibly he stepped back from further female
domination.

"I'll tell him myself," he said.

Kate said nothing more, but her eyes held a shine that was new to them.

Aunt Fritzie spoke up in forthright approval. "Good!" she said. "It's high time this house had a man at the head of it. It has been a matriarchy long enough."

Wayne was watching me. "You're shivering," he said suddenly.

"It's not the birds." At least I could tell him that with assurance. "I went into the conservatory when they were loose, and it wasn't the birds that frightened me. But there's so much that I—I don't understand."

"There's time to talk before anyone gets here from Shelby," he said. "Come along with me."

He led the way to the drawing room and there I sat with him on the sofa, where only a little while ago I had sat beside Grandmother Julia. I listened while he explained what had happened long ago when Henry Gorham had brought Fritzie home from New York and Grandmother had learned that her daughter was pregnant.

"Julia worked out the whole scheme," he said. "The plan was made before the baby was born. My doctor father knew, as Julia did, that Nina could never bear a child. But Julia had to have a blood heir—and here was her chance, though she wanted no scandal and illegitimacy. She bullied my father and everyone else into carrying out her scheme. She even bullied Diah. I gather he was against the whole thing from the beginning—but he was caught so that he had to go along with what she wanted. Nina was eager for a baby. She was quite willing to see Gerald taken away from Fritzie so that the deception could be perpetrated and he could be raised as her own child. Fritzie was obviously cracking up then, and they told her the baby had died."

"What was my mother's role in what happened?"

"Gerald was born right here at Silverhill, with my father attending, of course, and falsifying the records. When he was a few days old, your mother took the baby secretly to

Vermont, where Nina was staying. Nina had gone there
some months before, supposedly pregnant and unable to
stand the trouble here at home. Henry, of course, knew
everything, and he went to bring his wife and 'son' home after a suitable interval, so that everything became official.
Unfortunately Henry could never stand the boy. He never
gave Gerald a chance."

"And all the while Aunt Fritzie knew she had been
cheated?"

"That proved to be the danger. She made the baby dress
in secret, and when Nina brought the child home, she
claimed to Diah that it was hers. That day on the stairs she
tried to show him the dress she had made to prove the baby
was the one she had seen in its crib. Diah was brokenhearted
about the whole thing, but he had to keep her quiet or else
risk a far greater scandal. And he really didn't believe
Fritzie was competent to bring up a child. So there was a
quarrel—and you know what happened. You can see the
fear under which Nina has existed all this time. She lived
for Gerald until she almost believed that he was her natural
son. At the same time she always knew the danger of ex-
posure, and that he would turn on her if he discovered the
deception she had played. He was never much attached to
her anyway. She wanted him to be Julia's heir, but she also
wanted him to live his life out believing he was her son."

I was beginning to see the whole sorry picture now.

"Nina always hated Fritzie," Wayne went on. "She was
jealous of her as Gerald's real mother, and she blamed her
for Gerald's arm. But she was afraid of her as well. She was
at Julia constantly to have her sent away because she was
never sure how permanent her loss of memory would be.
Then you came—and everything began to happen. Your
mother had apparently run away from Silverhill to escape
the whole situation—a situation she could do nothing about
because she could never stand up to Julia Gorham—as
you've stood up to her, Mallie. I suppose she was never

able to free herself of a feeling of guilt, and the letter she wrote Julia just before she died was an attempt to make some late amends to Fritzie. But she didn't live long enough to tell you the contents of that letter."

I could ache for my mother too—carrying so hurtful a secret for all these years.

Wayne left the sofa and went to stand before the portraits of Diah and Julia. My hand touched something hard on the cushion beside me and I picked it up. It was my grandmother's ruby ring. I could wear it for her now. I slipped it on my finger and went to stand beside Wayne. The youthful face of the woman in the portrait meant more to me than when I had first seen it. There was pride and determination in that young face, but there was also the promise of courage and strength. If only she had not used those qualities in her own willful way.

"What a waste," I said sadly.

Wayne put an arm about me. "Yes, a waste. And we've all contributed to it. All of us who live here. Until you came in from outside and pulled the truth out of us. The only thing you've tried to cover is that cheek of yours, Mallie—and I think you know the truth about that too, by this time. You brought everything into the open with your own honesty, and—"

"And Grandmother Julia is dead," I mourned.

"By her own doing. By what she brought upon herself inevitably. Just as it will be with Nina."

I stared at him. "Nina?"

"Where else will she go but down to the pond?" he said. "Do you think she could live to face the same fate she wanted for Fritzie? She's been hiding the wild course her mind has taken for a long while, I think. And she's fooled us all while this was brewing. By the time Elden finds her, it will probably be too late."

He opened his arms and I went into them. He kissed me with love and tenderness and I wept against his shoulder as

I clung to him. I wept for all of them—for all except myself. But not at all for myself—who had everything!

At one of the drawing-room windows the curtains blew in and there was an odd whisper of sound—like wind in the branches of a tree. We turned together, Wayne and I, and went to pull the curtains apart to the tinkle of falling glass.

"The Silverhill legend!" Wayne said, smiling ruefully.

Lightning had indeed struck close. One of the tall white birches had been split down the center and its falling head had broken through the window so that its top, with all the leaves and twigs intact, barely protruded into the room. There it whispered and rustled contentedly, not knowing it was already dead, but as though it had come at last to the place where it belonged. The smell of scorching was bitter in the air.

Wayne saw my face. "We'll leave Silverhill as soon as we can," he said. "I'm free to move away now, though I'll still be a country doctor. Fritzie may never be completely stable, but I think she will improve steadily. Today she has matured more than she's been allowed to in the last forty years. And Gerald will be his own man now. Once he is, I don't think Kate will need to wait much longer. So we can leave them all to work out their own lives as Mrs. Julia never permitted them to."

Yes, I thought—we could leave them to work out their lives, while we started somewhere else, working out our own.

"Let's go find Chris," I said. "Let's talk to him together."

Wayne's arm was strong about me as we left the room to the birch tree and went upstairs.